During the entire time h   the garage, only one c   nothing. Only the garish   in the parking garage, the fumes and exhaust of long-departed commuters, and the absolute silence.

With his gloves still on, he opened the attorney's brief-case and searched around, looking for her business cards. They were there, in a gold metal container underneath some papers. He used one of the attorney's pens to write on the card, just below the lawyer's printed name, the message that he'd memorized:

The first thing we do, let's kill all the lawyers.

That made him smile. He never much cared for Shake-speare, but he'd heard the phrase before and he certainly agreed with the sentiment. Using it here, he thought, was perfect. The cops would know that they weren't dealing with someone who was ignorant. They'd respect him.

He bent over the dead woman's face, or what was left of it, and placed the card gently inside her mouth so that his message and the lawyer's name were clearly visible. He stood, took one last look at the woman, then turned and walked into the shadows. . . .

KILL ALL THE LAWYERS

MARC BERRENSON

ZEBRA BOOKS
KENSINGTON PUBLISHING CORP.

ACKNOWLEDGMENT

The following lawyers I consider my friends, despite the fact that they're lawyers. Each in his own way has contributed to the writing of this book: Sheldon Brown, Gerry Cohen, Burt Denmark, Steve Flanagan, Jack Gold, Danny Kallen, Tom Kascoutas, David Kurtz, Curt Leftwich, Mark Lessem, Gary Polinsky, Trudy Robinson, Mort Rochman, Alex Ross, Marshall Rubin, Jack Rudofsky, Ira Salzman, Jack Smith, James Tolbert, Fred Warner, Lewis Watnick, Jeff Wiatt, and David Ziskrout.

Also, I must thank the following two relatives, Jack Jacobs and Brian Raffish, for their help in describing to me exactly how they bag the animals.

DEDICATION

This one's dedicated to The Group: Edna and Tom Gordon, Diany and Ron Klein, Carolyn and Bobby Lee, Carol and Gary Mark, and Marty and David Uslaner.

And to my wife, Karen, for giving me the perfect gift.

Part One

One

It was a Tinseltown late summer afternoon, when the congested streets chopped downtown skyscrapers into grids of steel and concrete canyon cliffs, splintering the sun. The smog, like the big picture, was there, but only in the distance.

Focus on something close—like the winos sleeping on the grass outside the Hall of Records or the gangbangers wandering between cars in the parking lot, throwing their signs—and you didn't see it. It wasn't there.

The San Gabriel Mountains were there, like a brown smear, somewhere in the distance. You knew that. But it was easier not to look, not to risk disappointment.

Focus on something close. It was less painful that way.

"All right, Crystal, we're rolling."

She jerked her attention from the small crowd of attorneys, the court personnel in business suits, and a bum trudging behind a shopping cart filled with old clothes and discarded metal junk, took a deep breath, raised her eyes to the camera, and smiled.

"This is Crystal Pelotas reporting live from the Criminal Courts Building downtown. *Real News for Real People* has learned from confidential sources that the police are about to disclose the name of the suspect captured in the Metro Matador murders, the series of brutal slayings that have terrorized and held hostage the citizens of Los Angeles for nearly a year.

"Real News viewers will recall that the Matador first struck nearly one year ago. He has until now eluded capture by the Metro Matador Task Force, a combined effort of Los Angeles County sheriffs and L.A.P.D. detectives, formed after the Matador's third victim was found in a culvert near the Hollywood Freeway interchange.

"The body of the Matador's first victim, Mary Jo Miles, was discovered in the early morning hours of September 7, 1991, fully clothed, on an embankment adjacent to the Temple Street off-ramp of the Golden State Freeway, just a few short blocks from where I now stand. The following weeks and months brought the discovery of further bodies."

Crystal Pelotas paused, then looked down at her notes, as if she, along with every other citizen of Los Angeles, hadn't already memorized the body count.

"Sixteen in all," she said. "All marked with the Matador's bizarre signature of death: the fatal bullet wound to the head, the knife embedded in the neck, and the red cape covering the body of each of the victims."

The cameraman lowered his camera, placed it at his side, and removed a pack of cigarettes from his shirt pocket.

"We're on tape now," said the director. His eyes were fixed on a small television monitor inside the equipment van parked at the curb. The monitor displayed pictures of each of the victims, both before and after death. Smiling, unsuspecting faces beaming from the pages of high school annuals and family photo albums, followed by coroner photos of heads with sightless eyes, each with the same small black hole above the bridge of the nose, and the knife handle protruding from the neck marking the place where the carotid artery had been severed, as if the killer was somehow less than satisfied with blowing out the brains of his victims. It was a ghoulish slide show of bodies in the early morning gloom, splayed out on dirty hillsides covered with rusted beer cans, soda bottles, Styrofoam coffee cups, and other freeway garbage.

As the tape ran, Crystal Pelotas allowed herself to be patted with makeup, while the cameraman held a cigarette to her lips for her to inhale.

"Colin," she said, directing her comments to the director, "if this is all we've got, we're in deep shit. I don't see why we couldn't just put all this on tape and get it together later at the studio."

She patted at the sides of her head, smoothing back a few errant strands of golden hair, then hiked at the metallic lace pantyhose under her Adrienne Vittadini ivory satin coatdress, the one with the rhinestone buttons.

"This live bullshit isn't worth the trouble," she muttered, snugging her foot back inside her three-inch pumps and wincing at the pain. She angrily blew cigarette smoke from her mouth, as if trying to rid herself of some small insect that had inadvertently flown inside.

"We'll be fine, Crystal," said Colin Archer, the director, in a voice that sounded at the same time placating and weary. He spoke with an English accent; at least everybody thought it was English. Colin Archer promoted that misconception. In reality he was born in Wichita and had spent a year in Australia working as a beach lifeguard before returning to Kansas and taking a job as a gofer at the local television station. He had recently been placed in charge of *Real News for Real People,* a daily half-hour of sensationalist tabloid reportage featuring Crystal Pelotas.

Archer said, "They're running your bit with Powell."

Crystal remained on her spot at the top of the steps. On the TV monitor in the van, the station was running the tape of Police Chief Francis Powell's press conference earlier that afternoon. Powell and the D.A., Otto Durning, appeared agitated by the questions, most of which were from Crystal and had to do with law enforcement's certainty that they had, in fact, arrested the right guy. Both Powell and the D.A. said that they had.

As the tape of the press conference drew to a close, Colin Archer resumed his previous position poised behind the camera, one hand in the air. He pointed a finger at Crystal as he said, "And, back to you, Crystal."

"*Real News* viewers will recall that it was only after a second artist's rendition of the Metro Matador was prepared by *Real News* artists, in consultation with *this* reporter, that the suspect was identified by a *Real News* viewer who had been following our coverage of the Matador slayings and had seen the artist's composite of the killer on our show."

Crystal paused momentarily, seeing Colin Archer's gesturing outstretched hand. She turned, then grabbed the elbow of a man who was slowly making his way up the steps behind her.

"This is noted criminal defense attorney Gerald Isaacs," she said, maneuvering the attorney in front of the camera.

"Rumor has it, Mr. Isaacs, that you've been consulted by the suspect's family."

Crystal thrust the microphone at Isaacs' face, as if she were sharing an ice cream cone with him.

"Do you have any comment for our *Real News* viewers?"

Isaacs, without pausing, wrapped one hand around the microphone while moving closer. He opened his shoulder so that Crystal fit into the picture just to the side and under his chin. What the camera couldn't see was Isaacs' right hand resting softly on Crystal's backside.

"Until formal charges are filed," said Isaacs, "I can, of course, make no comment. I will say this, though, Crystal. I have been contacted by certain people pertaining to the Matador case."

"Would that be the family of the suspect, Gerry?"

Isaacs smiled calculatedly for the camera.

"I'm not at liberty to disclose that information now," he said. "As you and your viewers are aware, Crystal, my office is often consulted on such serious cases. We did receive a call earlier this morning concerning the Matador on our 800 number. That's 1-800-LAWSUIT." Isaacs paused, wondering if he could get in another plug before the camera was turned off.

Crystal grabbed the microphone, saying, "Thank you for your time, Mr. Isaacs." She turned to the right, away from Gerry Isaacs, who remained hovering in the background.

"Well, ladies and gentlemen. That appears to be all the information we have for now. *Real News* will stay right on top of this late-breaking story. We'll make sure that *Real News* viewers are kept abreast of any developments in the Metro Matador investigation as they happen."

"All right, cut. That's it. Great work, Crystal."

"When's this going to be shown?" said Isaacs. He was shadowing Crystal, following her back to the van.

"It's live, Gerry."

"You mean that was it? That's what everybody saw?"

Crystal smiled. "What'd you think? You got your plug in. What're you bitching about?"

Isaacs smoothed his silk tie inside his jacket, then nervously adjusted the knot. "You should have called me, Crystal. I could have prepared. I could have given you a real story."

Crystal stood at the curb, near the rear door of a silver Mercedes that was parked behind the equipment van. Her driver waited patiently behind the wheel. She had placed a pair of wraparound sunglasses on her face, and was sucking on the end of a cigarette that she held between outstretched fingers that never got farther than six inches from her lips.

"Yeah," she said, "And then you could have made up some more of your bullshit about representing this guy."

Isaacs' expression took on a hurt look, but then he smiled.

"From what I heard," said Crystal, "this guy's got no money, which means, as we both know, Gerry, that he's going to get stuck with the P.D., unless you've changed your tune about doing *pro bono* work, which, from looking at that Italian suit and those lizard slippers of yours, I doubt. What did that suit set you back? Fifteen, sixteen hundred?"

Isaacs flashed a grin, then looked down at his feet, admiring himself. He brushed a piece of imaginary lint from the front of his Alan Fusser double-breasted peak-lapelled pinstriped wool suit.

"For your information, Crystal," he said, "it's not Italian. And it's *twenty-two* hundred, not fifteen." He held up one foot, wiggling the toe. "The shoes are Italian, though. Lorenzo Banfi. You like them?"

Crystal tossed her cigarette into the gutter. "Great,

Gerry. I bet your clients are real impressed." She opened the rear door of the Mercedes and slid inside.

"Listen, Crystal," said Isaacs. He rested his forearms on the passenger door. Even with the window rolled down, the backlighting from the sun made his face look dark, indistinct. "I'm having a few close friends over this Saturday. Why don't you join us? You know, nothing formal." He smiled and started to laugh, then cut it short, seeing her response.

"Like last time, Gerry?" Her voice was even. Not angry, just serious. She made him look away first.

"Uh, yeah, babe," he said, shuffling his feet. "What, you changed your stripes or something?"

Crystal put her hand to her forehead, then shook her head.

The driver whispered, "Shall we leave now, Ms. Pelotas?"

"Gerry," she said, "Ya know something? You're a real piece of work. What's the matter, you got a cold or something? I can see your nose running and that little pink spot right below your nostrils."

Isaacs stepped back from the car, quickly pinched at his nose, snorted, then wiped the back of his hand across his upper lip.

"Yeah," said Crystal. "That's what I thought."

The car slowly pulled away from the curb. Crystal pressed the button of the power window and watched as Gerry Isaacs' image clouded in the glare of the afternoon sun, then became smaller.

It was that picture of Gerry Isaacs that she carried with her for a few moments as the driver maneuvered the Mercedes through the tangle of commuter traffic.

But it was not the image of Isaacs, his twenty-two-hundred-dollar suits, or his Italian slippers, or even his

out-of-control cocaine habit that stayed with her. That
was everyday bullshit, the kind of thing she'd learned
from experience was unimportant, unless she could make
it work for her, maybe work a trade when the time was
ripe.

Now her mind was back on the story. The cops and the
D.A. said that they had the Metro Matador. Crystal
wasn't all that sure that they did. Not that it mattered
much either way. She'd slant the story one way or the
other to garner the most interest. The facts were secondary, something she thought about but didn't dwell on. She
needed an angle with this one. A way to get herself personally involved in the coverage.

All of L.A. was watching her now. The Metro Matador
had worked wonders for the program, increasing the
show's ratings steadily over the last month. The network
suits had their corporate eye on her. She had success by
the shorthairs and it was now just a matter of when, and
how hard, to pull. It was time to make a move, to do
something that would get everybody's attention.

Crystal reached for the car phone and punched in
Francis Powell's number.

If he hadn't been paying such close attention to the small
portable TV, he would have observed the cat quickly
finishing off most of the canned tuna. As it was, Nestor
Stokes absentmindedly poked at the fish with a fork, his
eyes riveted on the screen, watching Crystal Pelotas reporting from the Criminal Courts Building. When the
news report concluded, Nestor noticed that only a few
small morsels of oily fish lay at the bottom of the can, and
Eleanor, his black and white cat, named after his mother,

was lounging on her side atop the fold-out kitchen table, licking at her whiskers and purring.

"Now what's Daddy supposed to do for supper, you bad cat, you?"

Nestor ran the palm of his right hand over the head of the purring feline, pulling her closer to him.

"That's right, Ellie, you bad cat, you," he baby-talked, caressing the cat, which was now on his lap between himself and the edge of the table.

"Daddy's got to go to work soon, while you, you fat, terrible, lazy cat, you get to lounge around the trailer all night. Isn't that right? Isn't that right?"

Nestor placed Ellie back on the table and made his way to the back of the trailer. He removed his lab coat and hung it neatly inside the closet. His first cat, Gracie, lay on her side on a shelf inside.

"How you doin', Gracie?"

Nestor lifted the cat from the shelf, looked into its eyes, and smiled, thinking he could have worked the Sculpal a little better to get more of a glassy wet look.

He put Gracie back on the shelf, pushing the three-chain-and-hook gambrel to the side to make room. He noticed that there was still blood and tissue residue on the gambrel, and made a mental note to thoroughly clean it when he returned from work.

From a hook inside the small closet, Nestor retrieved his security uniform: brown pants with matching shirt, his name stenciled over the logo of the security company on the chest pocket; his hat, like a cop's, except brown to match the rest of the uniform; his Sam Browne belt, which most of the other guards didn't wear, but Nestor liked and had treasured ever since he bought it second-hand at the Army-Navy Surplus a few months before.

No gun.

They wouldn't let Nestor carry a gun. That didn't matter, though. He already had plenty of those.

Nestor got into the uniform, gently nudging the cat out of the way with his toe. He slipped his feet into his shoes, thinking for a split-second, as he almost always did, about the collision, and the surgery that had followed.

It was the shoes, with their uneven elevator soles, that inevitably brought back the painful memories. He let the anger quietly simmer for a moment, his mind quickly clicking on the images of twisted metal, the blood-spattered clothing, the pain, and the smell of alcohol when both he and the other driver were placed inside the ambulance.

It was always like this, having to relive the years since the accident whenever he saw those shoes, whenever he caught a glimpse of himself in the pitying eyes of others.

Nestor let the memories run their usual breakneck course through his psyche, gritting his teeth and trying to focus on something other than his pain, while his mind poked one last salty finger in the wound by flashing a picture of the lawyer and his client—that drunk maimer of men, destroyer of lives—smiling and shaking hands as they left the courtroom, as if nothing had happened. As if Nestor Stokes sitting in court awaiting vindication, the giving of an eye for the taking of his, was no better than a pathetic postscript to the expeditious administration of justice. Merely the grimy residue of some lawyer's money-making machine.

Nestor headed down the narrow corridor of the trailer toward the kitchen. He caught a glimpse of himself in the mirror, that up-and-down bob of the head, shoulders jerking rhythmically as he limped.

The TV was still on, but he was no longer interested. He removed one of his photo albums from the shelf over

the stove and sat down at the table. He automatically
fingered the spot in the album and flipped it open.

On the opened page Nestor had neatly stenciled the
name, "The Metro Matador," and then below that, the
date when he had started making his entries. Over twenty
pages followed the title page, each of which contained
newspaper and magazine accounts of the Matador, which
Nestor had carefully cut out and pasted inside. This
album also contained Nestor's accumulation of articles
dealing with Richard Ramirez, "The Nightstalker." The
album was one of six that he had set up to contain his
collection of media accounts of famous killers.

Nestor reviewed the descriptions of each of the Matador killings. He had most of the facts memorized, having
gone over the album so often. Still, he liked reading about
the bodies, how they always found them with a knife
sticking out of the neck and covered with the Matador's
red cape. Nestor liked the Matador and his red cape,
maybe more than any of his other serial killers. Nestor
thought that the Matador had style,

"Poor man," Nestor said, finally closing the album and
returning it to its place on the shelf. "Poor, poor man."

He turned and bent down, allowing the cat to jump to
his shoulder.

"That's a kitty," he whispered. "They think they've
caught our Matador," he said, stroking the arched back
of the cat. "What do you think, kitty? Do they have him?
Did they catch the Big Bad Matador?"

Nestor smiled, then chuckled in a low throaty rasp that
sent the cat jumping to the floor.

"Bad girl," he said, still smiling, playful.

His mind focused on Crystal Pelotas. Nestor liked the
woman, Crystal. The one that said she had helped capture the Matador. Nestor doubted that. Crystal was too

beautiful and much too smart to become involved in something like that. Nestor had toyed with the idea of reserving a section in one of his albums for Crystal. Just pictures of her. He still thought that he might do that someday.

Crystal Pelotas drifted in and out of his thoughts, especially at night, when he lay in bed, Ellie purring at his side. Like a movie that he couldn't leave, Crystal was there in the darkness, reflected on the screen inside his eyelids, more vivid and more real than on television. And no matter how he had tried at first to think of something else, Nestor found that he could not rid himself of the woman's image; her long golden hair, the soft shoulders, her full breasts. Nestor wanted to place his hands, just for a moment, on her hips and legs, just to know what it felt like.

But then reality brought him back.

Who was he to believe that such a moment would ever come? He knew how he must appear to her, just a little, unknown man who walked with a limp. He was a nobody to her. Crystal Pelotas wouldn't give the time of day to a man like himself.

Not like she would the Matador.

If Crystal could only see him like that, Nestor thought, then his dreams of being with her, of sharing the things he wanted to share with her, would no longer be just dreams. He'd no longer be forced to do what he had to do at night just to satisfy himself, just to sleep.

Nestor grabbed his car keys from the counter and left the trailer, still thinking about Crystal Pelotas and the Matador. He walked over to the Nissan and put his dinner inside the cooler that he always kept in the trunk.

The photos from his albums raced through his thoughts, killers and victims finally merging into one indecipherable image. He felt the tingling pressure of the secret that he kept inside, like when he was young and had spent all his money to buy his mother that special brooch, the one of the cat with the rhinestone eyes. And he had almost exploded Christmas Eve, knowing how happy she would be to see it, and how hard it would be for him to wait until morning to give it to her.

Nestor checked his watch and told himself he better get on the road. He'd have plenty of time later to think about himself and Crystal.

He closed the trunk of the Nissan, but not before he made sure that the knife and the red felt material he had bought the day before were still inside the plastic bag underneath the floorboard of the trunk.

Two

"You sure you're ready for this?"

Curt merely shrugged his shoulders, smiled, then bent over the bed and kissed her.

"You look good," she said.

Jamie propped herself up on one elbow and massaged her eyes with her fingertips.

"I forgot how sexy those tight little shorts could be."

"Keep that thought," he said.

"Sure, like you're going to be in any shape for *that* once you get back. Just be careful, Curt. Those muscles aren't in the condition they used to be."

Jamie was sitting up now, reclining against the headboard. The T-shirt that she'd slept in was hiked up just below her breasts, revealing what struck Curt as an amazingly flat, firm stomach. She wore a skimpy pair of salmon-colored briefs that were cut low at the waist and high on the leg, accentuating her hips.

Curt found himself wondering if perhaps he was wasting his time going on this bike ride, feeling that he would just as soon stay in bed with Jamie this morning and benefit from a different sort of exercise.

"I'm putting in my reservation now," he said, kissing

her again. She hooked the back of his neck with her hand, holding him there.

"Why don't I just stick around for a while," he whispered within inches of her ear.

He loved the way her auburn hair fell over her shoulders like fine silk. Even without makeup, Jamie had a sort of natural girlish beauty. An innocence about her. Sure, the small spider-like lines were beginning to show at the corners of her eyes, and the skin around her chin and neck seemed slightly looser than it once had, but he rarely noticed such things. When he thought of her, he pictured the way she looked an hour or a day or even a week ago. In that way, she always looked the same, never changed. He could look back at pictures of the two of them and see the change, but in his mind her beauty remained constant.

And it wasn't as if he didn't realize that his appearance had changed right along with hers. That was part of the reason for getting back on the bicycle. He'd always had the beginnings of a spare tire, a few extra pounds around the waist. Recently, though, the restaurants and the martinis had taken their toll. His spare tire was taking on the appearance of something off a PeterBilt truck.

Five years had passed since Darren's death. During that time Curt had managed to weather a suicide attempt, a nervous breakdown, a couple of mini-breakdowns, and the daily self-doubting and uncertainty that followed in the wake of his son's murder. He knew that had it not been for Jamie's support, even in the face of his rejection of her, he would probably have ended up in some looney bin somewhere, or living in a trailer out in the desert, collecting rocks and counting grains of sand.

"You came in late last night," she said.

"Francis called."

"The Matador?"

"Yeah."

"He wants you to handle it?"

"No. Not yet, anyway. Besides, there's nothing special about prosecuting this case, except for the publicity. Francis is undoubtedly looking forward to that, what with the way the media has been hounding him lately. Now that they've finally caught this . . . Daniel Lopez, Francis can relax and bask in the glory."

"Then why'd he call?" said Jamie.

"I guess he was just feeling good and wanted to share it with someone. We've been through a lot of similar situations, high publicity media circuses. I think by the time he called, Francis had already tossed down a few and was feeling no pain. He just wanted to shoot the shit, let his hair down a little. The Matador's been a thorn in his side for a long time. He deserves to celebrate, now that they've finally snagged the guy."

Jamie said, "That TV reporter isn't so sure that Daniel Lopez is the right one."

"Yeah, Francis mentioned that. It's just so much bull-shit, according to him. Crystal Pelotas has been on his case for months. She's pushing for an interview with him. Anything to stir up the waters, create a little viewer appeal. Powell says it's nothing to get worked up over. In fact, the D.A.'s already filed murder charges against Lopez. He's set for arraignment tomorrow."

"What do you think?" she said.

"It's got nothing to do with me," said Curt. "I only know what I read in the papers and see on TV. Crystal Pelotas is not exactly Edward R. Murrow, ya know. And *Real News for Real People* is a far cry from the *MacNeil-Lehrer Report*. If Francis says that Lopez is the Matador, than I've got to go with that. Besides, Francis must be damn sure

Lopez is the one. I think he's going to give Pelotas that interview she's been dying for as a sort of reward for helping capture him."

"They did that drawing, the one that identified Lopez?"

"That's right. Lopez made the same stupid mistake that a lot of these guys make. He let the publicity go to his head. Another serial killer that read too many of his own reviews. Started telephoning the studio and talking with Pelotas. Even described himself to her, enough to fine-tune that composite so that one of their viewers picked him out."

"At a drug store, wasn't it?

"Yeah," said Curt, chuckling. "Lopez was standing in line to buy lottery tickets. Well, he's definitely going to get his wish. He'll be partaking in the Big Spin, only now it'll be to find out whether he spends the rest of his life in prison or takes his place on death row."

Curt headed for his bike, which he kept on the deck at the back of the house. He figured he'd put it out there, look at it every so often, see if he was ready to handle the memories.

The bike was practically new. He and Jamie had bought it over a year ago in the hope that he might finally be over the trauma of his suicide attempt. But the time hadn't been right. It remained under plastic on the back deck of Curt's Laurel Canyon home, gathering dust. Every time he took off the cover, he felt the same paralyzing depression and fear that had become a regular part of his life since Darren's death.

Now he was ready for another try. The bicycle had been wiped down, the tires inflated, and while seeing it still brought back agonizing memories, he felt stronger now.

Curt told himself that it was time. That he could manage the execrable images that had swirled in his mind, tormenting him: That day, riding his bike up through the overgrown brush of the fire service road; gazing down from the bluff at his house tucked into a corner of the serpentine canyon; believing that the vodka and Seconal would lift him from himself, from his memories. He now remembered only snatches of those moments, seeing himself hollow and without dimension, like a kite floating above the canyon. Then looking back at his own body, a motionless shell, sprawled on the bluff amid the weeds and tall grass, the empty beer bottles and rusted car parts. Like something thrown out the window of a passing car, or left by the side of the road. Useless. Wasted.

The nightmare had stayed with him: The deceptive feeling of ending; the sense of unfathomable defeat when he awoke in the hospital and realized he had, once again, failed at what he'd set out to do. Then there was the struggle to regain some crumb of his former life, after it had become apparent that the suicide attempt was to be a onetime deal, and that his true punishment was to spend the remainder of his days walking the face of the earth branded not only for a life replete with mistakes and misjudgments, but also for his impotence at ending it.

Jamie had always been there. Just as she was now, standing inside the house looking through the sliding glass doors, watching him. Curt knew what she was thinking. He knew that she was fighting to remain calm, to project confidence in him, while in reality, she churned inside with the fear that once on the bike, he'd flash back to that moment five years ago.

Curt felt like rushing inside and taking her in his arms, squeezing her so tight that she'd almost break. He felt like telling her that he'd never leave her again, that it was only because of her love that he'd made it this far. He wanted to hold her and never let go, make her a part of him forever.

And then, seeing Jamie standing in her T-shirt and panties, holding a cup of coffee, watching him, he decided to do just that. He had already held back too much. He determined in that one quicksilver moment of recognition—when the millions of transitory experiences of a lifetime are suddenly and cataclysmically reduced to their essence, to the unavoidable and incredibly simple truth—that he would go to her, tell her of his love.

But when he looked up, the moment had passed. Jamie was gone. All that remained was the ephemeral picture of her in his mind, the muted hiss of the shower, and her soft melodic voice carrying out the bathroom window, echoing in the quiet stillness of the canyon.

Hector kept telling his little brother Juvenal that it was no big deal. What the judge had said about them being on probation and not breaking any laws, especially no more graffiti, was just words. It didn't mean anything.

They would never catch him again, that was for sure. It was only because Juvenal had run the wrong way and got caught by that cop that they'd arrested him. And Juvenal was so young, he didn't know that you didn't have to talk to the cops, even if they threatened you and started pushing you around.

But it was no big deal.

Just like stealing the Toyota was no big deal. Just like getting the old-timer to buy them a few six-packs at the 7-Eleven was no big deal.

Now he and Juvenal, and Loco and Little Spider and Flaco, could kick back behind the parking garage with the brews and wait for the traffic to die down. He had a job to finish, the one he'd been working on when they were busted. He was going to be famous, his name would be on the freeway sign in giant letters for all his homeboys to see.

It was nearly two in the morning when the five of them had finished the beer. Hector and Flaco climbed up the pole that supported the overhanging steel freeway sign, maneuvering their way onto the narrow platform that ran its length.

From where he stood at the edge of the sign, Hector could see the Golden State Freeway stretching past Griffith Park into downtown. By turning and pressing his back against the steel sign supports, he could take in Burbank and the twinkling lights in the foothills to the east.

"You guys keep a lookout," he yelled to the others, who stood at the base of the support pole. "Spider, go down by the street, behind those bushes. If you see the cops, yell and start runnin', man."

Hector removed the cans of spray paint that he kept inside the canvas bag that hung from his belt. His name was already there in large block letters from the last time. He took his time, as Flaco watched and handed him the cans.

"You gonna be famous, man. Like Chaka, ya know, man. Maybe even more famous than that."

Hector smiled. "Chaka's in jail, man," he said. "They say they gonna keep the dude there forever."

"You shittin' me?" said Flaco. "Cops gotta do somethin', man. Can't keep the dude locked up forever. Shee-it, man, he gotta right to go to court, don't he?"

Hector just nodded. He liked the feeling of standing high over the freeway in the cool night air. Out there for anyone to see, like those trapeze guys he'd seen on television.

Hector said, "Chaka's lawyer says he's crazy. Can't try no crazy guy."

"Chaka ain't crazy, Hector. Not that dude. Fuckin name's all over the place. My cousin lives up in San Luis Obispo, man. Fuckin' Chaka got his name big as shit on a water tower a few miles from my cousin's house. Chaka's famous, man. He ain't crazy."

Hector had two more letters to go. He was filling in the outline of the letters with day-glow red paint so that it would reflect off the headlights of the cars at night. He wasn't paying close attention to Flaco.

Hector already knew all about Chaka. Chaka was the most famous of all the taggers. His tag was everywhere, from San Diego to San Francisco. They finally caught him, but not before he'd placed his name on everything from freeway signs to water towers to what seemed like half the mailboxes in L.A. And that wasn't even counting all the bus benches and buildings.

But now Chaka was in jail. The TV said he'd flipped out, gone berserk after they put him in a cell. Hector knew that jail could do that to you. Hector had been in the Hall a few times himself. He didn't like it, and was determined never to return.

Finishing the last letter, Hector said, "Okay, man. Let's split."

The two boys gathered the unused spray cans and put them back inside the bag, leaving the used cans on the steel platform to eventually blow off in the wind onto some unsuspecting driver.

About twenty minutes later, Hector and the others found themselves with another couple of six-packs out behind the parking garage again. From where they were, they could see Hector's name in large red letters, outlined in black, on the back of the sign that overhung the freeway.

Juvenal said, "I'm goin' up with you next time, man. I'm gonna be famous too."

The others laughed and tugged on the end of their beers.

Hector could feel the beer filling his stomach and making his head spin. He felt good, and a little crazy. Like a celebrity, a movie star with his name in lights. He felt he could stay there forever, looking at his name. He was famous now. Maybe not as famous as Chaka, but that would come pretty soon. And at least *he* wasn't in jail.

"I gotta take a piss," Hector said, standing.

He stumbled through the brush and debris at the back of the garage, looking for a good place. After walking about twenty yards, he stepped between two bushes, unzipped his pants, and started to urinate. He could hear the laughter of the others and the sound of broken glass as they threw the empty bottles against the side of the garage.

Hector had finished and was zipping his pants when he saw something funny in the darkness on the other side of the bushes. He took a few steps closer, cursing himself for stepping in his own piss.

"Jesus!" he muttered, bending to get a closer look. Then he said "Jesus" again, but much softer this time. He thought about calling the others. He knew what he was looking at. He'd seen the pictures on the TV.

But they said they'd caught the guy?

Hector shoved the bush to the side and held it there with his shoe. There was a funny smell, like cheese that had gone bad. The knife was there, just like in the pictures. And so was the red cape, crumpled and draped over the face.

Hector felt something turn in his stomach, then found himself bent over, retching the beer from his system. When he finished, all he could think of was how he hoped that nobody had seen him throw up.

And how he'd act really cool, like the dead guy was no big deal, when he told the others about it.

Three

She would go conservative. At least conservative for her. After all, it wasn't every day that she had the chief of police on the hot seat.

And even though it was taped and she'd agreed to let Francis Powell and his press people put in their two cents as to what to include and what to cut from the interview, Crystal knew that the final decision would be hers, and that when it came time for the final cut, there wouldn't be any juicy parts that found their way to the cutting room floor, chief or no chief.

So she took one last glance at herself in the dressing room mirror before heading for the set.

She had, she thought, chosen her outfit wisely. She didn't want to shock Francis Powell. On the contrary, making him relax, feel comfortable, not threatened, was her goal. Some might say she was setting him up for the kill.

She wore a black merino wool ribbed tank top that accentuated her breasts, revealing only the hint of nipple. Her medallion-printed brocade skirt was a metallic rayon and fit snugly over her hips and thighs. It was cut high enough that when she sat during the interview, the side slit would show just enough leg to keep her male viewers interested, even if the chief proved to be a bore. A velvet blazer, to pick up the purple highlights in the skirt, finished off the outfit and provided the token gesture toward a businesslike appearance.

"Francis," she said, offering her hand as she approached the grouping of chair and couch and coffee table that served as her set. Francis Powell was already seated on the couch.

"I see you've been taken care of. Is there anything else I can get for you? Coffee?"

Powell shook his head No.

"Are you comfortable?

"About as comfortable as I can be," he said.

Two stage hands fiddled with a microphone clipped to his lapel.

"Just before we start . . ." said Powell. "This is taped, right? I mean, we'll have the chance to go over everything before it airs, just like we agreed?"

Crystal smiled, then took a sip of coffee from a mug that had been placed on the table in front of her.

"Of course," she said, hiding her expression while looking over the edge of the mug. She had a twinkle in her eye that Powell missed.

"Good," grumbled Powell, looking stiff and uncomfortable.

One of Powell's aides whispered something in his ear, then walked to the edge of the set to watch. The director counted down, then motioned for Crystal to begin.

"Good evening, ladies and gentlemen. Tonight's guest is Los Angeles Chief of Police Francis Powell." Crystal nodded toward Powell. "Thank you, Chief, for taking a few moments from your busy day to be with us tonight."

Powell smiled and said, "My pleasure, Crystal."

The aide had whispered for him to remember to smile and to use Crystal's first name as often as possible. They had talked about it in the limo on the way to the studio. The aide had said that it would make him look warmer, less like the cardboard figure that the media liked to portray.

"Now, Chief, I suppose there isn't a resident of this city, by this time, who isn't aware that your department has captured Daniel Lopez and that Mr. Lopez has been charged with the Metro Matador murders. You should be proud of the hard work that your Matador Task Force has done over the past months. I know, speaking for everyone at *Real News*, that we all feel a lot more comfortable about walking the streets now that the Matador is securely behind bars."

Powell smiled. He wasn't quite sure what to say, whether there was a question pending or not. It seemed to him that Crystal Pelotas had paused, inviting his response. And he didn't want to seem like the hard-edged cardboard figure that the aide had warned him about.

"Well, thank you, Crystal. I am very relieved that after months of hard, conscientious police work, we have finally solved this heinous case. Now, of course, I am limited in what I can say at this time, since the suspect is still pending trial and—"

"Excuse me, Chief, but that's a subject that I wanted to touch on with you."

She had interrupted him with a slight wave of her hand. After she'd done it, Powell realized that he should have kept talking and finished his statement. Now he was beginning to feel that he had somehow been placed on the defensive. There was an aspect of Crystal Pelotas' expression that he'd caught—a raising of the eyebrow, an anxious twitch at the corner of her mouth—that he found unsettling.

Crystal said, "There have been reports circulating, merely unconfirmed rumors at this time, but still enough of them to demand some attention, that Mr. Lopez is perhaps the wrong man. That the Metro Matador is still somewhere out there, perhaps having himself a good laugh at the expense of the D.A.'s Office and your department."

Powell felt his heartbeat pick up. He told himself to remain calm, yet he suddenly felt uncomfortable and began to adjust his position on the couch. He felt something lightly tickle his temple and hoped it was merely a stray wisp of hair and not a bead of sweat.

He said, "I'm not sure who your sources are, Crystal." The repetition of her name clicked in his mind and made him feel better, like he was back on the right track. "But let me take this opportunity to assure you and your viewers that we have every confidence in the fact that the Metro Matador murders are over, and that as a result of the concerted efforts of the Los Angeles Police and Sheriff's Departments, we have arrested the proper suspect."

Powell paused, unsure whether he should elaborate. Something inside told him to hold it right there, that he was right on the edge. Yet he saw a look of expectation in Crystal Pelotas' face, like there was more to his answer that everybody expected.

"Mr. Lopez," he said, answering that look of expectation, "we are convinced, *is* the Metro Matador. I have no doubt that he will be convicted of the Matador murders."

Powell flashed a quick smile, then nodded his head as if to signal that he had spoken the final word on the subject. He was too pleased with his response to notice his aide, standing off to the side, wincing at his boss's last statement.

Crystal, smelling blood, said, "And, Chief, do you expect this to be a quick trial? Do you expect Mr. Lopez will receive the death penalty for his horrendous crimes?"

By this time, Powell sensed that he might have taken his last comments too far.

"Well, Crystal, as you know, Mr. Lopez will have his day in court. I don't want to prejudice his trial. I'm sure you're aware of the many defenses and appeals that criminal defendants and their lawyers have at their disposal. I don't want to be accused at some later point of having prejudiced Mr. Lopez's ability to obtain a fair and impartial jury." Powell paused. He could see his aide nodding in agreement.

Crystal said, "But, and I'll leave it at this, you are convinced, are you not, that the residents of this city need no longer fear being attacked by the Metro Matador? You can at least assure us of that, can you not?"

Powell paused only a moment. "Yes," he said. "That I definitely can do."

Crystal swiveled a quarter-turn away from Powell toward the camera.

"Well, thank you, Chief Powell, for your comments. You heard the chief, ladies and gentlemen. The Metro Matador has slain his last innocent victim, and while we should all be cautious of the dangers of big-city life, we can rest a little easier this night knowing that our chief of police is right on top of things."

"All right, cut."

Crystal removed her microphone and handed it to the stage hand.

"Great interview, Crystal." Colin Archer nodded toward his star, then turned to Powell. "It went well, Chief. Don't you think?"

"Uh, yes. Sort of stumbled a little there at the beginning. But I suppose we can edit all that out later?"

Colin Archer hesitated for a moment, flashing an inquiring look at Crystal, then said, "Uh, yeah, no problem. It'll all come out looking smooth as English cream by the time we air."

"Good," muttered Powell. "About that business concerning Lopez and his trial . . . I'd like to take another look at that on tape before we finish here. I'd hate to think that I said something that might cause this trial to be moved to another county. I mean, it probably wasn't that bad, but it doesn't take much for these damn defense lawyers to start ranting and raving about not being able to get an unbiased jury. Jesus, if they can do it when Reagan and Bush open their mouths, they sure won't hesitate when it comes to me."

Archer waited for Crystal to respond. He looked like he wanted no part of the current discussion; a not-entirely-committed coconspirator.

Crystal said, "This won't air until tomorrow evening, Francis. We'll get the final taped version to your office in time for your review. Just call us and let us know what you might want streamlined or modified. How's that?"

Both Powell and the aide nodded their approval.

Crystal watched as Powell and his entourage left the set. A few moments later, she found herself back in her dressing room on the telephone.

"Got something you might be able to use."

Crystal recognized the voice as one of her runners, one of the group of people who provided her with information, story tips. She paid for the information whether she ended up using it or not, insuring that the tips flowed to her regularly, and not to her competition. In this way she kept her informants on a string by doling out minor favors and small amounts of cash.

"Go ahead," she said. She was touching up her makeup, flicking at her eyelids with a tiny black-bristled brush.

"They found another body," the voice said. "Near a parking garage off the Golden State. We were bird-dogging one of the Task Force units. You know, trying to get something on Lopez. They got called to the scene, and we followed. Before they roped off the place and kicked everyone out, I saw the body. Just like the others, the gunshot to the head, the knife, the cape, the whole thing. It was the Matador, no doubt about that. I think the cops were a little embarrassed, us being there after they made such a big deal about catching Lopez."

Crystal said, "You're sure about the knife and cape?"

The interview with Francis Powell was being played back in her mind. She had that tingling feeling, like an electrical current being released in her chest, that she always got just prior to a big story breaking.

"Jesus, Crystal. Give me some credit. It was the Matador, just like the others. I knew it, the cops knew it. That's why they were in such a hurry to get us out of there."

"You didn't by any chance manage to snap off a few pictures before they closed up shop?"

"We tried, believe me, we tried. I don't think we got much, though. As soon as they saw the body they started moving us out. Maybe something from a distance. I don't know, we're working on the roll now."

Crystal said, "Get the pictures to me as soon as they're ready."

"Uh, sure, Crystal. No problem."

There was a short pause in the conversation. Crystal knew what was coming next.

Her informant broke the silence: "This is worth a lot, wouldn't ya say?"

Crystal was not thinking about the informant. She saw herself doing a live spot at the end of the show. She saw herself announcing to her millions of viewers that what they'd just heard from Francis Powell about capturing the Metro Matador just might not be true. She would then relate the story of the Matador's most recent victim, maybe use some of the still photographs, announcing to the world that the Metro Matador was still out there, preying on the innocent citizens of Los Angeles.

"Yes," she whispered into the telephone, "It is worth a *lot* of money."

"Your comment didn't do us much good, Francis."

"Otto, I don't see how what I said to Pelotas makes much difference right now. They'd be out there like piranha at feeding time whether I said what I said or not."

Otto Durning District Attorney, looked away from Powell, toward the press room that was rapidly filling with reporters and equipment. The image that struck him was not of piranha. Something more like African killer bees with an attitude. He knew that Powell was right, that his comment hadn't helped matters, but probably had made little difference. Pelotas would have broken the story about the Matador's latest victim, and it would have had the same frenzied effect, whether Powell's interview had run or not.

Still, it was something they'd have to deal with during the press conference and beyond, at least until the media and their simple-witted stepchild, the viewing public, were convinced that this latest murder was merely a copy-cat crime and not the work of the Metro Matador.

Durning had confidential information that, had he been able to reveal it to the public and the press, would go far in eliminating the Matador as a suspect in this most recent killing.

The victim had been an affluent attorney, which was a change of pace for the Matador, whose previous victims tended to run to the middle and lower-middle classes.

But that wasn't the main point of distinction. While the victim had been found with a single gunshot wound to the head, like the others, the attorney's tongue had been removed, cut out, which was something totally new. The knife in the neck and the red cape were there, but it was the tongue, Durning felt, that was the telling distinction.

Besides, Durning was sure that Daniel Lopez was the Matador. It was more than just the feeling of a thirty-year veteran in law enforcement. Lopez matched the artist's composite, and he had not presented anyone with a reliable alibi for the dates in question.

Whoever it was that had taken on the Matador's identity for this killing, Durning surmised, had decided to disclose a bit of himself, to ad-lib. Removing the tongue was the sort of thing that serial psychos thought was cute. Something they could read and hear about in the media. It was a signature act of bravado, like an artist signing a painting. But more important to Durning and Powell, it was something that could provide them with a motive and a possible suspect.

"No mention of the tongue, right?"

Powell shook his head. "It's all we've got to filter out the crazies who are going to come out of the woodwork now claiming they're the Matador."

"I'd like to mention the tongue," said Durning, frustrated. "Just to shut those bastards out there up. They're gonna jump all over us, Francis, yelling and screaming that we arrested the wrong guy." He wiped a hand over his face. "Jesus. I can just imagine what Lopez's lawyer is going to do with this."

"A united front," said Powell. "Come on, Otto. Let's get this over with."

Both men walked from the short hallway into the press room, which was ablaze with lights. Two chairs were set up at a small Formica-covered table that was partially covered with electrical cable of various sizes. More cable snaked from the microphones mounted atop an adjacent podium onto the floor, where it was haphazardly taped to the linoleum.

The initial entry of the two men brought an explosion of flashes from the army of still photographers. A half-dozen voices shouted questions at the same time. Powell sat down, took a deep breath, then crossed his legs.

They'd decided that Otto Durning would give a short preliminary statement and then would field all questions that weren't specifically addressed to Powell. The room became a sea of waving arms. The press were like anxious schoolchildren stretching their hands in the air to get their teacher's attention.

"Before I answer any questions," said Durning. "I'd like to make a short statement."

There was a low-level groan from the audience as the reporters lowered their hands and listened. Someone in the back was rattling one of the folding metal chairs that had been set up for the conference, and two reporters in the second row were jockeying each other for position.

"Most of you know that yesterday the body of a thirty-eight-year-old male Caucasion was discovered near the Griffith Park area adjacent to the Golden State Freeway.

The body has been indentified as that of Brad Philbin. Mr. Philbin was a local attorney whose offices were located near where the body was found.

"While there are certain similarities between Mr. Philbin's death and the crimes attributed to the person you of the press have termed the Metro Matador, there are also substantial differences. I am not at this time at liberty to specify those differences for obvious reasons. The investigation into Mr. Philbin's death is ongoing. Suffice it to say that we are convinced that Mr. Philbin's death is a separate incident, and not, I repeat, *not* related to the Metro Matador investigation."

Durning paused, girding himself for the expected onslaught.

"I'll now take a question or two," he said.

Half of the reporters in the room jumped to their feet, yelling. The flashes popped again in unison, disorienting him. It was like looking into a bank of lights at a sporting event. Durning pointed to a female in the front row.

"My question," said the reporter, a petite brunette that Durning didn't personally know but recognized from one of the local news shows, "is directed to Chief Powell."

Durning told himself to remain steady. He fought off the almost uncontrollable urge to audibly groan. He had been surprised at Powell's gaff with Pelotas. It was the type of thing that a seasoned politico like the chief should have seen coming. It made him think twice about trying to play nice guy with the media, about going out on any limbs himself.

The reporter continued, "Chief, most of us saw your recent interview with Crystal Pelotas on *Real News for Real People*. I was wondering if, as a result of this latest victim being discovered, you are still as confident that you actually have the Metro Matador in custody? Doesn't this open up the possibility that you've arrested the wrong man, and that Daniel Lopez is not the Matador?"

Powell, still seated, looked up at Durning. In that split-second, they each understood that their worst fears were about to come true. An entire city had been held hostage for nearly a year. The capture of a suspect had given everyone a chance to catch their breath. Things were just starting to slow down. They could actually go to a dinner party now and discuss something other than the Metro Matador.

And now this.

Powell got up and took Durning's place at the podium. He looked directly at the audience for a moment, then at the brunette. "Barbara," he said, grateful that he remembered the reporter's name. At that moment, had Crystal Pelotas been in the room, Powell felt he could have very calmly and dispassionately strangled her with his bare hands. He tried to push such felonious thoughts from his mind.

"I will merely reiterate what Otto Durning has just told you. The two investigations are separate and ongoing. There is no reason to believe that this latest murder is the work of the Matador."

Durning moved toward Powell, placing a hand on the chief's back.

"Now ladies and gentlemen," he said, gently nudging Powell toward the hallway and out of the room, "if you'll excuse us, there are things that both Chief Powell and I have to see to."

Both men headed for the door, trying not to notice the expressions of shock and disappointment. Questions flew at them from across the room. Durning turned quickly, just before backing out, and said, "We'll provide you with a written statement within the hour."

With that, both Powell and Durning exited the room to the media's screams and shouted questions, most of which sounded more like threats.

He could see on the television that they were unsure of themselves. Powell and Durning and the rest of them.

They wanted to sound like they knew what they were doing, like they had everything under control. But he could tell by their faces, the way Powell hurried away from the reporters, that they were worried.

That made him feel good.

They had looked so arrogant when Lopez was caught. They'd demeaned the Matador, not acknowledging his accomplishments, not respecting the opponent whose craftiness they'd underestimated from the beginning.

Now Powell and Durning were feeling the pressure being screwed down on them, and as far as Nestor Stokes was concerned, that was just fine.

Nestor changed the channel on the small portable TV that he'd brought to work.

The building had been set up with surveillance cameras on each floor, each camera feeding into a central console at the security desk in the lobby. From where he was seated, Nestor could view each floor of the building by merely punching a button. The video surveillance was a godsend on those nights when he just didn't feel up to actually walking each floor. He was supposed to do that at least twice each shift, but he, along with the other guys who worked the night shift at the Century Bank Building, always fudged that part. It was easier to sit behind the desk and let the cameras do the walking. Besides, nothing ever happened at night. The most difficult thing was trying to stay awake.

On the TV they were showing an old movie with Clint Eastwood as Dirty Harry. Nestor's thoughts were still on the Matador, and the press conference of Powell and Durning.

He had seen Powell's interview with Crystal Pelotas earlier, and was surprised at how Powell could have been so stupid as to paint himself into a corner.

Crystal had done that, though. Nestor understood how that worked. One look at her, Nestor thought, and like Francis Powell, he too might have lost his senses and started babbling something stupid, mesmerized by her beauty.

A commercial for an attorney appeared on the television. A face flashed on the screen saying, "Gerald Isaacs got me 1.3 million." Then another with a Spanish accent: "Geraldo Isaacs won seven hundred and fifty thousand dollars for me." Nestor recognized the attorney as the one Crystal had interviewed a few days before. Nestor had seen the attorney's ads on television, and wondered what the sleazy lawyer had paid those people to lie for him on TV.

Nestor was sure they were paid. It was just like lawyers, he thought, to try something underhanded like that. Anything to get your trust then take your money. To Nestor they were all crooked, immoral, money-hungry vultures.

Nestor pushed the chair back from the desk. He slowly walked toward the bank of elevators. The building's directory took up an entire wall near the elevator doors. He methodically went down the list of names. He knew where the lawyer's name was, but he liked to work his way there slowly, thinking about what he would do and how he would do it.

When he reached the T's, he stopped.

TAYLOR & CROCKETT, A PROFESSIONAL LAW CORPORA-
TION.

Then he saw the lawyer's name below that, in a group
of twenty or thirty others. The lawyer was an associate in
the law firm, or so the directory specified.

It was cool and quiet in the lobby. The only noise was
the regular ticking of the clock in the marble-faced wall,
and the muted sound of Clint Eastwood coming from the
TV.

What would Dirty Harry do in this situation, Nestor
wondered?

*Probably blow the slimebucket a frontal asshole with his .44
magnum, the most powerful handgun made.*

Nestor chuckled, then shaped his hand into a gun,
pointed it at the elevator doors, and said, "Go ahead,
make my day."

Yeah, that was it. That's how Harry would handle the
lawyer.

Nestor ran the attorney's name through his mind, letting his thoughts drift back over the three years since he'd
last spoken to the lawyer.

It was at the state bar hearing. The lawyer had been
there represented by another lawyer. All of the hearing
officers, the judges, were lawyers. They had all seemed to
know each other, to be friends.

Or maybe that was just in his mind?

Nestor had read his complaint at the hearing, not wanting to look at the lawyer or the judges. He had wanted to
get it all right, perfectly clear, because he thought once
they heard what the lawyer had done, the case would be
over. He would win and the lawyer would be punished.

Nestor told the judges of his invention, a special process
for injecting plastic, and of taking his invention to the
lawyer. He said that the lawyer guaranteed him that he

would obtain a patent, and that Nestor could be assured that he and he alone would realize the fruits of his labors.

Nestor then related the story of how the lawyer had sold the invention to a local company for a paltry few hundred dollars, telling Nestor that it was worth only that, and that despite his efforts, nobody was willing to pay more.

"Take the money," the lawyer had said, adding that he was waiving his usual fee because he felt so badly about not making Nestor rich.

Nestor remembered how his voice had cracked as he told the judges of his discovery a year later that his invention was earning the company millions, and that the lawyer was now a vice president of the company, the same company that had cheated him of his invention.

At the hearing, Nestor had been sure that everyone would agree with him. That it was all just a formality. That justice would prevail.

But then the lawyer spoke. He spoke through his attorney, who told the judges a lie. All of the facts were changed. The truth got lost in the prevarications and slimey-smooth lawyer-talk.

And Nestor's former lawyer had just sat there, not saying a word. He didn't have to argue, or get angry or impatient with the stupidity and shortsightedness of the court. He looked confident, like he'd known the outcome all along.

The lawyer had even offered Nestor his hand in some mock gesture of reconciliation after the decision was rendered. As if, now that some review board, some tribunal of lawyers protecting their own, had stamped the kangaroo-court proceedings with their imprimature of legitimacy, his theft, the lawyer's rape of what rightfully belonged to Nestor Stokes, had never happened. A dream. Some horrendous misunderstanding, but a misunderstanding at best.

Now, staring at the name on the directory, Nestor felt better. His careful planning was about to pay off. He'd take it slowly, though. After all, the lawyer wasn't going anywhere. The time had to be absolutely right, he had to feel it in his blood.

Like he had with the drunk driver's lawyer.

It had surprised him, that godly feeling of retribution, revenge, and righteousness. He hadn't planned on that. An unexpected bonus. Like coming home from the store with a bag of groceries and finding a package of steaks inside that you hadn't paid for.

Now revenge was all that Nestor thought of. It was as if the lawyers continued to exist for that purpose, and that purpose only. Revenge for the months he'd spent alone in the convalescent hospital. The doctors had said that he was severely depressed. That the patent lawyer and the hearing had put him over the edge. He remembered getting into a fight with that clerk in the supermarket, but could no longer remember why. They'd forced him into the convalescent home because he'd lost it, flipped out. Mentally unstable, they'd said.

Even now he had those same feelings every once in a while. Like he was on the edge of the volcano about to jump in, and not really giving a damn what happened.

The clock ticked off its seconds, marking time like a death watch. There would come a moment, Nestor told himself, when he'd know that the lawyer was his.

Nestor read over the name one more time: "Taylor & Crockett."

It made him smile.

Just like Dirty Harry would smile right before he gave the bad guys a frontal asshole.

Four

"And what did he say, Officer, when you asked him about the pager?"

The D.A. stood to the left of the undercover narcotics officer, between the witness and the jury box. At the counsel table sat a young black man formally dressed in a charcoal gray suit with pale ivory pinstripes, a freshly starched monogrammed white shirt, paisley tie, and matching gray woven leather shoes that looked like a cross between expensive Italian leather slip-ons and Mexican sandals. The young black defendant wore no socks, showing only dark, coffee-colored skin, like satin, at the ankle. His hair was cropped in a short afro, clean cut, except for a three-inch ponytail, tied with a sequined red rubber band, that hung down the back of his neck. A pair of burgundy Vuarnet sunglasses with mirrored lenses dangled casually from the pocket of his suit coat.

"Objection, your honor. I fail to see the relevance of any response my client may have given this witness. In addition, I would point out to the court that at this point in the officer's testimony there are definite Miranda problems."

The attorney remained standing at the counsel table

awaiting the judge's response. Curt looked over from his seat at the other end of the table. The public defender making the objection stood before the court dressed in a pair of faded stone-washed Levis. He wore a red-green madras shirt under a tattered copper-colored corduroy jacket with patches on the elbows. The top button of his shirt was open, showing a healthy sprig of squirrely brown chest hair. A wrinkled dark-blue knit tie, loosely knotted at the collar, separated in an inverted V and hung down over his chest and pot belly. Mousy brown hair, lighter than what was thrusting its way up from his chest, dangled in ringlets over his ears and shirt collar.

As he spoke, the public defender gestured, jabbing his finger in the direction of the witness. His head jerked backward every time his finger jabbed at the air, as if there were an invisible piece of elastic connecting head to finger.

Curt sat at the counsel table eyeing the young black man who exuded an air of calm confidence just short of arrogance, absentmindedly picking at the sole of one of his imported leather loafers. Curt thought that somebody just walking into court and unfamiliar with all the players would probably figure the defendant in the suit as the lawyer and the P.D. as his client. An honest mistake.

"Mr. Stein," said the judge, weighing each word, speaking slowly and building up speed as he spoke. "I fail to see how a person with your great . . . *expertise,* shall we say, cannot appreciate the relevance of the paging device in question. This is a sale-of-cocaine case, is it not?"

"But your honor—"

"Mr. Stein, please take your seat."

The judge turned to the D.A., who had been resting against the rail separating the jury box from the rest of the courtroom, whispering and laughing in hushed tones with the defense attorneys who were seated in the jury box waiting for their cases to be called.

"Please continue, Mr. Feller. I'll hear the witness's answer, subject to a motion to strike should I agree with Mr. Stein that the evidence is irrelevant."

"Do you remember the question?" asked the D.A., looking at the witness.

"Yes, sir," said the officer. He referred to a crumpled police report that he held in his hands. Part reading and part ad-libbing, he said: "When I asked the defendant why he carried the beeper, he said so that he wouldn't be late for dinner."

The few people seated in the audience section of the courtroom began to laugh. There was also a slight titter from the attorneys and police officers seated in the jury box.

With feigned incredulity, mimicking the public defender's finger gesturing, the D.A. asked: "He said 'so that he wouldn't be late for dinner'?"

"That's right." The undercover narc, sporting a three-day growth of beard, wiped a smile from his face with the back of his right hand. But just as quickly as the smirk disappeared, it returned. The narc looked away from the counsel table toward the carpeted courtroom floor and cleared his throat, attempting to regain his composure. "Excuse me," he mumbled, adjusting his seat in the witness box.

The narc continued: "He said that his mama wanted to be sure that he was home on time. That's why he wore the pager on his belt."

Curt rolled his eyes. He looked at the defendant, who was trying very hard not to laugh. The judge looked down at the public defender, smiled, then shook his head slowly back and forth.

"May I take this witness on *voir dire,* your honor?" The public defender had shot straight up from his chair and was gesturing with his finger once more. He was the only one in the courtroom without a smile on his face.

"Be my guest, Mr. Stein," said the judge, leaning back in his chair and clasping his hands behind his neck.

"What type of pager was this, Officer?" barked the public defender, moving quickly around the counsel table toward the witness.

"A Motorola, digital display with tone. Twenty-four-hour capability, with a vibrator option," said the cop. The smirk returned. The narc readjusted his position in the wooden chair, shooting his arms, both at the same time, from the sleaves of the faded denim jacket he was wearing. He'd been in the middle of an undercover investigation involving one of the local motorcycle gangs when he received the call to come to court. Aside from the heavy black beard-stubble, the narcotics officer sported a small gold hoop in the lobe of his left ear. Underneath the denim jacket, which was emblazoned with the skull and crossbones insignia of the biker club, he wore a pale yellow nylon tank top with the words "Fuck You Asshole," stencilled in biker-script across the chest. The narc held the denim jacket closed in front so that all you could see was the "You Ass" part of the tank top.

The witness decided to take a chance, sensing that the P.D. was wading into unknown waters. During a pause in the questioning, he volunteered: "It's the beeper of preference, you might say. Among street dealers in the greater Los Angeles area, that is. It's got a vibrating option that allows them to turn off the beep if they're in the middle of a sale, or"—the cop smiled toward the D.A., then back at the public defender—"if they feel they're being surveilled by undercover."

"Motion to strike," shouted the P.D. He was pointing again. "That answer is totally nonresponsive, your honor."

"Very well, Mr. Stein. Everything after 'vibrating option' will be stricken. By the way, Officer . . ." The judge rocked himself forward in his chair and leaned toward the witness. "Did this beeper ever go off during the time you were arresting the defendant?"

"Yes, your honor. My partner and I turned it back on audio beep and the thing went crazy. The digital display lit up like a Christmas tree. We called the first few numbers back."

"And was it the defendant's mother, Officer, on the other end of the phone, paging him for dinner?" The judge let his wire-rim glasses drop to the tip of his nose and peered over the frames at the counsel table. He smiled benignly down at the public defender as the witness gave his answer.

"No, sir, it was not. They were different people calling the defendant, your honor. Each said they were looking for a dove."

"And," said the judge, "for the benefit of Mr. Stein and the court record, Officer, can you tell us what a 'dove' is?"

"It's the street name for rock cocaine, your honor."

"Thank you, Officer. Mr. Stein, do you have any *further* questions?"

"Uh, not at this time, your honor."

"Very well," said the judge, shuffling some paperwork in front of him. "I find that the People have presented sufficient probable cause to hold the defendant to answer in superior court. The motion to suppress is denied. Mr. Denmark, are you going to follow this case?"

Curt looked first at the judge, then at the D.A. He raised his palms upward.

"The defense has no further need for Mr. Denmark," said the P.D. "I will note though, your honor, that the presence of Officer Jack Kempton will be required for the adjudication. My client intends to assert that his constitutional rights were intentionally and violently violated by Officer Kempton shortly after his arrest."

"Fuckin' crazy asshole," mumbled the young black man under his breath. Only Curt heard him.

"We'll make sure that Officer Kempton is available for the next hearing," said the judge. Curt got up and motioned toward the D.A.

"Kempton's on medical leave, I think," whispered Curt. "Went I.O.D. shortly after he arrested this dipshit."

"Don't sweat it," said the D.A. "Let Stein rant and rave all he wants. He's not going anywhere with that constitutional rights bullshit. Though, I can sorta see his point on this one. Seems like Kempton put this asshole's head through a plate glass window. That's the real reason they got the guy's beeper."

Curt shook his head in disbelief, though he believed every word of the story. He'd known Jack Kempton off and on over the last twenty years. They'd crossed paths years ago during several homicide cases where Curt was the court-appointed defense counsel. The last case they'd had together was during one of Curt's special-prosecutor stints for Internal Affairs. They hadn't talked much since then.

The only reason Curt was in court this day was because he'd been investigating some of the Administrative Narcotics officers making buys in the Mid-Valley area and was listed as the investigating officer on a few busts just to make the paperwork look legit. There had been reports that cash and dope were missing from the station evidence locker and that some of it had never actually found its way there. The suspicion was that the cops were selling it on the street themselves. As the chief's legal affairs liaison, Curt had been asked to look into the allegations on the Q.T., under the guise of a routine Internal Affairs investigation.

The D.A. said: "This asshole voluntarily absents himself from the jurisdiction for nearly two years, then has his lawyer talk some referee into releasing him pending the preliminary hearing because his poor mother is supposedly near death in some hospital. Total bullshit, pure and simple. My guess is that Stein will stretch this thing out as long as possible hoping that the evidence will disappear or the wits will die.

"Or the narc who made the bust gets indicted."

Curt let his comment remain there for a moment, watching the D.A.'s reaction. The D.A.'s Office had already been forced to dismiss over twenty drug cases due to the indictment of a half-dozen narcotics officers in federal court. It had been front-page news for over a month, and the downtown brass still squirmed whenever it was mentioned. Now that the cases were coming to trial, the whole thing was being dredged up once again by the media.

"Yeah," muttered the prosecutor. "And all the time this jerkoff will be out on the streets making more money on a bad day than either of us will ever see in a month!"

Curt tossed his paperwork back into the manila file folder and headed for the public telephones in the hallway. He was glad to be finally clearing up the loose ends of his job with Internal Affairs. Once this case, and a couple others, finished winding their way through the courts, his business with Internal Affairs and L.A.P.D. would be finished. Not that the chief had let him leave without first extracting a promise to make himself available should his services be needed in the future. Curt was glad to make his friend that promise.

But now, Curt had decided to take some time off from the cops and Internal Affairs, and go back to the private practice of law, at least part time. He'd determined not to get caught up in the rat race of taking every case that walked through his office door, like he had before. And he'd decided to play it low-key, opting not to take an office in one of the high-rises on the boulevard, but instead to operate out of his home in Laurel Canyon, midway between the San Fernando Valley and West Hollywood. It was one of those old canyon boxes on stilts that were quickly being replaced by scores of guard-gated mansions and luxury condo communities carved into the hillside.

In the corridor outside the court, a young child sat on the other side of the hallway. Curt stood at the pay phone, receiver in hand, listening to the rings, waiting for the tape-recorded message. The child held a large burrito in both hands and every time she took a bite, a lump of mushy brown goop would squirt out the other end. The child's mother sat on a wooden bench next to her, rocking an infant in her arms, oblivious to the mess her daughter was creating.

Curt pressed in his code numbers and listened to the tape rewinding, then to the messages played back. First, a broker from Dean Witter who'd been badgering him to buy mutual funds. Next, a voice that he didn't immediately recognize, with a name that he did. Richard Lassar, a friend of a friend, asking to meet with him about a "spot of trouble that he'd fallen into." Those were his words. Curt connected the voice and the name with the face. White, middle-aged, like himself. Business suit. Accountant. The spot of trouble was probably a deuce. The accountant had probably gone to a party, had a few too many, then got popped by the Chippies driving home. Blow into the machine: Wham, you're guilty!

The third message came while he was still thinking about the second. He missed the first few words, and once he realized who it was, cursed himself for never having learned how to rewind and relisten to the tape once he'd played back the message. Francis Powell, the chief of police, was inviting him to lunch. Hell, inviting wasn't really the right word. Ordering him was more like it. Command performances were the chief's specialty. Powell wanting a word over a sandwich and a beer, purchased by the chief, could only mean one thing. Curt sighed, wondering what favor Francis wanted from him this time.

Art's Deli on Ventura Boulevard in Studio City was famous for its sky-high pastrami and corned beef sandwiches, the crowds at lunch, and the total indifference of its waitresses. When Curt walked through the door late Thursday morning, the breakfast regulars had already filtered out. A group of retired studio workers traded war stories and sipped coffee near the front window. Two college-age young men were wolfing down pancakes and eggs at the counter. One of the chefs had taken off his white hat and had come around from the grill to kibitz with the waitresses. A balding, overweight man with a neatly trimmed black beard stood at the cash register diligently counting money. Curt immediately spotted Francis Powell seated at a booth in the back.

"Hey, Curt. Thanks for coming down."

Powell put down the newspaper he'd been hovering over and shook hands. Black coffee in a heavy brown ceramic cup stood untouched near the table's edge.

"Keeping up with the bad news?" said Curt.

Powell muttered and shook his head. "Jesus, 'bad news' ain't the word for it." He flicked at the newspaper with his finger as he spoke. "Fucking paper! You'd think these guys'd give us a break every once in a while. Now they're starting all over with this Matador crap. It's that damn Pelotas and her bunch stirring up trouble. I know she's behind this. Man, if I could just get my hands on that bitch, I'd . . ." Powell was making choking gestures with his hands.

"Relax Francis. If it wasn't Crystal Pelotas, it'd be someone else. You gotta admit, this last murder really throws a monkey wrench into your otherwise smooth-running machine. And just when you figured you had Danny-Boy Lopez with one foot in the gas chamber."

Curt motioned to the three waitresses who were talking to each other behind the counter. He kept waving until he finally caught the attention of one of the women, who, with a resigned look, put her coffee down and slowly trudged her way to their table.

"I see," said Curt, "that the service in this place is still as good as ever."

Powell paused momentarily, then said, "Wha . . . ? Oh yeah." He glanced at the matronly woman approaching. "They must be union or something. Like they're doing you a favor by taking your order."

"What'll it be, hon?"

The woman, Curt guessed in her fifties, with hair the color of copper tubing, stood at the edge of the table staring down at her order pad. Her jaw moved in perfect rhythm, destroying a very large piece of gum. Curt was reminded of the talking cow he'd seen on a milk commercial on TV.

"Lox and eggs," said Curt. "Easy on the onions." He

looked to Powell, who was still consumed with the newspaper. "Francis. You want anything?"

"Uh, yeah." Powell looked away from the paper. "Maybe some toast. No, wait a minute. A bagel. Yeah, a bagel with cream cheese."

The waitress kept chewing as she repeated the order. "That all?" she said.

"Coffee, please," said Curt, handing her the menu.

After the waitress left, Powell said, "The thing that really gets me about all this is that I think Pelotas knows that Lopez is the Matador. I know the woman has sources inside the department. I don't know who, but rest assured, if I ever find out who's feeding her information, heads are going to fucking roll, you can be sure of that."

"You figure she's pushing this angle just for the publicity?"

"Exactly," said Powell. "Why else? She must know that we're sure Lopez is the one. I don't know what she knows about this lawyer's death, but if her sources aren't jacking her around, they must've told her that Lopez is still our man."

The waitress brought a cup of coffee and placed it on the table in front of Curt.

"What do you have on the attorney?"

Powell looked around quickly, then leaned over the table.

"Very similar to the Matador. You know, the knife in the neck, the cape . . . Guy was shot once in the forehead." Powell pointed to a spot on his face just above the bridge of his nose.

"Except," said Powell, "this time the victim's tongue was cut out."

Curt had the cup of coffee poised at his lips. He stopped blowing over the rim and put the cup down.

"A copycat?"

Powell nodded.

"Maybe the Matador's decided to branch out, be more creative?"

"Don't think so. Guy goes almost a year doing people. Same way every time. Never varies." Powell shook his head. "I don't think so. It ain't the same guy."

Curt sipped on his coffee.

"And there's more," said Powell. "Matador never used anything but a thirty-eight. Always a thirty-eight. The lawyer's got himself a new twenty-five-caliber eyeball."

"And you're holding back on the gun and the tongue?"

"Got to. We're already getting calls from every psycho wannabe serial killer in the city. Some of them we know and just kiss off. But it's still work, and I can't afford to have a couple guys wasting their time listening to all these crazy assholes that want to get their picture on TV."

Powell continued, "Now Pelotas is saying that our department isn't in the position to fairly evaluate this latest murder. That we're so locked into Lopez as the Matador that our eyes are closed to any other possibilities. She's saying this latest murder could be the work of the Matador but that we'll never admit it because it'd make us look bad."

Powell leaned back against the Naugahyde cushions and crossed his arms. There was a whoosh of air as his weight was redistributed. He said, "There are times when I truly believe I could kill that woman. Jesus, like our department is so lacking in integrity that we're going to overlook a serial killer just because we don't want to look bad? I've been in fucking law enforcement my entire life. There's no way I'd be a part of any cover-up. If I honestly felt that the lawyer had anything to do with the Matador, believe me, I'd be the first one to say it. I'd fucking go down to County myself and set Lopez free."

It was taking Powell a while to get around to why he'd asked Curt to join him. While the two men had been friends for over twenty years, Curt knew that there must be a reason for this meeting. There almost always was with Francis Powell. In the past, it had usually been because Powell needed a favor. Though back in private practice now, over the past several years Curt had spent time working as legal liaison for L.A.P.D. Internal Affairs, and had handled some high publicity prosecutions for the D.A. at Powell's insistence. Curt had been at a number of these informal little get-togethers before, and realized that thus far he had heard only part of the story from Powell. He was waiting for the chief to drop the other shoe.

"I want your opinion, Curt." Powell was about to continue when he spotted the waitress approaching with their breakfast. After she'd left, Powell leaned across the table and said, "Whadya think? I mean, I could stonewall this whole thing. Act like Pelotas and her crowd don't even exist. That's worked before."

Curt lifted a forkful of lox and eggs into his mouth, then washed it down with coffee.

"That's dangerous, Francis. She's not going to just go away. The more you fight her, the more she'll find a way to fight back."

"You think she's right?"

Curt shook his head. "Whether she's right or not is not important. I know you, Francis. We go back a long way together." Curt smiled, then chewed off a piece of bagel covered with cream cheese. "You may be a lot of things, Francis, but you wouldn't risk the safety of this community just to preserve your own ego."

Powell snickered. "Jesus, Curt . . . Thanks for the glowing vote of confidence."

The waitress returned to the table to refill their coffee.

"You know what I mean, Francis. It's not the reality of the situation that matters, it's what people perceive looking in from the outside. Some people might think that you and Durning are so firmly locked into Lopez being the Matador that you aren't willing to look elsewhere, to consider other suspects. I'm afraid that Pelotas can take that and run with it all the way to the bank. It's the sort of paranoid conspiratorial theory that people love to believe, especially considering the similarity of the crimes."

"Okay, okay," said Powell. "I got ya. Let's just say you're right." He tossed a piece of bagel in his mouth, slapped the crumbs off his hands, and slurped his coffee. "I have an alternative plan."

Curt stopped in mid-sip. "Why is it that I don't like the sound of that, Francis?"

"It's perfect. I get the D.A. to go along with assigning you to handle the dead lawyer's investigation, what's his name . . . Philbin, Brad Philbin. Durning won't have any objection to that. In fact, he'll probably welcome it. That way we look like we're being fair. We say that because of our desire to avoid even the appearance of impropriety or conflict of interest, we are appointing you to handle the Philbin murder investigation separate and apart from Lopez. That way nobody can say that our preconceived notions about the Matador are affecting the Philbin case, or vice versa. Whatdya think, Curt? A pretty good idea, right?"

Curt hesitated before deciding. He owed Francis Powell a lot. Perhaps more than he could ever pay back. It was that part of his relationship with Powell that grated at him. Powell would never admit to it, but Curt felt that his friend had taken advantage of him over the last several years. Without really thinking about it, Francis Powell had played on their friendship and on what he perceived as Curt's feeling of obligation.

Yet it was Powell who had been there when Curt needed him most. During those long dark days when Curt felt that the slightest setback would knock him over the edge, it was Francis who extended his hand to help keep him from falling. Anyway, what was so bad about feeling obligation to a friend—even if it did stick with you for life? If he turned down the offer, he knew that Francis would understand. It wasn't hurting Francis Powell's feelings that Curt was concerned about. The man was an armadillo when it came to that.

"Just Philbin, right?"

"That's the beauty of it, Curt. You know how the system works, all the ins and outs of the department. And this isn't like those other cases. Just a straightforward murder. The copycat thing'll probably make it easier to find the guy. We'll be working on it too, believe me. But for the press, for the appearance of propriety, this is the perfect solution."

Curt considered Powell's last comment. Over the last several years he'd handled a number of serious high-publicity investigations that proved to be far less than simple, unless you considered nearly losing your life to deranged killers just a walk in the park. But this one, Curt had to admit, seemed to be different. And, in actuality, L.A.P.D. would be working both cases, which would make his job a lot easier.

"I'll come down and take a look at the file," said Curt.

Powell jabbed his hand across the table, holding it there for Curt to shake.

"This is great," said Powell, pumping his hand. It was

like a weight had been lifted from Powell's shoulders. His expression became more animated, his entire body seemed more relaxed.

"So," said Powell, leaning back in the booth with one leg draped casually across the seat. "I almost forgot to ask about Jamie. How the two lovebirds doing?"

Curt pursed his lips, then smiled. He hadn't told Francis anything about his intention to ask Jamie to marry him. He wasn't sure himself if he'd consciously arrived at the decision. Someplace in the back of his head he still wondered whether he was being old-fashioned about the whole thing. Didn't people today just live with each other? Was it necessary to go through the antiquated convention of blood tests and marriage vows? Wouldn't they look at one another the same way regardless of whether they were bound by a bunch of artificial legalities?

"I believe I'm going to ask her to marry me," said Curt.

Powell's face was expressionless, but only for a moment. He broke into the type of wide-eyed grin that Curt remembered from when the two of them had been cadets in training at the police academy.

"That's terrific, Curt."

"You don't think it's old-fashioned?"

Powell waved his hand. "Who cares," he said. "It's what you want, right? Then do it. A guy doesn't get lucky like you very often. Jamie is a real prize." Powell flashed a sly little grin. "And for some weird unexplainable reason, she seems to like you."

They both laughed.

Powell again leaned across the table, his voice taking on its conspiratorial tone.

"Listen, Curt. You of all people I don't have to lecture about grabbing on and not letting go of all the good that happens to fall into your life. This is good, Curt. About as good as it gets. Don't screw it up. You do whatever makes you happy, and the rest of the world can go fuck itself. Right?"

There was a twinkle in Powell's eye that Curt couldn't remember seeing before.

"You'll be my best man?"

Powell looked indignant for a moment, then smiled and said, "Shit, I'd be pissed as hell if you didn't ask!"

He liked her to watch. She picked up on that the first time they'd slept together. So now she sat on the edge of the bed, her eyes darting back and forth from his penis to his face, then back to his penis. And she'd raise her eyebrows and giggle like a young schoolgirl, as if she'd never seen one quite that big before.

But of course, she had.

It was what Crystal knew she had to do, making Detective Felix Axel think that she lived her life for these moments, when he would practically suffocate her with his sweaty overweight body.

"Now it's your turn," he said, standing nude in front of her, gently massaging himself. She grabbed his penis in her fist and slowly kissed the tip, then ran her fingers down the shaft, caressing his testicles.

"Jesus," he moaned. "You're good. You're so . . . damn . . . good."

Crystal got up and began to remove her clothes. She had to remind herself to do it slowly. Her mind was elsewhere. She was growing tired of these weekly couplings.

"Slower, babe. You know how I like it." He was seated on the bed, still massaging between his legs.

Crystal smiled, then deliberately played with the hook on her bra, as if she were having trouble getting it off. She came close to him, her arms behind her back, thrusting her breasts at him, pouting like she wanted something from him.

"You like that?" she said, finally allowing the bra to fall from her breasts, land on his face. She looked at him, then down at herself, lifting one breast and licking at the nipple with her tongue.

"God, I love that," he said. He was ramrod-hard now, stroking himself quickly. His hips moved rhythmically, thrusting up and down to meet his hand.

Crystal was formulating what information she still needed about the Matador. These afternoon sessions, she thought, were about to come to an end. Detective Felix Axel had just about shot his wad with her, literally and figuratively. Besides, he was due for a transfer out of Parker Center, and would be unable to provide her with inside information very much longer.

He motioned for her to straddle him. She did as she was told, the same way she always had. After inserting him inside, she rocked forward, letting her breasts brush against his face.

"Smother me with tits," he moaned. "Jesus, I love your tits."

Again, she did as she was told. After a few seconds, he cried out, then again, and she felt him warm, sticky and limp inside her. Crystal planted a kiss on his forehead, like a mother seeing her child off to school, then headed for the bathroom.

"So Powell's still holding back with the information on the severed tongue and the caliber of the bullet?" She was washing herself at the sink, talking into the mirror.

"He's got to," said Axel, his voice still heavy with fatigue. "It's S.O.P., you know that."

"Even though releasing that information would get him off the hook on the Matador case?"

"I don't think he looks at it quite the way you do, babe."

Crystal appeared at the door to the bedroom, rubbing between her legs with a towel.

"Whadya mean?"

Felix Axel reclined on the bed, still naked, smoking a cigarette.

"I mean, Powell's taken care of that. He's bringing in someone from the outside to handle the lawyer's case."

"You mean Philbin?"

"Yeah, whatever. Friend of Powell's. Curt Denmark.

She flashed him a questioning look. "Wasn't he the one who lost his son?"

"Yeah," said Axel. "Tough break. The kid was shot in a robbery. On his way home from school. Stopped to buy some baseball cards or something. Denmark took it pretty bad. Flipped out for a while."

Crystal let this new information play in her mind. She liked the idea that she had pressured the chief of police into action. But now that she'd accomplished that, she'd have to look elsewhere to find something that would titillate her viewers.

She was pretty sure that Daniel Lopez was the Matador, and that Brad Philbin had been murdered by someone trying to copycat the crime. The different caliber gun and the removal of the last victim's tongue, while not eliminating the Matador altogether, did argue strongly for Francis Powell's theory that the crimes were committed by two different killers.

Except, her viewers weren't interested in some lawyer

biting the dust, even if his tongue were removed. She knew that deep down, in a place where it couldn't be seen, only felt, people wanted to believe that the Matador was still out there. Like going to a horror movie knowing you were going to be scared. They wanted to hear about other people, people not as careful as themselves, who had become the Matador's victims. They wanted to huddle around the television and look at the pictures of the bodies draped in red. They wanted violence and mayhem and gore, as long as they could turn it off when it was time to go to bed. Having the Matador on the loose did just that. It was scarey and exciting, and it beat the hell out of watching Dan Rather or Peter Jennings do the evening news.

"Hey, babe . . . ? There's something I always wanted to ask you." Felix Axel stubbed out his cigarette in the ashtray on the nightstand. He reached for his pants while he spoke.

"I thought all you Mexican babes were natural brunettes." He smiled and brought his eyes to the level of her pubis.

Crystal looked down at herself for a moment. The golden blond hair between her legs still glistened with water. She'd spent her childhood thinking of herself as being different from the woman that cleaned her parents' house, or the laborers that worked at her father's factory. She remembered how in the exclusive boarding school that her parents had sent her to, the other girls had teased her and whispered behind her back. She was always the Mexican. The beaner. All her father's money hadn't been able to change that.

It was only later, after she'd entered college, that Crystal realized how to make her ethnicity work for her. Now she didn't hide it. She rolled her *r*'s and stretched out her *s*'s, leaving no doubt as to her Latin origin. And it had worked. It had landed her a spot on *Real News* when the corporate suits put out the word that they wanted to see a minority face on the screen.

Crystal decided she'd had her fill of the fat sweaty detective. This last comment of his was like a sign, she thought. The end of the line. If she needed to, she'd find someone else to funnel her information. Maybe a nice young undercover narc whose idea of bathing took in more than merely dousing himself with Aqua Velva.

She put one foot atop the bed and rested her weight on her knee. She allowed her breasts to hang freely on either side of her leg, letting him ogle them.

She looked Felix Axel straight in the eyes and said, "Well, asshole, I guess you were wrong."

Five

"I just don't see what you've got against it. It's just your damn pride that's getting in the way."

Susan Lampley pulled the tray containing the Stouffer's macaroni from the oven and set it on the sink. "I don't like the way we live, Terry. You know that."

"How could I not," he said, then regretted snapping at her. "Please, hon. Not so loud. Jeff'll hear."

She stood motionless for a moment, fixing him with that cold stare that he'd grown accustomed to. They were in the sixth year of marriage. He'd married Susan while still in college. Susan had said that two could live cheaper than one, and didn't they love each other? They'd shared a small apartment in Culver City while she worked for an insurance company and he studied for his classes.

Susan's analysis of their financial condition proved overly optimistic. When it became obvious that they needed two incomes to live the lifestyle that Susan wanted, he dropped out of school and signed up for the police academy. Though disappointed at not getting his degree, Terry told himself he'd finish up by taking night classes.

They were going to wait a few years before they had

kids, but then Jeff came along a month before Terry graduated from the academy. Now he felt trapped. He hardly ever saw his wife or his son. With Susan, he was saddened that he no longer really cared. They'd grown apart and hadn't even noticed.

At least not until now. All they seemed to do together lately was argue. Their marriage had turned into a high-wire act, with Terry riding the bicycle over the crowd, supporting Susan on his shoulders. Except now they were losing their balance and each was grabbing for the wire instead of each other.

But with Jeff it was different. Terry lived and breathed for the moments he spent with his son. It had become the only thing that made the hardship, the long hours, the otherwise pitiful existence with Susan worthwhile.

"If you really cared about us," said Susan, plopping the aluminum container in front of him. "You'd take that job that Daddy offered. At least you'd have regular hours, no more of this going off to work in the middle of the night, then, just when everyone gets used to that, you're back on days and we all have to switch. It's no way to raise a family."

Susan was behind him, banging the plates around, taking out her frustrations. When she got in these moods, Terry had learned it was better to just stay out of her way.

"And maybe then," she said, still talking about her daddy's job, "we could afford a few more things around here, instead of having to save every penny just to make the mortgage."

Terry tried to restrain himself. The idea of buying the house had been hers. Now she was throwing it back at him, using it as a lever to demean him into moving back East with her parents. Making him feel that he was somehow to blame because he worked two jobs to provide for his family.

"We've gone over this a million times," he said, looking down at the rectangle of noodles in a greasy yellow sauce. He tried to keep his voice down, fearing that Jeff would hear them arguing. He didn't want his son to think that this was how all men and women related to each other.

"I'm working two jobs, Sue. And I like what I do, at least the police work. Sure, I'd like to quit the job at the bar. Pouring drinks until two A.M. is not my idea of a life's work. You know that. But I can't quit, at least not for a while. We need the money. You said you wanted a house, a place where Jeff could grow up in a nice neighborhood. So we have a house. In a nice neighborhood. I never complained about practically killing myself trying to make the payments. Things'll get better. Just give it a little while. If I get that promotion, maybe I can cut down on the hours at the bar. Believe me, I'd like that as much as anyone. As it is, I have to fit Jeff in between coming off day-watch and working the bar at night."

He shrugged, "Heck, the other day I swung by his school just to say hi while he was out on the playground. It was the only way I could see him."

When he looked around, Susan was gone. Terry put his fork on the table, got up, and headed down the hall. Jeff was in his room, playing with the hand-held electronic game that they'd bought him for his last birthday.

"How's it going, partner? You getting any better at that?"

"Just watch, Dad."

Jeff was seated on the edge of his bed, furiously working his fingers on two small black buttons that controlled the game. "I almost got it. I just need to get this guy, here, the Ninja, to kill that other guy, and I'll get to the next level."

Terry sat down next to his son, thinking about what his wife had said. His father-in-law had, on several occasions, offered him a job at his plant. The position would mean more money and regular working hours, to say nothing of safety. But it also carried with it a boss who considered himself the patriarch of his family, and who didn't hesitate to direct each of his children's lives, married or not. Two weeks during the summer, when Susan's folks came to visit, was about as much as Terry thought he could handle.

Until recently, he felt that the money problems would eventually work themselves out. Now it was as if the money wasn't really the problem between them, but more a symptom of something deeper. Money was what they talked about, argued about, but it was merely a vehicle for Susan to vent her disappointment and anger.

"I'll be right back, partner."

Terry patted Jeff on the head and started for the bedroom. Susan was standing near the bed, folding clothes.

"I'm sorry," he whispered, coming up behind her and wrapping her in his arms. She pulled away, moving toward the closet. He wasn't sure what to say next.

"I'll think about the job," he said, wanting her anger to leave, wanting something of what they'd had before.

"No you won't" she said matter-of-factly. She stood in front of the closet with her back to him. "You won't," she said, still looking away, "because you just don't care. You love that job more than you love me and more than you love Jeff."

"That's not true," he said. He felt anger and guilt rising from his stomach. This was the way she always turned their discussions. "You know that's not true, Sue."

"Then prove it," she shouted, spinning and pointing an accusatory finger at him.

He was aware of her raised voice, as if he were in his son's body listening to it. He was aware of the hatred in the air, in her words and thoughts. He felt it was something that would eventually poison his son as it was poisoning him. He grabbed his jacket and headed for the front door.

"Where do you think you're going?" she shouted after him.

He wanted to tell her to lower her voice, that Jeff would hear. But he knew it would do no good. It felt like something small in his heart had just died.

"Sure, just leave. Go ahead," she shouted. "You're real good at that."

He could hear her shouting at him from the front porch as he backed the car down the driveway. The anger churned inside him, but he kept his mouth shut. It didn't do any good to try and trade punches with her, he'd learned that long ago. He just wanted out of there.

Before heading up the street, he took one last look at the house. Upstairs, with the window open, Jeff was there waving to him. The small child's face in the window, with his arm slowly moving back and forth, made him want to run upstairs and hug the boy and never let go.

Terry thought about getting home after midnight, then having to leave at five the next morning to start his shift. As he drove away, he was planning on when he'd see his son next. Maybe, he thought, he'd sneak in and sit with Jeff tonight. He'd gently kiss the boy, not disturbing his slumber, listening to his soft, innocent breathing. Then sit by him for a while, dreaming of his son's future.

*   *   *

She found him in the canyon where the dirt trail became obscured by brush. He was sitting atop an outcropping of rock, gazing off in the distance.

The sun had half-risen behind the mountains, creating a jagged electric-gold line along the edge and lighting up the canyon with an iridescent glow. Where Curt was seated, though, was still partially shielded from the sun and remained shrouded in morning shadow.

"I thought you might be here," she said.

Jamie reached down and lifted a small smooth stone, rolled it in her palm as if gauging its weight, then casually tossed it into the canyon.

Curt smiled and motioned for her to come closer. Her hair was still wet from her morning shower, and the sunlight glistened in streaks as she moved in and out of the shadows.

"You know what day it is?" he said.

Jamie nodded. They were both silent for a few moments.

"I think Darren would have liked this place," she said.

Curt looked further into the canyon. Early morning commuters snaked their way along Ventura Boulevard. In the distance, like insects, he could see the cars stacked up on the freeway.

Curt said, "I think so, too."

His mind drifted back to thoughts of his son. With Jamie's help, he'd gained some control over the guilt and shame that had almost led to his destruction. There was a place in his heart—in the cracks, he thought—where he kept his most treasured memories of Darren, and of Jamie.

"You came to this place because of Jackson, didn't you?"

Curt shrugged, then smiled. "Am I that transparent to you?"

"Not transparent," she said. "Anything but transparent." She moved closer, resting her head on his shoulder.

She said, "You know how most people remember their dead by visiting their graves? Except with Darren, it's different. Besides, I don't think it would have the same meaning for you."

Curt pulled away, turning to face her.

"How come you're so smart when it comes to me?" Jamie smiled.

"I've had a lot of experience watching you, Mr. Denmark. I know this place holds a lot of memories for you, bad and good, but mostly, I think, good."

"You're right," he said. "As usual."

"You almost died here," she said, then stopped, momentarily crippled by painful memories. "But you didn't," she continued. "Your confrontation with Travis Jackson was more than just physical. It was more than just Jackson. I think you found out something about yourself that day, something that you've been denying ever since."

Curt thought for a moment. "Maybe you're right."

Jamie slowly nodded. "It's been five years, almost to the day, since Darren's funeral. He'd be what, sixteen?" She paused, as Curt nodded, lost in thought.

"Driving," he muttered, shaking his head slowly back and forth. He thought about what Jamie had just said. It had been on his mind for weeks. He'd found himself suddenly wide awake this morning, as if some cosmic alarm had sounded, replaying the last five years of his life. Francis Powell had told him to stay out of the investigation into Darren's death, that they'd catch the bastard who shot him if it was the last thing he did. And Powell had been good to his word. Travis Jackson, a parolee from Folsom, was arrested for the murder, only to be ultimately released on a legal technicality. It was then that Curt decided he could remain on the sidelines no longer. He tracked Jackson down, not letting Powell or anyone else know what he was doing. It had ended in a shallow ravine behind the Laurel Canyon house, just him and Jackson. The way Curt had wanted it.

"You'd think," he said, "That I wouldn't want to hang around here because of what happened with Jackson. But you're right. I settled something that day. Not just with Jackson, but with myself. Something that will always be bound together with my memories of Darren. A sort of . . . reconciliation, if that makes any sense . . ."

Jamie placed his hand in hers, rubbing her fingertips along his knuckles.

"I used to just worry about you," she said, still stroking at his fingers, not looking at him. "I still do, except not as much. Not in the same way. Everything's been so good for so long, I . . ."

"Nothing to worry about," he said, once more doing what he'd become so adept at doing, suppressing his grief behind a mask of acceptance. But Jamie knew better. She let him hide behind the mask because she knew he needed that. She could see the real man was there, just beneath the surface, peering out from behind the mask.

He brought her hands to his lips and kissed them. The sun had cleared the ridge and was illuminating their spot in the shadows. Curt put his arms around Jamie and pressed her close. He could smell the sweet smell of shampoo in her hair.

"As long as I have you," he whispered, "Everything will be okay."

Six

When he got back home, his mind was filled with images of the lawyer, and confused as to what he should do next. He unlocked the door to the trailer, his thoughts still back at the Century Building.

Something had gone wrong. Without his knowing, the lawyer had left the firm.

Inside the trailer, the first thing he saw were tufts of hair on the floor and kitchen table. He knew immediately what had happened. He closed the door behind him, then slowly made his way toward the back.

"Ellie, my darling? I know you're back there, you bad cat, you."

On a shelf in the back of the trailer, he found the cat. She had the remains of Gracie, most of the body and three legs, resting comfortably under her front paws, and was gnawing on the neck. Gracie's head had already been torn off.

Nestor thought of striking the cat. For a split-second he visualized himself raising his hand and bringing it down on Eleanor's head. But then he decided that he couldn't do that.

"You're a bad, bad . . . *very bad* cat," he yelled, and the cat whined loudly, then quickly jumped from the shelf and scurried to the other end of the trailer.

Nestor searched the floor on hands and knees for a few seconds, finally finding Gracie's head and missing leg. He picked up the body parts, inspected them for a moment, then took them, along with the rest of the cat, to the kitchen table. Ellie still whined in the corner, afraid to approach.

"You better just stay there," he said, directing his comments and his anger toward Ellie. "I warned you about this, Ellie. What did Gracie ever do to hurt you?"

He shook his head slowly back and forth, checking to see what sort of work would be needed to repair the cat. He placed the head on the body, thinking about the type of stitches that would be least likely to show. Finally, after deciding that he could mend Gracie, he put the cat, in parts, in an old shoe box on the shelf. He wrapped four heavy rubber bands around the box to keep Ellie from doing further damage.

It had been nearly a week since the attorney died. Nestor had read all the newspaper accounts of the killing, along with catching Crystal Pelotas' reports on TV. The police were still holding to their theory that the attorney had been killed by someone other than the Metro Matador. Crystal, and a few of the newspapers, were busy working up the story that the Matador was still on the loose.

Nestor crooked his finger at Ellie, motioning for her to approach. The cat was wary, waiting for a good deal more coaxing from him.

"Come on you bad cat, you," he whispered. He was sweet-talking the cat now, no longer angry with her. "Come on, come on," he repeated as the cat slowly made her way toward the table, paused, then jumped into his lap.

"That's a sweet girl," he said, stroking at her fur.

He had decided that fixing Gracie wouldn't entail that much work after all. He could restitch the head and the leg, then reset the wires inside to cover the creases in the pelt. A little fresh hide-paste and Gracie would look as good as new. Still, he'd make sure from now on that he kept Gracie in a locked cupboard, at least while he was gone from the trailer.

Nestor began sifting through the newspaper, looking for articles to cut. At first the attorney's death had made the front page. Now there was just a short article in the back of the Metro Section of the *Times* dealing with Francis Powell's appointment of a special investigator to handle the case.

The drop in coverage disappointed Nestor. But more than that, he'd been thinking over the last few days that perhaps he'd made a mistake. Perhaps it was wrong for him to adopt the Matador's style with the lawyer. Wasn't it an affront to the Matador? Didn't all the truly famous serial killers have their own personal style, something that made their murders unique to them?

And what did he have?

He'd used the Matador's style in part as a means of paying homage to the man, and in part to confuse the police, cause a stir in the community. He'd accomplished what he'd set out to do. Crystal and the others already had the city convinced that the Matador was still out there. There were even sightings, women claiming they'd seen men carrying red capes wandering along the freeway embankments and behind public buildings at night.

Yet, even with the publicity, Nestor felt something was missing. The excitement of taking the lawyer's life had filled him to near bursting the night he'd done it. In the days that followed, he'd basked in the glow of the power that committing the murder had imparted. At the dental lab, he'd even had the feeling that the women were looking at him differently, almost as if they knew what he'd done, and were surprised how they'd underestimated him. He knew that was impossible, but he still liked thinking about it.

But now his memory of the details was becoming blurry. The passage of time had rearranged priorities. Everyone in the media seemed to have put the murder behind them. Nestor felt that it was time for him to establish his own identity. It was time for him to do something, to make a statement that would put him among the pantheon of serial killers.

The patent lawyer would have to wait. He'd ask some more questions, subtley, of course. He couldn't have anyone wondering why he was interested. Eventually, though, he'd find out where the lawyer had gone.

But for the moment, there was someone else who would nicely fit the bill.

The divorce lawyer was still in town. Nestor had seen his name mentioned in a magazine. They had a picture of the lawyer—older and heavier, and, Nestor thought, a lot richer—emerging from the hot tub in his office, wearing a bathrobe and sipping champagne. That's how he interviewed prospective clients, or so the magazine had claimed.

The picture in the magazine made the lawyer look different from what Nestor remembered. Of course, he told himself, the last time he'd seen the lawyer had been over five years ago. When he and Belle had split. Belle had told Nestor that she'd tired of him, and his trailer, and his stuffed animals. That she was cut out for better things.

She had sworn to him that there wasn't anyone else, that it was nothing sexual. But he'd found out afterwards that it was. Nestor found out that she had been seeing the lawyer, even sleeping with him.

Nestor continued to stroke the back of the cat, digging his fingers in gently at her neck and making her purr with every stroke.

"Belle was a bad girl, Ellie," he said. "A very bad girl."

He thought of his ex-wife sleeping with the lawyer. Of the two of them sitting in the lawyer's hot tub, sipping champagne. It was the same picture he'd had a million times over, his wife in bed or in the hot tub with the lawyer.

"But it wasn't Belle's fault," Nestor said. He felt the anger like a mild electrical jolt reach into his chest. He dug his nails in deeper and the cat jumped from his lap. "Belle was just such a pretty thing," he said, gazing into space, his mind back to when they were married. "The girl just didn't know what she wanted."

He got up and went to the locked cabinet above the stove. He removed the padlock and reached inside, taking down a covered wooden box. He placed the box on the kitchen table.

"It's unfair to blame Belle," Nestor whispered to himself as he lifted the cover on the box and removed the Sterling Model 300 .25-caliber semiautomatic. Just holding it in his hand made him remember about the attorney, and how good he felt when he saw the look of recognition on the attorney's face just before he pulled the trigger.

Nestor started to pack the gun into the small sack that he would take with him, when it struck him that he'd forgotten an important part of his plan. He took the bag containing the Sterling and put it aside. He'd have to figure a way to get rid of the gun. After all, it was cheap.

Certainly not costly enough to risk having some cop fire-arms expert determine that he was the killer by running a ballistics test. Nestor knew they could do that. He'd seen in a movie how they examined the lands and grooves on a shell casing and matched it to the inside of the gun barrel.

Nestor removed his H&R Defender .38 from the box, and ran his fingertip over the four-inch barrel. He'd bought the gun two years before in the parking lot of the swap meet from a guy who said he was hard up for cash. At sixty-five dollars, no questions asked, Nestor consid-ered it one of his better investments.

Nestor removed the Sterling from the bag and replaced it with the H&R Defender. He then found a brown paper sack, into which he placed the Sterling. He checked the bottom of the wooden box, making sure that the .25-caliber Bauer Stainless was still there, then replaced the lid and put the box back inside the storage cabinet. There was a freeway overpass they were doing work on nearby. Nestor figured he would drive by one morning, before work started, and toss the Sterling into one of the concrete forms, then cover it with dirt. That way they'd have to destroy the whole freeway if they were ever to find the gun.

Nestor started to think about what he was about to do. Each step clicked in his mind's eye. The divorce lawyer would get something special. Nestor liked the bit about cutting out the tongue. He thought it was incredibly clever of him, and damn symbolic. It had come to him after he'd blown a hole in the drunk driving lawyer's forehead. He just wasn't satisfied with plunging the sword in the pig's neck. He had looked at the lawyer laying there in his own blood, and decided that he needed to make a statement, something that would tell the world of the harm the lawyer had inflicted.

The more he thought about it, the more he figured that even then, he was branching out, getting away from the Matador's style. Developing one of his own. He wondered what they'd call him, once the TV and the newspapers realized there was a new kid on the block. He tossed some names back and forth in his mind, envisioning them in bold letters across the front page of the *Times*. He saw Crystal Pelotas mouthing the name on TV.

The new killer's name.

His name.

As he drove toward the lawyer's office, Nestor felt a surge of power, like all of his senses had been sharpened. His memory of killing the drunk driving lawyer had come back. He was grateful that he'd been able to re-create that moment. He felt he was on the right course now. That this was just the start of something big. He saw himself, sitting at the kitchen table in the trailer, telling Ellie and Gracie what he'd done, and cutting out magazine articles about himself. He'd fill his own album to overflowing.

He'd be one of them.

"Tell the cocksucker that if he wants to play hardball, he's come to the right guy. I'll fucking cut your client's nuts off and feed them to him for breakfast."

Bernie Berkowitz took a deep puff of his Macanudo and slipped further down into the bubbling hot tub. He had another attorney on the speakerphone, so he could eat the caviar, chopped egg, capers, and onions on the little rye toasts that his secretary had brought for him before leaving. From the tub, Bernie could gaze out his picture window into the night, taking in the red, white, and amber glow of the car lights on Sunset, and the silvery iridescence from the backyard pools of the mansions in Beverly Hills.

"Babe," he said, his mouth full of food, "you know I don't operate that way." He lifted the champagne bottle from the silver ice bucket and topped off his glass. The other lawyer sounded like a small child whining over Bernie's speakerphone. It was all Bernie could do not to laugh at the guy. He knew he had the guy by the shorthairs.

"You talk to your client," said Bernie. "You tell him the facts of life. Believe me, you'll both feel a lot better doing things this way. You don't want a big messy custody battle on your hands, right? Of course not. Your man's a big corporate exec. Can't afford having any messy shit hit the papers about his divorce. Trust me on this, babe. I'm not just thinking of myself. I'm thinking of both our clients."

Bernie carefully layered some caviar and egg atop a piece of rye toast, then tossed the entire thing in his mouth.

"That's right," he garbled, as the other attorney agreed to terms. Bernie gulped at his champagne. "We should do business more often," he said, smiling and sucking on the end of the Macanudo. He blew rings of smoke into the air over the hot tub as he scrubbed at his back with a loofah.

After hanging up with the attorney, Bernie took one last bite of caviar, scooping it from the bowl with two fingers then thrusting the fingers into his mouth and sucking on them. Then he let himself slip under the water for a few seconds before coming up for air. He carefully stood and removed his terry robe from the edge of the tub, then wrapped it around his soft, pink, flabby lawyer's body.

Once back on dry land, Bernie made an effort to touch

his toes, reaching a few inches below his shrunken genitals before slipping into a pair of sandals and shuffling toward the bathroom.

He dressed, then left his robe and the plate of food on the floor for the help to clean. He finished off the champagne and headed for the parking garage.

Bernie had just opened the door of his all-white Rolls-Royce Corniche when he sensed someone standing behind him. He turned, and in a second, saw the face of a little man whom he thought looked only vaguely familiar.

Bernie was just about to ask the little man what he wanted when the man pulled a small stubby gun from somewhere, levelled it at his forehead, smiled, and before Bernie could say, "Hey, babe," blew from Bernie Berkowitz all recollection of the little man, the hot tub, the caviar—and life itself.

Seven

"The court calls the matter of Eunice DuPont."

Curt got up from the jury box where he had been waiting for his case to be called, motioned to the attendant seated with his client in the back of the courtroom, and took a seat at the counsel table. A few moments later, the attendant from Metropolitan State Hospital sat Curt's client next to him, then returned to the audience.

"Will both counsel please approach the bench for a moment."

The judge swiveled to the right a half-turn, waiting for the lawyers to make their way up to the side-bench. The judge was Peter Ramsey, a recent appointee of Governor Pete Wilson. Ramsey had surprised everyone by requesting assignment to Department 95A of the Los Angeles Superior Court. 95A was the mental health court, generally considered less than a plumb assignment by judicial officers.

"Now Mr. Denmark," said Ramsey, whispering to both lawyers at the side-bench. "We're only going to get in a couple hours of testimony today. I have to break early, and I believe you mentioned something about a juvenile court appearance later this afternoon in East-lake?"

Curt nodded.

"Okay," said Ramsey. "Let's get started and see how much we can get done."

Both lawyers returned to the counsel table. The county counsel, an old veteran who Curt had seen around the courts for years, was prosecuting the matter representing the Public Guardian's Office. He called as his first and only witness Dr. Michael Genser, the treating psychiatrist for Curt's client, Eunice DuPont.

The hearing was being held under the Lanterman-Petris-Short Act to determine if Ms. DuPont should be placed under a conservatorship. The issue was whether she suffered from a mental disability that rendered her a danger to herself and unable to provide for her own basic needs. Curt had been appointed a few years back by his old friend Harry Cohen to represent Eunice DuPont. Harry had since retired from the bench and moved to Palm Springs.

The DuPont case, like all mental-health conservator-ships, came up annually for review. At each such yearly review, the conservatee had the right to contest renewal of the conservatorship in a court hearing, which is exactly what Eunice DuPont was doing this day.

After Michael Genser had testified to his qualifications as a psychiatrist, it was up to the county counsel to lead him through the standard question-and-answer designed to prove that the patient, in this case Ms. DuPont, was so gravely disabled that she could not provide for her own basic food, clothing, and shelter.

"Doctor Genser, what is your diagnosis of Ms. DuPont, and upon what facts do you base that diagnosis?"

A good portion of Dr. Michael Genser's practice was

treating psychiatric patients at state hospitals, then testifying in court under appointment by the court. Eunice DuPont was just the first of four or five cases that he was scheduled to testify on this day.

"The patient, Ms. DuPont," said Genser, "suffers from schizophrenia, shizo-affective type. This is a serious mental disorder and affects her thinking, feelings, and behavior. Ms. DuPont has a long psychiatric history and has been under conservatorship for approximately twelve years. She has had numerous psychiatric hospitalizations, including two in the last twelve months."

Genser continued, "Prior to her being placed at Metro, Eunice was living in a locked facility, Idle Acres Sanatorium. She was administered six hundred milligrams of lithium and eight hundred milligrams of Mellaril per day. Also twelve and a half milligrams of Prolixin Decanate every three weeks, and two milligrams of Cogentin twice a day. Despite the medication and the fact that she was in a locked facility, Eunice continually AWOL'd from Idle Acres, the most recent AWOL resulting in her placement at Metropolitan State Hospital."

Genser adjusted his position in the witness chair and straightened his tie. Judge Ramsey had his head down, taking notes on a yellow legal pad. The county counsel seemed to be following his witness's testimony from the written doctor's report in his file.

Curt put his hand gently on Eunice DuPont's shoulder, telling her that everything would be all right. Eunice DuPont merely smiled, continually saying, "Hi, Dr. Genser," during the doctor's testimony. A few times during his testimony, Michael Genser would pause momentarily and wave back.

"Eunice," said Genser, "has a mild tardive dyskinesia of the mouth. She has demonstrated delusional thinking, rambling speech, disorganized ideas, and inappropriate affect. During my interview of her, her speech was pressured and tangential. She manifested delusions of persecution and grandeur. She stated she murdered John F. Kennedy with a silver bullet in New York City."

"That's right," Eunice yelled. "I did it, I did it." Then she laughed, and as suddenly, went sullen, rocking back and forth in her chair, staring at the tabletop and mumbling to herself.

Genser continued, quoting from a copy of his written report that he held on his lap. "Eunice said that she would like to be locked up at the women's jail, Sybil Brand, and get surgery performed on her by their *famous* doctors, in her words. She said she could take care of herself, and that she has a job lined up if she were released. She could not explain, though, why she hasn't been able to work in the past eighteen years. She denies having a mental disorder."

"Is she," asked the county counsel, his nose still in the file, "in your opinion, Doctor, able to provide for her own food, clothing, and shelter outside of a locked facility?

"No," said Genser. "Definitely not. When left to her own devices, Eunice often fails to eat for days. Also, she has great difficulty in bathing; apparently, she doesn't like it. Even the staff at Metro has to fight to get her to take a shower."

"I have no further questions," said the county counsel.

"Mr. Denmark?" said Ramsey, looking up from his notepad.

"No questions."

"Very well," said Ramsey. "You may be excused Dr. Genser."

As Genser walked from the courtroom, Eunice waved

at him, saying, "Bye, Dr. Genser. I love you." Genser smiled and waved back.

The county counsel said, "We have no further evidence. your honor."

"Mr. Denmark," said Ramsey. "Do you have any evidence to present to the court?"

"Yes," said Curt. "We would call the conservatee, Eunice DuPont, to the stand."

The courtroom bailiff helped Eunice from her chair, then escorted her around to the witness stand on the other side of the courtroom. The court clerk then stood and asked Eunice if she swore to tell the truth, the whole truth, and nothing but the truth, so help her, God? Eunice started giggling. Ramsey motioned to the clerk that it was okay, and told Eunice to have a seat.

"Ms. DuPont," said Curt. "Is there anything you want to tell the judge?"

Everyone looked at Eunice. It was customary not to demand that the formal question-and-answer procedure normally used in the courtroom be followed when examining conservatees. Curt figured he'd let her ramble on for a while, give her her day in court. He had no hope of actually winning this case, since it was obvious to everyone that Eunice DuPont was more than two tacos short of a combination plate, and had been that way for most of her adult life.

"Well, yes," said Eunice, warming to the task.

The court reporter smiled at Curt. She'd been smiling throughout the hearing. She was a slender young woman in her late twenties. Not the regular 95A reporter, though Curt had seen her there once or twice before. She sat directly below the witness stand, just a couple of feet from the witness. She seemed to find the entire idea of such courtroom proceedings humorous.

"I want to get out of that hospital," said Eunice.

"And why is that," said Judge Ramsey, monotone. His attention was focused on something inside another case file. He didn't look up for Eunice's response.

"That place is dangerous," she said. "The people in that hospital are crazy."

Curt looked at the county counsel, who was in deep conversation with the representative of the Public Guardian's Office. Neither appeared to be paying any attention to Eunice DuPont's testimony. The court reporter was still smiling, hands poised over her machine.

"Eunice, is there anything else you want to tell the judge?" asked Curt.

"Yeah." Eunice looked around for a moment, then stood up. She spread her legs, then lifted her dress, exposing her thighs and genitals. She wore no underpants, and their was a yellowish stain dripping down the inside of one leg. Eunice started fanning the dress in front of her. A sour stench quickly permeated the courtroom.

"I been pussy-snatched," Eunice yelled. "Those people in that place pussy-snatched me."

She continued to fan her dress until the bailiff, quickly moving from his desk on the other side of the courtroom, came to her side and forced Eunice to retake her seat.

In the commotion that was going on inside the court, Curt failed to notice that the court reporter had apparently fainted. She lay in a heap at the base of the witness stand, right next to her steno machine.

"We'll be in recess," said Ramsey, his face expressionless. He'd seen it all before. He stood and pointed to the fallen reporter who was now being helped to her feet by the county counsel. "Is she all right?" he asked.

The county counsel nodded, then helped the reporter from the coutroom.

"I think I've heard enough," said Ramsey. He was waving his hand in front of his face, trying to clear the air. He looked at the clerk and said, "Do we still have that bottle of Lysol?"

Curt was still seated at the counsel table. Eunice DuPont was on the witness stand, smiling. She looked at Curt and said, "Am I guilty, Mr. Denmark? Tell 'em I don't wanna go to no more hospitals. Tell 'em to send me to the women's prison, so I can get those operations from those famous doctors that operate on the stars. Yeah, I wanna have those breast implants that all those beautiful movie stars have."

She then looked at Judge Ramsey and said, "Ain't that right, your honor?"

That afternoon, Curt found himself sipping a cup of coffee in the hallway of the Eastlake Juvenile facility. He was having a hard time ridding himself of the image, and the scent, of Eunice DuPont. Another in the long list of crazy 95A stories. He would have to remember to tell Jamie this one.

Curt was in Eastlake for the disposition of one of his juvenile clients. Aurelio Mercado was to appear before the court for sentencing on a residential burglary. The judge had previously continued the sentencing at Curt's request. The recommendation of the probation department was that Aurelio be sent to camp.

Curt had convinced the judge to give his client another month to see if he could get his act together in school. Today's hearing was to determine whether Aurelio had attended school during the last month and whether he was passing his classes.

Curt was still thinking about Eunice DuPont when he

spotted Jamie approaching down the hall. They'd arranged to meet at Eastlake, then go out to an early dinner.

"How was your day?" she said, grabbing his shoulder and brushing her cheek and lips across his.

He would save the Eunice DuPont story for dinner, he thought. Or maybe after dinner.

"Fine," he said. "How about you?"

Jamie sat on one of the nearby graffiti-scarred wooden benches, plopping her briefcase down next to her. Curt thought she looked a bit frazzled.

"Okay," she said, reaching into her purse and removing a small mirrored compact. She spent a few seconds checking her appearance in the compact, then snapped it closed and tossed it back inside her purse.

"Being a partner isn't all it's cracked up to be," she said, letting herself lean back against the wall, relaxing for a moment. She blew a wisp of hair from her forehead.

"More money, but when something goes wrong, the buck stops right at my desk. Now we're shorthanded, and I have to redistribute the work to the associates, most of whom are already putting in sixty-hour weeks."

"Someone leave? Get sick?"

"Ron Jacobs," she said. "Left a file cabinet full of active cases."

"You can handle it," said Curt, tossing his coffee cup in the trash. He stroked her chin with his finger, lifting her head toward him. The delicate gold stick-pin that Jamie wore on her lapel seemed almost electrified in the overhead fluorescent light. The pin was in the shape of a cat. It was set with sapphires for the eyes. The stones glittered and commanded attention. Curt had given Jamie the pin on her last birthday.

"You know how much I love you?" he said.

She looked around. The courthouse was almost empty,

most of the cases having been resolved earlier in the afternoon. Still, Jamie felt uncomfortable about possibly encountering some gangbangers, or auto thieves, or rapists, or any one of the typical sleazeballs that Curt represented.

"I know," she said, grabbing his hand and holding it in hers. "You must have had a very good morning," she added.

Curt laughed. "I'll tell you about it at dinner."

A young man in a sheriff's uniform stuck his head out the door. "Curt," he said. "They're ready for you."

Curt walked down to the snack bar and got his client, then returned and entered the courtroom. The court commissioner was already on the bench.

"This is the Mercado matter," the commissioner said, not waiting for confirmation from either Curt or his client. He read his notes from the previous appearance.

"I continued this matter to check on the minor's school attendance and performance. Do we have anything from the school liaison?" The commissioner looked at the court probation officer, who was seated at a small desk to his left.

"Your honor," said the probation officer, not bothering to stand while he addressed the court. "My information is that this minor has missed a total of fourteen school days since he last appeared in court. The school liaison reports that there have only been twenty-three actual school days that the minor could have attended. That means that the minor has missed sixty percent of school since this court last continued his case."

Curt had the school records before him. He'd already reviewed them with his client.

"Well," said the commissioner, snickering while he wrote something in the court file. "Perhaps, Mr. Denmark, your client would benefit from a short sojourn in camp?"

"Your honor," said Curt, standing at the counsel table. "My client, Mr. Mercado, does have an excuse for being absent." He saw the commissioner smile and quickly glance at the probation officer, as if they'd heard this routine about a million times before.

The commissioner said, "Go ahead, Mr. Denmark. I can't wait to hear this one."

Curt cleared his throat. "Well, your honor, Aurelio was stabbed shortly after his last court appearance. Some rival gang members spotted him on his way home from school. There was a fight, and Aurelio was stabbed in the chest." Curt looked down at his client, who was in the process of lifting up his T-shirt to show the commissioner his scars.

"The minor was in intensive care for nearly a week, and then couldn't return to school for another week-and-a-half." Curt could see the commissioner peering down at his client's chest. The probation officer also got up and came around to take a closer look, nodding as he inspected the still bright red gash and purple stitch marks just below the minor's heart.

"You might say," said Curt, winking at Jamie, who had slipped into court to watch, "that the fight has cut into my client's education."

The commissioner didn't laugh, but Curt did get a giggle from the court clerk, and from a young police officer seated a few seats away from Jamie. Curt didn't know the officer, but had earlier noticed him staring at Jamie's pin.

The commissioner agreed to give Aurelio Mercado another month to prove himself, then declared the court to be in recess until the following day. As they were leaving, Aurelio said to Curt, "Hey, man, thanks. You did a good job."

Curt threw up his hands. "I had nothing to do with it. You fuck up again and you'll go straight to camp."

Aurelio flashed an easy smile. "Got ya, man." He turned and headed for the door, then suddenly turned back.

"Hey, Mr. Denmark," he said, completely serious now. "What's a *sojourn*, man?"

After sitting together on the sand and watching the sun go down, Curt and Jamie had dinner at the Petite Boulangerie in Santa Monica. Curt had wanted to go someplace more fancy, or at least dine in the restaurant's main dining room. But Jamie had always liked the open-air atrium cafe.

Though the atrium dining area, with its wood-and-wrought-iron tables, was only half-full, there was a steady stream of people during the evening, coming to the restaurant for everything from a cup of coffee and some conversation with friends to full-course dinners in the wood-paneled dining room. The place bustled, as usual, with shoppers who had come to purchase take-out food or partake of the exotic cheeses and deli items. The restaurant, which stretched for almost a block on Main Street, also had a large selection of wines, which filled several floor-to-ceiling racks. The wine vaults were located adjacent to a small bar where cocktails, hors d'oeuvres, and deli sandwiches were served.

Curt told Jamie his story of Eunice DuPont, and they both had a good laugh over it. He wanted to talk with her about their future, about getting married, but in the noisy hubbub of the restaurant, the moment just didn't seem right. After dinner, they decided to move to the bar and have a B&B before going home.

"I don't know if this is the right time," said Curt, aware that people were strolling through the bar on their way in and out of the restaurant. There was a small television mounted on the wall behind the bar. A few of the locals were sipping on beers, talking with the bartender, and watching the TV.

"A good time for what?" she said.

Curt paused, his eyes drawn again to the jeweled brooch.

"I remember when I bought you that," he said. "The jeweler said it was one of a kind. The eyes reminded me of yours."

Jamie glanced down at the pin. "I love it," she said. She placed her hand on his. "And I love you."

"Maybe we should do something about that," he whispered, and then paused, leaving the comment there in the air between them. Jamie flushed slightly, and a smile started to turn up the corners of her mouth.

"Maybe you should be a little more specific," she said. "I've got all kinds of ideas running through my mind. I . . . well, I thought you wanted to wait with that. Do you mean what I think?"

Curt nodded and gripped two of her fingers, rubbing his thumb gently around the nail.

"You don't think getting married is too old-fashioned," he said, "do you? I mean, it wouldn't change things . . . You know, at least not the important . . ."

Jamie put a finger gently to his lips. She got up and leaned across the table to kiss him.

"Change is something we've had a lot of lately," she said. He could see her eyes glass over. She sat back down, then looked away for a moment. "A little more," she whispered, turning back to him, "won't hurt." She smiled, locking her eyes on his. "Don't you think?"

He felt light-headed, but relieved all the same. "I was, well . . . a little worried, you know . . ."

There was that smile again, the look that told him everything was all right.

They spent the rest of the time at the restaurant talking and making plans for the wedding. Jamie was excited, like a young girl. It made Curt happy to see that. Francis was right; who cared what anyone else thought? What they had was good, too good to waste. There were dozens of lists to prepare and scores of people to talk to. They had to decide on a date, and whether they should simplify matters by getting married in a judge's chambers or deplete their combined savings and throw an all-out bash at some hotel.

When they left the restaurant, they hadn't decided on anything. They were both so consumed with their plans and with each other that neither noticed the news report on the TV. Had Curt paid closer attention, he would have learned that another lawyer had been found murdered. And that this lawyer, like the last, had had his tongue cut out by the killer.

Eight

"You look like hell," said Powell. He stood in the doorway of Curt's office at Parker Center. Powell had arranged for Curt to have the use of the small office during the Brad Philbin murder investigation.

"Thanks, Francis. I suppose you've heard?"

Powell nodded, looked down the hall, then slipped inside, closing the door behind him.

"I got the call last night," said Curt. "Jamie and I were just returning from dinner. Apparently Crystal Pelotas' informant was right on top of this thing. There was a camera crew already at the scene by the time I got there."

Curt watched Powell grind his teeth in anger.

"I'll find that sonofabitch," he muttered, "if it's the last thing I do."

"Right now," said Curt, "Crystal Pelotas and her informant are not our main problem."

"Yeah, I heard," said Powell, shaking his head in disbelief. "Just what this city needs, huh? Another serial killer. Where the fuck do these assholes come from? You'd think they had some sort of spawning grounds or something so that as soon as we catch one of these guys, they just release another. Like the serial-killer-god is just sitting up there playing games with us."

"You gotta admit," said Curt, handing Powell the preliminary crime reports, "this one's pretty unusual. Only picks lawyers."

"Mm." Powell quickly rifled through the paperwork. "Same as the last one," he said, "except this time he decides to get cute."

"He or she," said Curt.

"You just yanking my chain or do you have an angle on this?"

"I've got nothing more than you see there," said Curt. "I'd bet we're dealing with a male. Still, I don't want to rule anything out."

"Someone who maybe knew both these lawyers."

"Right," said Curt. "I've got a couple guys cross-referencing the records now. Maybe we'll get lucky and come up with a name. Who knows. The problem is that lawyers don't keep client records forever. This guy could be an old client."

"A very dissatisfied customer, I'd say."

Curt laughed. "Francis, every lawyer's got a long list of dissatisfied clients. It's the nature of the biz, you know that. Person comes into your office and tells you he's pissed as hell at somebody. He's got all this hatred and animosity built up, and he says, 'Here, let me put all this bullshit on your shoulders, Mr. Lawyer. You go out and do battle for me.' "

Curt continued, "Sometimes you're lucky and things work out, everybody's happy. But most times everything doesn't get tied up in a nice little bow. The way the courts work, the delays, the astronomical lawyer fees, as a client, even when you win, you don't. People are expected to compromise. Except, some clients don't want to do that.

It's all or nothing for some people. So when they lose, or things don't turn out the way they thought, they get pissed off and blame their lawyer."

"Pissed off enough," said Powell, "to kill them?"

Curt thought a moment. "Tell you the truth, Francis, I've had more than a few clients who I worried about. Still do, every once in a while. This is America, Francis. The most litigious country in the world. Instead of asking the next guy to discuss your differences calmly and rationally, Americans pull out their constitutionally protected weapons of death—the Saturday Night Special or the nine-millimeter that Uncle Harry keeps in the night-stand—and blow each other to smithereens. Either that, or you do a lot of yelling and threatening, then go and visit your local legal clinic the next morning and sign up for about four years of depositions, interrogatories, and court hearings."

"This guy's real cute," said Powell. He ran his fingertip over the face of the page, reading to himself.

"The business card?"

"Yeah. Can you believe this bullshit?" Powell shook his head slowly, then said, "He shoots the poor sonofabitch, then cuts out his tongue. Then leaves the lawyer's business card sticking out of his mouth with a little note claiming that he killed Philbin, and this other mumbo jumbo written underneath. Jesus! Where the fuck do they get these guys?"

"He's developing, Francis. The Matador was always the same from the first victim on. Always the identical M.O. This guy, on the other hand, isn't sure what he wants, or who he is. He did the first lawyer, Philbin, as a Matador copycat. And even then, he added something of his own by removing the tongue. Now he's branching out, feeling his oats. This calling card business is classic stuff.

It all means something to the killer, just like cutting out the victim's tongue, just like selecting only lawyers. He's painting a picture of himself, Francis."

"You been hanging around the shrinks too long, Curt."

"Maybe so, but you have to admit, it all fits."

Powell shrugged and said, "Pelotas is floating a trial balloon about Philbin and Berkowitz being the work of the Matador. She's saying that the Matador did the two lawyers to throw us off the track."

"Yeah," said Curt, waving his hand in the air. "That's bullshit, and she knows it. And so do most sane people. She's looking for a story. As soon as she gets an angle on the attorney killer she'll drop this Matador stuff, you watch."

Powell snickered. "You're probably right. The Matador is better for ratings. I hate to say it, but it's hard to get too worked up over a couple of lawyers biting the big one."

"Remember who you're talking to, Francis. I've already been contacted by the county bar. They're concerned."

"I'd be concerned too," said Powell with a sly grin. "Though I can think of a lot of sheisters, present company excluded, of course, who I wouldn't miss at all. Hey, what's this?" Powell asked, gazing down at the crime reports and furrowing his brow, looking confused. He spoke haltingly. *"Qui parcit nocentibus innocentes punit?* What is that, Latin?"

"It's a legal term," said Curt, "It was written in handwriting on the business card they removed from Berkowitz's mouth. It means, 'He who spares the guilty punishes the innocent.' "

"Oh, that's cute. That's real cute. Now we have a serial psycho-killer who quotes Latin. You know, Curt, it's things like this that make me wonder whether I've been in this business too long."

Curt smiled. "Well, that might be the case, Francis." He waited two beats for Powell to get the joke. "But we should be thankful that this guy's leaving us these little clues to his identity. It's pretty obvious that whoever killed Philbin and Berkowitz had a major-league grudge against both of them."

"From what I know about Philbin," said Powell, "that could include about seventy-five percent of the D.A.'s Office, the entire police department, and half the criminal court judges."

"I know," said Curt. "Philbin wasn't about to win any popularity contests.

"And Berkowitz," said Powell, "is probably not much better. If half of what I read about the guy is true, he was your typical high-profile, flashy legal mouthpiece. Some said he was asking for trouble, hanging himself out there with all that publicity about his hot tubs and his million-dollar settlements. A lot of ex-husbands probably wouldn't mind getting a piece of his hide."

"I've got S.I.D. going over the handwriting and the business card. Latent Prints came up with nothing."

"Doesn't surprise me. A guy that spouts Latin is not gonna be stupid enough to leave his fingerprints all over the fucking card."

Curt got up from behind his desk and said, "I'm going down to S.I.D. to see if I can speed things up. The ballistics reports should be completed by now. Our killer changed to a thirty-eight with Berkowitz, so now we're looking for two guns instead of one. The coroner's supposed to put a rush on the body. For whatever good that'll do. Probably not much. Not much doubt that it's the same guy who did both killings. And if he used gloves, there won't be any prints."

Both men walked into the hallway outside Curt's office. Curt watched Powell glad-hand the troops before getting on the elevator. Curt stopped for a drink at the water cooler, gulping at first, then letting the icy liquid trickle down his throat. He was not optimistic about breaking this case anytime in the near future. The way it looked, they were dealing with a definite serial-psycho, but a psycho who was clever enough to cover all the usual tracks. Leaving the note on the business card was taking a chance, but without something to compare it to, the handwriting on the card was meaningless.

Perhaps the only aspect of the investigation that gave Curt cause for optimism was the apparent pattern of the killings. The psycho was after lawyers. Maybe the killings would end with Bernard Berkowitz. If that happened, Curt knew it would be unlikely that the police would ever solve the case. The killer might make a mistake, maybe brag about what he'd done, and that could lead to his discovery. But without more to go on it was unlikely that they would be able to crack the case on their own. All they could do now was follow each and every lead and hammer the scientific evidence for all it was worth.

And wait for the killer to strike again.

All the message said was that she had had enough. Just two or three sentences from Susan saying that she'd taken Jeff and moved back with her folks. He could call, if he wanted.

Terry Lampley sat inside his son's now empty room, trying to make sense of what happened. Jeff's closet had been totally cleaned out. The baseball-clock he had bought Jeff at the Dodger game was still there, along with a small framed picture of the two of them playing catch in the backyard.

He'd called Susan's parents and let the phone ring ten or fifteen times before giving up.

How could she do this?

His first thought was to hop a plane and bring them both back. Then he ran through that scene in his mind, seeing himself at a disadvantage in Susan's parents' home, trying to coax his own wife into returning to him. He felt demeaned and small just thinking about how it would probably turn out.

And then there was Jeff. He would have been happy just to have the boy back. If Susan needed a change, that was fine. But why take the boy? Surely she must realize that disrupting Jeff's home and school life would be doing him no good?

Terry Lampley checked his watch, reminding himself that he had a little over an hour before his shift started. There really wasn't time to do anything, other than to try and get Susan to hear him out on the phone. And nobody was answering. He wondered whether they were all there, sitting in the living room, sipping at coffee, watching and listening to the phone ring, knowing it was him and not wanting to have any part of him.

He thought about calling the station, telling the watch commander that he was sick and wouldn't be coming in. But he couldn't do that forever. Eventually they'd find out that he was having problems. If he was to go back East, he'd need time off. Then they'd find out for sure. He'd have to tell them about Susan, and Jeff, and the fact that his marriage was going down the crapper.

Terry went to the kitchen and took the bottle of whiskey down from the cupboard. He had a policy of never drinking any booze before a shift. But this was different.

He measured out three fingers of the amber liquid into a glass of ice, then brought the glass to the kitchen table. All he could think of was what was going through Jeff's mind. What Susan was telling him about his father.

He took a swallow of the whiskey, then another longer one. The first swallow made him wince and smack his lips. He finished off the whiskey, slamming the glass on the table. The glass shattered in his hand, opening a gash across his palm. He watched as the blood dripped from his palm onto the table, creating a small puddle of water and whiskey and blood.

Terry took the rest of the whiskey with him into the bedroom. He'd try and call Susan again later.

He grabbed his car keys, took one last look at the picture of himself and his son, swigged the rest of the whiskey until the bottle was empty, and left for the station.

Nine

The TV was on inside the trailer. Crystal Pelotas was reporting on the latest lawyer killing. The VCR had already been set to record the show so that Nestor could watch it again later.

Nestor had the squirrel that Ellie had caught attached to the three-chain-and-hook gambrel, and with his curved skinning knife was spinning the squirrel, peeling the skin downward from the incision he'd made at the breast bone.

"Crystal looks particularly beautiful tonight, don't you think, Ellie?"

Nestor kept working at removing the skin as he watched television and spoke to the cat.

"And you know, she's talking about us, kitty. Yes, we are famous, kitty. Yes, my sweet little baby, do you like that?"

Nestor had peeled the squirrel's pelt down, inverting it from the carcass. He cut the claws off, then carefully pulled the pelt over the head.

"There," he said, holding the pelt in his hand. "That came off rather nicely, don't you think, kitty?"

Nestor removed the skinned carcass of the squirrel

from the gambrel and wrapped it in some old newspapers.

"I'd bet you'd like to play with this, wouldn't you, Ellie?"

Nestor smiled, holding the wrapped carcass over the cat, teasing it as it stood on its hind paws, reaching and clawing at the package.

"Not for you," he said. "This goes in the trash."

Nestor placed the carcass inside a gray plastic bag and tied the end with a twisty, then tossed the bag in the trash. He then returned to the kitchen table, where he spread the animal's hide on a piece of newspaper.

Crystal Pelotas had finished her report on the lawyer-killer and was now on to a new subject. Nestor rewound the tape in the VCR and played it back from the beginning.

"I like the part," he said, "where she calls me the 'Barrister Butcher.' " Nestor giggled, then reached inside the cupboard and removed a container of Wasco Dry Preservative.

"That's what the English tabloids are calling me. Can you imagine that, Ellie. England! We're already famous all over the world. And it's only the beginning."

Nestor applied the preservative to the squirrel's pelt, his mind spinning with excitement. It was more than he could ever have expected. The whole world knew what he'd done. The whole world was watching, waiting for the Barrister Butcher to strike again.

"I like that," he said, "much better than what the *Enquirer* called me." He made a sour look with his face. "I think that 'Barrister Butcher' sounds alot more important than 'The Attorney Assassin' or, God help us, 'The Sheister Slayer.' "

Nestor set the treated pelt aside. He would give the preservative time to do its work before he stitched and pasted the pelt to the small urethane foam body. Then he'd work on the mannequin for another couple of days, pinning the pelt to the underbody to accentuate the squirrel's natural musculature. The last step would be the eyes and teeth. This time he'd pay more attention to working with the Sculpal, making sure he had the animal's expression just the way he wanted before painting.

Nestor dusted the pelt lightly with puffed borax and set it aside. He rinsed his hands in the sink, one eye still on the taped television program. Crystal Pelotas was on the screen, standing in front of the Criminal Courts Building. Her voice echoed inside the tiny trailer.

"The Barrister Butcher, or Attorney Assasin, as some media have come to refer to him, has struck again. This time, the body of well-known divorce attorney Bernard Berkowitz was found shot to death in the parking garage of his office. Authorities say that they believe it is the work of the same killer who just last week took the life of Brad Philbin, another local attorney.

"So far," said Pelotas, "authorities have refused to comment on any leads they may be pursuing in this investigation. As I reported previously, Chief of Police Francis Powell has appointed Mr. Curt Denmark, a local lawyer and former investigator for Internal Affairs, to head up the investigation of the Butcher. Some of you might remember Mr. Denmark as the one whose son was murdered in a liquor store robbery several years ago."

Nestor eased himself onto the fold-out bed. Ellie joined him at the head of the bed, positioning herself at his shoulder, licking the side of his face.

Nestor took the remote control in one hand and pointed it at the VCR, rewinding the tape. He then undid the top button of his pants and pulled them down to just above his knees. His mind filled with the bloody television images of the two attorneys as he began fondling himself, while watching Crystal Pelotas on the television.

"We're famous," he whispered to himself. He couldn't get his mind off the fame that killing the lawyers had brought him. He couldn't get his mind off Crystal. As she moved on the screen, he saw himself with her. He closed his eyes for a moment, letting his mind float off into dream. In his dream, Crystal was naked, standing before him, telling him of his power. She wanted him, more than she'd ever wanted any man. Those were the words she spoke to him in the dream. She came closer, and he could feel the hard nipples of her breasts against his chest. She wanted him.

Nestor felt himself growing hard in his hand. In the dream, Crystal was kissing his chest, working her way down until, on her knees, she took him inside her mouth. He felt the fire between his legs ignite, then explode.

When he had finished, he lay on his back, trying to catch his breath. Ellie moved from the head of the bed to between his legs, sniffing at the milky liquid on his stomach, then moving away.

Nestor saw a vision of himself inside the Century Building, standing in front of the large double doors that led to the lawyer's suite of offices. His eyes filled with the oversized gold lettering on the doors, the firm's name: Taylor & Crockett. He saw himself looking down at the lawyer after he'd used the Bauer to blow away the top of the lawyer's head. He saw himself placing the lawyer's business card inside his mouth, just like he had with Berkowitz.

He already had the legal saying. Thinking about it made him feel good. And afterwards, he'd tape Crystal on the TV, talking about him and what he'd done.

And he'd paste his articles into the album, knowing that

the Nightstalker and the Son of Sam and the Hillside Strangler and all the others would be envious of him.

The Barrister Butcher . . . He liked the sound of that.

"Just pee in the fucking bottle."

"I can't, man. I ain't had nothing to drink since last night."

"Yeah, I'll bet.

"Truth, man. My old lady and me had a fight. Bitch threw me outta the house."

"Listen, just pee in the fucking bottle. I ain't got time for none of your bullshit. You ain't gonna pee? Then I'll note that down in your file."

"Aw, shit, man. You be settin' my ass up. Don't run none of your bullshit on me, man. I seen it all before. You want my ass, fucking take it, man."

With that, Monroe Davis tossed the empty bottle at Randall Lawrence, his parole officer, zipped up his pants, checked out his Jheri curl in the mirror, and headed out the door. He took a second before leaving the building to look back. Randall Lawrence stood just outside the doorway to the men's room, holding the empty sample bottle. Lawrence was about six six and two eighty, so Monroe had been pushing it, throwing the bottle at the guy. But now that there was a hallway between them and Monroe was halfway out the door, the gorilla standing outside the men's room didn't bother him much.

"I'm gonna bust your ass," yelled Lawrence. Then he smiled the kind of wide, practiced smile that looked like he went to bed at night with a hanger in his mouth. Lawrence, Monroe thought, had the biggest, whitest teeth he'd ever seen. If Lawrence were in a dark room, the only thing you'd see would be those fucking teeth.

"Fuck you, man," said Monroe, heading out the door. "Fucker thinks he can mess with a man's head like that. Shit . . . Fucker's messin' with the wrong dude. Yes, sir, I ain't no chump he thinks can fuck me around with that shit."

Monroe had walked nearly two blocks before he realized he was still talking to himself. People on the street were looking at him funny. He wasn't sure whether he liked that or not. In the joint, there were ways guys looked at you like that. Monroe Davis had become an expert on the way guys looked at you. He had to. He had to know when his bullshit wasn't going to cut it. When to back down, find a place to lay low—or some other dude to lay it off on. Eight years in prison had made him an expert on guys' looks.

Monroe had been on the outs less than two months and was already in trouble. He'd tested dirty twice, and this last test was going to be the ball-breaker. Monroe knew that. He knew there was no way, if he did the test the way Randall Lawrence wanted, that he'd come out okay. He was floating now. Just marking time until the next thing happened. The next thing, Monroe knew, would have something to do with a bus with iron bars on the windows that would take him back to the joint.

Still, that wasn't so bad. Take a parole violation, maybe do another six months, then be done with it. If he kept his nose clean and didn't pick up any new beefs, that's all he'd be looking at. Six more months of playing queen-for-a-day.

Monroe stopped at the methadone clinic. Inside, lined up against the wall waiting for their little plastic glass of state-approved joy juice, were dozens of men like himself. Worn-out cons looking and feeling like E.T. on some strange planet. Wondering why the thing they'd wanted so badly in the joint, what they'd dreamed about, had turned out to be just an exercise in waiting. Freedom had amounted to merely passing time until the inevitable return. A joke. A trick that wasn't clever or cute, and that destroyed what little self-esteem they might have had when they got out.

So Monroe left the clinic. The guy he was looking for wasn't there anyway. He headed up the street to see a friend of his. *A friend?* At least, that's what the guy called Monroe. Except Monroe realized it was all bullshit. This guy, *his friend,* was no different from the cons in the clinic. The friend was looking at taking the express back to the slammer. He was tired of waiting. He didn't know it, but Monroe could tell.

The freedom dream . . .

Monroe knew the dream was something you bullshitted other cons about inside. Only fools took it serious.

The friend had said that he needed some help, a home-boy as backup, and that Monroe looked to be his man. There was this Korean market where the wife watched the counter in the afternoons. No big deal, the friend had said.

And Monroe smiled and nodded his head, thinking that maybe this friend had the right idea. Monroe thought maybe he'd take the express back himself.

No, not the express.

What was that train they had in Japan? He'd read about it waiting to see the nurse at the clinic. The bullet-train, something like that. Yeah, the bullet-train. Maybe he and his friend would jump the bullet-train back to the joint, fuck the dream altogether.

Monroe hurried his pace. He was starting to get a buzz just thinking about his friend, and the righteous speedball he'd cook up for the two of them.

Ten

The sergeant said, "Rough night, huh?"

Terry Lampley waved and cracked a smile, not stopping on his way past the desk.

"The kid was sick," he yelled back to the sergeant. "Up all night." He noticed the sergeant nod, as if he understood all about parents and sick kids.

The locker room was almost empty. Terry said hello to a few friends, then sat down on the narrow wooden bench that separated the rows of lockers. The room would soon fill up with the sounds of men working the 6 P.M. to 2:45 A.M. "Mid-P.M." watch.

He opened the metal locker, swinging the door back. Taped inside the door was a picture of Jeff. For a few moments Terry just sat there, staring at the picture, wondering if he'd ever see his son again.

It had been nearly a week since Susan had taken Jeff with her. He had finally gotten through, having to talk his way past his father-in-law in order to get to Susan. Terry had intended to start slowly, telling Susan how much he loved her and how hard he would try to make it work. He was, he said, even willing to think about a move, maybe back East. Except that he needed some time to see what sort of employment might be available, perhaps he could get on with one of the local police departments.

Terry had even written it all out, though when he spoke to her he didn't make it sound as if he were reading. He just didn't want to forget anything. He wanted Susan to know that he was willing to bend, that he'd try anything she wanted to put things back the way they once had been.

Susan allowed him to finish, not saying a word during his explanation, his pleading. He could hear her take a deep breath, just before she spoke. She said that Jeff couldn't come to the phone, and that she'd decided to start divorce proceedings.

Even now, sitting on the bench, slumped over in front of his locker, staring at the picture of his son, Terry remembered how matter-of-fact she'd been.

She had decided to start divorce proceedings.

Like two lawyers talking to each other; it was that cold.

Terry could still hear the sound of his voice as it cracked while he pleaded with her to reconsider. He recalled how it felt as if all the blood in his body had instantly rushed to his head, the fear of never seeing his son again.

Susan calmly explained to him how this wasn't something sudden, that she had been thinking about it for months. That it hadn't been good between them for years and that this was the best thing for everybody.

He remembered holding the telephone pressed against his ear and hearing the words, but not listening. His mind groped for something to grab onto, a lifeline to save him. He could hear the voice of Susan's father in the background, as if he were prompting her. A regular cheerleader, Terry had thought. They had never hit it off. And now, Terry figured, his father-in-law had one more of his children, and a grandchild—*his child*—to play daddy to.

Terry pulled off his sweats and started to get into his uniform. He noticed that his boots and Sam Browne belt needed polishing, and remembered the sergeant saying something about that at inspection earlier in the week.

He slipped into his pants, then sat on the bench, punching his feet into his leather boots. His mind drifted from the conversation with Susan and focused on the lawyer he had seen about the divorce. One of the guys had said that the lawyer was good, that he reduced his fees for cops. The lawyer told Terry to be patient. He said that courts almost always placed the child, especially one as young as Jeff, with the mother. Terry knew that, except he wanted to hear something else. He wanted the lawyer to tell him that it would be a piece of cake to get Jeff back living with him in California. He wanted the lawyer to make Susan suffer for the pain she'd caused.

But the lawyer just said to be patient. "These things," the lawyer said, "take time."

Terry slipped the front and back pieces of his bullet-proof vest over his shoulders and snugged down the straps. He put his shirt over the vest, slowly zipping the front.

After talking with Susan, he had gone from shock and surprise, to disappointment, then anger. Now the frustration was causing the anger to seethe inside him, like acid on an open wound. And it wasn't a feeling that was entirely unwelcome. It provided him with a sense of focus, something to take his mind off the fact that his reason for living had been taken from him. Things had gone bad, he now thought, but he would get even. He sensed that his aggression would carry him in the right direction.

Terry strapped on his Sam Browne belt, attaching the

Keepers to the inner belt of his pants to hold the Sam Browne in place. He made sure he had both leather handcuff cases, his R.O.V.E.R. holder, key holder, and baton ring. Then he adjusted the badge and placed his name tag on his shirt.

He removed the black nylon bag containing his notebooks and riot gear, and placed the bag on the bench. Inside the notebooks were preprinted divider sheets containing departmental policy for various field situations, along with blank crime and arrest report forms.

At roll call, Terry found a chair in back and waited for the lieutenant and the sergeants to enter. He occupied himself with his F.I. cards, discouraging conversation with his fellow officers. He wasn't in the mood for small talk. He still hadn't told anyone about Susan's leaving. The lawyer had suggested that he advise his sergeant of the problem, perhaps take some time off to go back East. But Terry felt uncomfortable doing that. They liked him at the station. He was a good cop. Something like this, he thought, would change the way the others looked at him.

"You okay, Terry?"

He looked up to see Cheryl Kent standing a few feet from the desk, fiddling with her badge.

"Uh, yeah, sure. Why, something wrong?"

"You just seem a little quiet lately. Walked right by me without even saying hi."

"Sorry. Uh, I'm a little out of it. My boy was up all night." He waited, watching her expression to see if the excuse would work again. She smiled, signaling that it had.

"I know all about that," she said. "Mine are at my mother's now, thank God. I tell ya, I gave that woman a ration of shit while I was growing up, but I don't know what I would do without her."

Terry smiled. "Most of us are like that."

"Yeah, guess so."

Normally, Terry would have welcomed Cheryl Kent's company. They'd gone through the academy together and had sat next to each other during the classroom part of their training. Cheryl had just made the minimum height requirement for entry, and during most of the physical training, had suffered due to the disparity in height and weight between herself and the other trainees. What she lacked in physical stature, though, she made up for in smarts. Cheryl had helped Terry work his way through the bookwork, courtroom procedure, and search-and-seizure law, and Terry had returned the favor, practicing martial arts and in-field exercises with her after class.

Though she was as quick and agile as any of the male officers, as Terry looked around the squad room, Cheryl Kent still remained the smallest person at the station. Most of the other guys, even the other females, harbored unspoken doubts about her ability to back them up in a physical situation.

The room grew quiet as the lieutenant and two sergeants entered together. Cheryl Kent gave him a quick wave and found a seat on the other side of the room. One of the sergeants began addressing the group of uniformed officers, referring to the large magnetic board set up in front. Roll was taken, the partners and cars were assigned according to the name plates on the board. One sergeant referred to the Rotator, announcing the names of suspects for whom warrants had been issued, while the other sergeant passed out a series of small pocket-sized photographs of some of the wanted suspects.

Terry looked around, seeing the others making notes in their field officer's notebooks as the sergeant spoke. Terry pulled out his notebook and made as if he were checking something, though his mind had already left the roll-call room.

After roll call, there was a fifteen-minute training session during which Terry thought of Jeff and planned how he would bring the boy back home. He figured he could fly back East on a day off, pick the boy up without Susan knowing, and bring him back to California. After all, he thought, why should Susan have any more claim over Jeff than he had? The lawyer would go through the roof, no doubt, but he didn't care. As long as he had his son back with him, everything would be okay.

Terry was assigned to an L-car this shift. That was good. All by himself with time to think and no other partner to have to make small talk. Not that he didn't normally like to have a partner officer in the car to break the boredom. But today was different. In fact, every day had been different since Susan had left with Jeff. Now all Terry wanted was to be alone with his thoughts, his plans. The L-car was the perfect place, just cruise around the city thinking about the future.

Terry went to the kit-room and checked out his R.O.V.E.R., a shotgun, car keys, a taser, and a print kit. He then carried all his gear to the car.

He knew he was supposed to perform a five-point check on the shotgun, but he didn't. He merely loaded the gun and locked it into the rack at the base of the front seat. He wanted to get on the road, and since there was no partner to check on his moves, he could do what he wanted. Instead of lifting the backseat and checking for weapons and contraband, he merely slid behind the wheel, and after filling up with gas, headed into the early evening twilight.

After logging in on the Mobile Digital Terminal, he

removed the R.O.V.E.R. from his belt and inserted it into the CONVERTACOM in the dash. His daily field activities report lay on the seat next to him, though he didn't plan on making many stops this shift. He didn't have the time or inclination to be filling out the log or making arrests. This was going to be six or seven hours to himself.

Terry pulled the patrol vehicle onto a side street in a small industrial park. The businesses were all closed and the parking lot empty. He reached into his nylon bag and felt around among his gear for the pint of Jim Beam, then removed the bottle and took three long pulls. He felt the whiskey going straight to his head, as his brain sizzled for a split-second with each pull from the bottle. Then the warm numbing sensation as the liquor hit his stomach, firing his anger and frustration, making him impatient with his own lack of action.

In the night sky he saw the running lights of an airliner and wondered where it was headed. He would soon be on a plane himself, he thought. He'd get his son back if it was the last thing he did. And more than that, he'd get even with Susan for what she'd done.

Terry looked around, making sure he wasn't being observed, then took one last pull before replacing the bottle in the bag and heading back to the street.

He felt his fingers in a death grip on the steering wheel and told himself to ease off. He draped his right wrist over the top of the wheel, trying to relax. But it was no good. Deep inside, somewhere in that part of his brain that was beyond his control, the flames of blind retribution were being stoked.

And there was nothing that Terry Lampley could do to control the blaze.

* * *

At first he was disappointed. Then once he realized that it didn't matter, he went about his preparations with the same excitement as before.

Nestor decided that he'd use the Bauer this time, and when he located the patent lawyer, he'd buy another gun. He would have to go shopping for another one eventually. This was just a small crimp in his plans, nothing to worry about.

He had called the patent lawyer's firm, Taylor & Crockett, asking for the lawyer by name, Ron Jacobs. He was told that the lawyer had left the firm, moved up north to the Bay Area. They weren't sure if he was even practicing law anymore. When he asked for the lawyer's new address, the receptionist asked Nestor who he was, and told him that the lawyer would have to return his call.

Nestor hung up after that. He didn't want to identify himself, and the receptionist sounded as if she'd been instructed to screen all of the lawyer's calls. Sure, he could have given her a phony name, but then she would have asked for his phone number and Nestor couldn't give her that.

He'd find the lawyer eventually. It was just a matter of time.

But his system had geared up for this one already. He had the gun and the legal saying. He had already envisioned himself placing the Bauer against the lawyer's forehead, smiling, then blowing the lawyer's brains from his skull. He had seen himself cutting out the lawyer's tongue, then writing his saying on the lawyer's own business card and placing the card in the lawyer's mouth.

Nestor felt like an athlete before the big game. Everything he had done or thought for days before had been designed for him to peak at this moment, the moment he took the lawyer's life.

The receptionist had given him a name, though. A new lawyer, one of the partners who had taken over the patent attorney's cases. "Could she," the receptionist had said, not wanting to lose a possible client for the firm, "possibly be of help?"

Nestor remembered being amused by that, how greedy the lawyers were. Even now, it still brought a smile.

The firm wouldn't lose him as a client, he thought. Not a chance.

Nestor waited in the shadows of the parking garage for the partner. He'd decided that it was the partner's law firm that had really benefited from his invention and the money and legal work it had generated. Nestor reminded himself that all lawyers were scum and double-dealers, not to be trusted. He thought that by killing the partner, he would not only be sending a message to all lawyers, but would be throwing the cops off the scent by choosing someone who didn't know him from Adam. He figured they were already knee-deep in the files of the other two lawyers, looking for a lead, looking for his name.

The last of the other lawyers had gone home over an hour earlier. Jamie realized she was running late, but the hearing was tomorrow and the paralegal had failed to Shepardize two key cases she had cited in her brief. She had the Shepards opened on her desk as she lifted the receiver to call Curt.

Running her fingertip down the list of citations, as she punched in the telephone number she discovered that, as of the most recent pocket-part update, her cases had not been overturned, they were still good law.

"Hi, honey," she said, hearing Curt's voice against the din of barroom laughter. She closed the *Shepards Citator*.

"Sorry, I'm running a little late. There were a few things I had to check. Last-minute stuff."

"I can barely hear you," he said. "The bar in this place makes T.G.I. Friday's sound like a convent."

"You started without me?"

"Sorry. I just felt like celebrating. Us, I mean."

"I'll forgive you then."

"I'll save a place for you at the bar," he said. "The food in here must be pretty good, the place is packed."

"Okay, I'm on my way out the door. And Curt?

"Uh-huh?"

"I love you."

"Me too."

It couldn't have worked out better. There she was, looking a little tired, her mind elsewhere. Dangling a set of car keys from her fingers, and lugging that big leather briefcase.

He slipped behind the lawyer as she stood at the driver's door. She had placed the briefcase on top of the car. Nestor thought he heard her humming something to herself as she fiddled with the lock.

That was sweet.

"Wha . . . !"

She turned, hearing him breathing. Jumped back against the car, dropping the keys to the pavement. They made a slight tinkling noise at his feet.

"Don't, please don't!"

She sprayed him with saliva as she spoke. But Nestor didn't mind. She was just scared, he thought, as well she should be. Her eyes were wide open and she'd withdrawn her arms and hands into her chest. It made Nestor think of the pose he had put the squirrel in, the one Ellie had caught.

Nestor raised the Bauer and placed the tip of the barrel against her forehead. He watched a tear trickle down across her cheek, and saw his own image in the murky center of her eye, holding the Bauer and smiling.

"No, please," she said, softer this time.

She knows it's useless.

"What do you want? I'll give you money. Please don't . . . Please . . ."

Nestor grew tired of her pleading and pulled the trigger, sending a spray of blood and bone and tissue out the back of her head into the air and against the side of her car.

She slumped against the driver's door, then fell to the ground, her face thudding against the side-view mirror, then cracking again on the concrete.

Nestor looked around, listening carefully.

Nothing.

During the entire time he'd waited for the attorney inside the garage, only one car had passed. Now there was nothing. Only the garish reflection of the overhead lights in the parking garage, the fumes and exhaust of long-departed commuters, and the absolute silence.

Nestor set to work, first placing the thin plastic surgical gloves on his hands, then removing the woman's tongue and placing it in the plastic sandwich baggy. Then he put the baggy and the gun back inside the cloth bag and pulled the drawstring shut.

With his gloves still on, he opened the attorney's brief-case and searched around, looking for her business cards. They were there, in a gold metal container underneath some papers. He used one of the attorney's pens to write on the card, just below the lawyer's printed name, the message that he'd memorized:

The first thing we do, let's kill all the lawyers.

That made Nestor smile. He never much cared for Shakespeare, but he'd heard the phrase before and he certainly agreed with the sentiment. Using it here, he thought, was perfect. The cops would know that they weren't dealing with someone who was ignorant. They'd respect him. And more important, Crystal would just love him for this.

Nestor bent over the dead woman's face, or what was left of it, and placed the card gently inside her mouth so that his message and the lawyer's name were clearly visible. He stood and took one last look at the woman before leaving.

In his mind as he turned and walked into the shadows, he visualized the quote he had written on the card just below the printed words *Jamie Sills, Attorney at Law.*

Eleven

They smiled at each other, like how easy could it get? They were right there on the boulevard, less than a block from the Century Bank Building when the call came through.

Jim Burnham nodded to his partner, then accelerated to the corner, where he made a quick left, squealing the tires. Another quick left brought them to the mouth of the parking structure. The patrol vehicle bucked as they took the raised entry ramp without slowing.

Burnham's partner for the night, Rick O'Meara, lifted the hand microphone from the dash and notified central dispatch that they were at the scene. He had a cup of coffee in a Styrofoam cup balanced between his legs as he spoke. When Burnham took the driveway at full speed, the hot liquid lapped over the edge of the cup, scalding his crotch.

"Jesus, Jim!"

Burnham glanced over and smiled. O'Meara dropped the hand mic and began wiping himself.

"Sorry, part."

"Yeah," muttered O'Meara. "I'll bet."

Burnham slowed the patrol vehicle once inside the

garage. The car's headlights illuminated the otherwise murky gray structure. The two officers looked intently out the windows as Burnham maneuvered up and down the aisles, slowly spiraling the car up the levels of the garage.

"There," said O'Meara, pointing to a vehicle that was parked toward the end of the aisle, near the elevators.

Burnham brought the patrol car to a stop opposite a late-model Acura sedan. A body was visible on the ground near the car. Even before exiting the patrol vehicle, they could see the pool of blood under the body. It followed the slope of the garage floor, running in a narrow trickle toward a metal drainage grate.

A man was seated near the body, bent over, his head in his hands. Both officers unsnapped the leather guard on their holsters and exited the patrol car.

"Just remain seated, sir," said Burnham, carefully approaching. "Rick," he said, then gestured toward the seated man. O'Meara approached, his palm resting on the grip of his gun.

O'Meara said, "Do you have some identification, sir?"

The man looked up. His eyes were red and his hair disheveled. He had the look of a small child, lost in a department store. Petrified. It was obvious to O'Meara that the man had been crying. The man gave O'Meara a blank stare for a moment, then covered his face and head with his hands and began throwing up. The wretching echoed in the empty cavernous structure.

"This one's dead," said Burnham.

O'Meara glanced over at his partner.

"Better call for backup," said Burnham. "Get a coroner's van out here, and call Homicide."

O'Meara wanted to look at the body, but didn't want to leave the man unguarded.

"Keep an eye on this one," he said.

Jim Burnham didn't know if he was dealing with a suspect or a witness. The call had come through specifying a shooting, with a male informant at the scene. Burnham had been around long enough to know that not every murderer did his business and then split. The man seated on the dirty concrete floor could be an innocent observer; then again, he could also be the killer. You didn't take chances in these situations.

"Sir," said Burnham, standing about six feet away. He'd drawn his service revolver and held it in his outstretched hands. "I want you to slowly lay facedown on the ground."

The face looked up, uncomprehending.

"Please! Sir," said Burnham, using his command voice. "Do as I say."

The man slowly got on all fours, then laid on his stomach.

Burnham approached, moving the man's legs apart with his boot, patting the man down for weapons.

"I know her," the man said, softly. "I'm the one that called."

Burnham slipped two fingers inside the man's coat pocket and removed a wallet. With his eyes still watching the prone suspect, Burnham flipped through the photos inside the wallet, looking for identification.

"They're on their way," said O'Meara. He had come back from the patrol car and was looking over his partner's shoulder.

In the stillness of the early morning, the wail of approaching police sirens could be heard. The only other sound was the echoed sobbing of the suspect, who lay prone on the concrete, no more than a foot from the dead woman.

O'Meara pointed to a photograph in the suspect's wallet.

"That's her," he said.

Both men compared the subject in the photograph to the woman on the ground. Burnham flipped to the next photograph.

"Jesus," said O'Meara. "Look." He pointed to the last picture in the plastic photo holder.

"That's Powell," said O'Meara.

Both officers took a closer look at the suspect.

"Jimmy," said O'Meara, staring into the hollow, vacant face of the suspect. "You know who this is?"

Burnham took one final look at the wallet, then closed it. He carefully placed it back inside the man's jacket, then said, "Yeah, I know who it is."

Both officers felt uncomfortable, like intruders, gazing down at the man and the woman. The man lay on his side, with his knees raised in the fetal position. He clutched the dead woman's hands to his lips, whispering and crying as he kissed her fingers.

"It's Curt Denmark," said Burnham.

Part Two

Twelve

"I'll have another," he said, handing the glass to the cabin attendant, a slender white girl who he figured was pushing thirty and trying not to look it.

"Thank you, sir," she said.

When she bent over to take his glass, he noticed her delicate white lace bra and creamy skin in the space where she had forgotten to secure one of the buttons of her blouse.

He was glad he'd decided to fly first class. Not that he usually didn't. But there were times when, for appearances, he'd have to buy an economy ticket and be herded on board the airplane with the masses, huffing and puffing in the stale, overcrowded cabin, jockeying for a seat. And then inevitably they'd stick some ill-behaved child or some dotty old woman next to him.

But this was great. A man of his size needed the extra room. When he flew economy, he could barely squeeze his hips between the armrests, not to mention the embarrassment of having to stand in the aisle, waiting for one of the bathrooms to clear, and nobody being able to get by.

"Here you are, Mr. Poindexter."

The cabin attendant handed him his drink. He didn't

immediately offer his hand. He waited for her to bend over and place it on his table. When she did, he again glanced at the opening in her blouse.

"Thank you, child," he said. "And it's *Reverend* Poindexter."

"Oh, I'm sorry, sir." She tilted her head to one side and smiled. Then she bent over again, this time wiping some crumbs from his table. "Just let me clean this up a little for you, sir," she said, trying to please.

"That's just fine, child."

The Reverend Lamont Poindexter took a sip of his drink. He was glad the young woman wanted to please. He wondered whether it would be too chancey to steer their conversation to a more interesting topic.

"Tell me, child," he said, looking around the almost empty first-class section. "Do you make your home in Los Angeles?"

"Why, yes, sir. Manhattan Beach. You familiar with L.A.?"

He shook his head, looking at her blouse over the rim of his glass. He continued to sip, his eyes focused on her chest.

"It's south of LAX," she said. "A little beach community. I've lived there all my life. My parents still do."

"That's nice," he said.

He could feel the sweat slowly running down his lower back. Even in the oversized seats of first class he felt pinched for space. He knew he would be in L.A. for only a few days, and that there really wasn't time to start anything with the young white girl. Besides, if he didn't play it right, that could lead to a lot of trouble.

"Ya know," the attendant said, wrinkling her nose. "Haven't I seen you somewhere?"

He smiled. "You may have seen me on television."

"That's it," she said. "You're that guy who's always leading those marches." She brought her hand to her mouth, then quickly added, "I mean, Reverend, you were involved in that big case in New York, right? The one about that girl that was raped?"

"Yes, I was. The Delilah Jefferson case."

"I thought so," she said, pointing at him.

Lamont Poindexter smiled and allowed himself a chuckle. The white girl, he thought, was stupid. So stupid that he might just be able to get away with what he'd been thinking.

"I'll be staying at the Bonaventure," he said, "while I'm in Los Angeles. If you're in the area, perhaps you'd care to stop by and say hello."

Then she said thank you, and gave him a smile and a pat on the shoulder that told him just how stupid she was. She didn't have the slightest idea what he had in mind.

He adjusted the seat and stretched out, his mind replaying his conversation with the girl. Yes, he thought, she had probably caught his action on the Delilah Jefferson case. He'd made all the network broadcasts the week that case broke. His picture was in *Time* and *Newsweek,* along with every major metropolitan newspaper in the country. He was flying high then. Movie stars and agents were calling him, wanting to appear with him at his press conferences, wanting to jump on the Delilah Jefferson bandwagon.

Then it had all turned sour. Delilah, against his counsel, gave that interview to one of the New York TV stations. She admitted telling a friend that she made up the story about getting raped to get attention. That she didn't mean anything by it, and that once the whole thing got going it was just too big for her to stop.

He'd had to lay low for a few months after that. But

after the first few weeks, his phone stopped ringing off the hook. He released a statement saying that he still believed in the young girl, and that interests antagonistic to the black movement in this country had gotten to the girl and were behind Delilah's recanting her story. The statement went largely unnoticed, which is what he intended.

Lamont Poindexter told himself that this time would be different. They had a video tape of the police. The whole world would see that this was not another Delilah Jefferson.

The attorney was planning a public spectacle. And who better, the attorney had said, then the Reverend Lamont Poindexter to spearhead the movement among the black community.

He snugged the seatbelt around his huge belly, as the overhead signs signaled that the plane was about to land. Within a few minutes, he felt a soft thud, then another, as the wheels came in contact with the runway at LAX.

"I'm glad you could make it on such short notice."

"When it comes to the suffering of my black brothers and sisters," said Poindexter, "I always have the time. Mr. Isaacs, I *make* the time."

"Uh, yeah," said Gerald Isaacs. The two men were walking through the airport to the limo that Isaacs had illegally parked outside at the curb.

As they descended on the escalator, Poindexter pointed out a proclamation from Mayor Tom Bradley that had been installed on the wall just above the escalator, welcoming peoples of all races, creeds, and beliefs to the City of Angels.

"Mayor Tom," said Poindexter. He flashed a grin at

Isaacs. "The white man's good ol' boy, and the black man's worst nightmare."

"Not a friend of yours, huh?"

Poindexter didn't answer. He didn't much care for the mayor, or the mayor's comments about his sensationalizing the Delilah Jefferson case. Poindexter figured the mayor would lay low for a while after this most recent example of police brutality against the black community. The mayor, Poindexter knew, liked to determine which way the political winds were blowing before he took a position.

They arrived at the limo, with the porter in tow. The porter quickly placed the luggage in the trunk, then remained at the curb, waiting.

Poindexter looked at Isaacs, then at the porter, then back at Isaacs.

"Oh, yeah," said Isaacs, reaching into his pocket and pulling out a fistful of change and bills. He picked a one dollar bill from his palm and handed it to the porter.

"Well, thank you very much, sir!"

The porter spoke loud enough to draw the attention of people who were waiting on the sidewalk. He held the bill up to the sunlight in mock admiration. "Yes, I do thank you," he said, thrusting the bill into his pocket. He then turned and headed back inside the terminal, clucking his tongue and saying something under his breath about "damn white folks."

"I've got a press conference set up at the hotel for this afternoon," said Isaacs. The two men were seated in the back of the limousine. Though the limo's air conditioner was blowing cool refrigerated air, Poindexter still felt hot. Under his coat, his silk shirt was stuck to his skin. He realized he should have dressed for warmer weather.

"All the major media will be represented," said Isaacs.

"Monroe will, of course, be there. They released him yesterday." Isaacs flashed a nervous half-smile. "D.A.'s not filing charges. At least not yet. If I know those guys, they're probably scurrying all over the Criminal Courts Building trying to do damage control." Isaacs pursed his lips and shook his head, then gave Poindexter a serious look. He said, "This is a career case, Lamont. It's okay if I call you Lamont, isn't it?"

Poindexter turned away from the window to face the attorney. He thought to himself that for some reason on this day it was to be his destiny to have to converse with stupid white people.

"Sure, Gerry," he said. He tried to keep his voice to a whisper. "Except, in public, it might be better if you referred to me as Reverend Poindexter."

"Oh, of course," said Isaacs, holding up his palms. "You got it, Lamont. No problem."

The two men rode in silence down Sepulveda Boulevard. It struck Poindexter that this part of Los Angeles had little in common with the picture-postcard images of Disneyland, or the magazine accounts of glamorous movie industry beautiful-people having lunch on Rodeo Drive. The decayed industrial buildings, traffic gridlock, and gray pollutant-filled air was not much different from New York, or Detroit, or any other big city.

"The tape," said Poindexter, breaking the silence. "Did you bring it with you?"

Gerry Isaacs put his hand to his heart, as if he were having an attack. "Jesus, I almost forgot."

He reached inside a briefcase that was on the floor between his feet and removed a cassette. "I made sure the limo had a VCR just for that purpose," he said as he fiddled with the TV console in the backseat.

"I tellya, Lamont. This case is big. Really big. If we work it right, we could blow the lid off this city."

"And get you a million dollar lawsuit, right, Counselor?"

Isaacs hesitated a moment. "Uh, well, yeah," he said, slightly embarrassed. "That's part of it. I mean, Monroe—that is, Mr. Davis—is entitled to damages. I'm only taking the customary fee in such matters."

"Forty percent of, what would you call it, Gerry? Five million, maybe more?"

"Uh, yeah. Maybe." Isaacs had the cassette in the machine. He was talking to Poindexter while looking at the controls. "But there's lots of work that needs to be done. There, I think it's ready."

Isaacs pushed a button on the TV console. The picture filled with snow for a few seconds, then cleared. A street scene flashed on the small screen, and in the corner of the picture were white letters noting the date and time the video was shot.

"You say a neighbor shot this?"

"Yeah," said Isaacs, adjusting the picture. "Guy was looking out his apartment window at the park across the street. Just our luck that he was there."

The two men watched the video as the limousine headed into downtown. When the tape had completed, Isaacs said, "You want to see it again?"

"That's a copy, right?"

"Hey," said Isaacs. "Would I be stupid enough not to keep the original safely hidden away somewhere?" He smiled. Poindexter also smiled, but not for the same reason.

"What do the doctors say about the injuries?"

"Multiple contusions," said Isaacs. "Fractured skull, broken nose. His leg is broken and the kneecap is shattered. He'll walk again, but not without a lot of operations. He's in a wheelchair now."

"And Mr. Davis?"

Isaacs looked confused. "What about him?"

"Is he going to present us with any problems down the road?"

Isaacs smiled. "You mean, is Monroe Davis likely to turn into another Delilah Jefferson?"

Poindexter winced internally, then nodded.

"No way," said Isaacs. "Monroe and I are like this." Isaacs crossed his fingers as if he were making a wish. "Ol' Monroe knows which side his bread is buttered on. He'll be just fine."

"My people tell me he's got a record."

"Hell, he's got a record, sure. Most of these damn people living in the street got records." Isaacs caught himself. "I mean, you know. Nothing to do with race or anything, but life on the streets is tough. A police record comes with the territory."

Lamont Poindexter thought about saying, "Yeah, tell me about it." Instead he just nodded.

"The tape is good," Poindexter said. "But as good as it is, we have to be ready for when the cops and the rest of the white establishment start making excuses. They'll say Davis is an ex-con who was in violation of his parole. They'll say he was on PCP, totally dusted, out of control. That the drug gave him abnormal strength. That the only way the cops could handle him was by doing what they did."

"What we need to do," said Poindexter, "is make sure that people get our side of the story. We need to rally the black community behind this thing, maybe call for the chief or the mayor to resign, or at least take a stand against the cops that did this."

"Cop," said Isaacs. "Only one cop."

"Okay," said Poindexter. "Lots of cops would be better, but one cop will have to do. My people have done their homework. We'll have a long list of police abuse victims at the press conference. This is an indictment of the system, Mr. Isaacs, not just one cop. The police will try to make it that way. Like this was an isolated incident. We can't let that happen. We're going to put the entire rascist establishment on trial here."

"Gerry. Call me Gerry."

Poindexter didn't respond. He could see where the attorney's head was and knew he'd have to deal with that later. For now, he needed Isaacs.

Poindexter turned to look out the window at the downtown Los Angeles skyline. The tops of the high-rise buildings were obscured by thick brown-gray clouds. The smog settled over the city like a deadly halo. The City of Angels, he thought, remembering the mayor's welcoming plaque at the airport. He turned to Gerald Isaacs and said, "My foundation will expect twenty percent of the gross settlement, plus expenses."

"I have the written contract right here," said Isaacs, not missing a beat. He reached inside his briefcase and removed a two-page document, then handed it to Poindexter.

"Just like we spoke of on the phone," said Isaacs.

"And Davis will agree to this?"

Gerry Isaacs laughed. "Monroe Davis," he said, "will do whatever I tell him to do."

"Good," said Poindexter.

He flicked at the paperwork with his finger. His mind had suddenly shifted away from Gerald Isaacs and Monroe Davis. He was back inside the airplane, staring at the soft white skin of the flight attendant's breasts.

Thirteen

Francis Powell had his driver wait at the curb. He knocked softly on the front door, then, getting no answer, rang the bell. A voice from inside said to come in.

Curt was seated on the couch in the living room, silently staring at the wall. He was dressed in a dark suit. His tie was loosened and the top button of his shirt was undone. He turned his head in Powell's direction for a moment, then went back to staring at the wall.

"It's time, Curt."

Powell moved closer, not wanting to intrude on Curt's thoughts. He stood near the arm of the couch, looking down at his friend.

"I can still see her," whispered Curt. He spoke without looking at Powell. His eyes were transfixed on a spot midway up the empty white wall. "Sitting out on the deck in back. The two of us. Watching the sun go down." He looked out the sliding glass doors, then swiped at his face with his fingertips.

"The car's outside, Curt. You need some help?"

Curt didn't answer. The picture in his mind had changed. In the two days since he'd discovered her lifeless body, the image of Jamie laying in her own blood with her skull splattered in pieces on the car and floor of the garage had occupied center stage in his mind. Try as he might, it was impossible for him to remember her alive, without thoughts of seeing her that last time intruding on his memories.

Yet, like a dream not remembered upon waking, certain details of the night Jamie was shot were hidden deep in his unconscious. He'd been told that the patrol cops had found the two of them, and that they had answered a call from an unidentified informant. Curt remembered being in the hospital afterwards, and Powell saying, "They've brought you here for observation. You're in shock."

That was the first time it struck him that he'd been through this scene before. That the emotional abyss it had taken him five years to crawl out of had swallowed him up once again, and that this time he was doomed to remain floating forever in the darkness.

"Come on, Curt," said Powell, helping him from the couch.

The two men walked arm in arm to the car. Neither spoke during the ride to the cemetary. As the car approached the entry, Powell spotted a large group of people standing on both sides of the driveway.

"What the hell is this?" muttered Powell, hunched forward, peering at the crowd through the window.

The driver slowed and said, "What shall I do, sir?"

"Just drive through, don't stop."

The driver did as he was told, not even slowing for a group of reporters and cameramen standing in front of them, who had to scurry out of the way to avoid being hit.

"Curt," he said, "I'm sorry about this. This was supposed to be a closed ceremony. Family and friends only."

Curt didn't answer. Through the window he could see

Minicam units running up behind Powell's car. Near the entry to the sanctuary there were additional camera crews shooting the mourners as they entered. It was the type of thing that should have angered him, he thought. But it didn't. Anger was not what he felt. In fact, the circus atmosphere made the whole scene seem like a bad dream, and he was very much used to those.

He was aware that he had been numbed by the last two days. He'd pulled within himself as a means of self-preservation, and because he knew of no other way to deal with the pain. Some people in time of great emotional hardship welcomed and found solace in the company of friends. He did not. As with Darren's death, he had retreated into his shell, closing his eyes and ears to the outside world.

Yet, while he tried to insulate himself from others, to convince himself that he no longer cared, he knew that he was on the edge, ready to crack. It was just a matter of time, he thought. The memories, the anger and hatred, the guilt could be held inside for only so long, until finally he'd explode, his psyche shattering into so many little pieces. Like the pieces of his beloved Jamie.

"Just stay close," said Powell, opening the car door. He waited at the door, keeping his body between Curt and the reporters. "No comment," he barked at the crowd. He grabbed Curt at the elbow and whisked him through the shouting reporters into the sanctuary.

The two men sat next to each other in the front row as the rabbi conducted the service. Powell had positioned a half-dozen uniformed officers in the back rows just in case the media got brazen and decided to step inside. As it was, the hum of their conversation and shouted greetings could be heard inside the sanctuary.

During the ceremony Curt's expression didn't change.

He sat motionless, stoically staring at the stage where the rabbi addressed the small crowd of mourners. Powell thought it was as if Curt really weren't there. As if he were still laying next to Jamie in the garage, trapped in time forever.

Curt had donned a pair of sunglasses, making his eyes invisible. The media, the noise from outside, the casket just a few feet in front of him, seemed to have no effect. Powell had the feeling that Curt was irretrievably slipping away. He noticed a single tear escape from behind the dark glasses, and trickle untouched down Curt's cheek.

Once the service was over, the two men, along with the other mourners, ran the gauntlet of reporters back to their cars. The cars moved in a slow procession up the hillside along the cemetery drive to a spot overlooking the sanctuary and the entrance. Chairs had been set up on three sides of the open grave. The casket was chauffeured up the hill in a hearse, and cemetery employees carried it to the grave site.

The media, like swarms of ants, traversed the distance between sanctuary and grave site on foot, trampling over headstones in the process. By the time the service began, the folding chairs had been surrounded on all sides by media people jostling each other for a better camera angle.

Powell felt his blood pressure rising as he tried to maintain control. He had Curt's well-being to be concerned with, and flying off the handle at this point, he knew, would do neither of them any good. He was relieved to see some of the uniformed officers working with the mortuary employees to keep the press further down the hill at a respectable distance from the mourners.

"You know, Francis," whispered Curt, staring at the dark black rectangle of moist soil, and speaking as if he were talking to himself, "I asked her. At least I did that."

Powell looked at Curt, not understanding for the first few seconds. Then he nodded, and put his arm around Curt's shoulders. "That's good, buddy, that's good."

When he had concluded his prayers, the rabbi announced that the mourners would be welcome at the home of one of Jamie's partners, and directions were made available. The mourners stood and began moving away from the grave site. Curt remained seated, laconically accepting their condolences, nodding his head in agreement with the clichéd apologies, the heartfelt sympathies.

After most of the mourners had filed by and were walking down the hillside back to their cars, Powell helped Curt from his chair. The two men stood for a moment, gazing at the polished wooden casket. Powell heard a commotion behind him, turned, and saw a group of reporters climbing up the hill toward them.

"Curt," he said, placing his hand on Curt's back and guiding him to the side. "We should be getting back to the car."

Curt didn't move. He remained staring at the casket, trying to make some sense of the foreboding hole that had been cut into the hillside.

"Mr. Denmark," said a voice from behind. Powell turned. It was Crystal Pelotas with a camera unit at her side. Powell put up his hand, trying to wave her off.

"Not now," said Powell through clenched teeth. "Don't you people have any respect?"

"Just a few questions," said Pelotas, undaunted. She looked to make sure that her camera crew was getting it all.

"Chief," she said, "now that Mr. Denmark has suffered

such a tragic loss, do you think it will affect your handling of the Barrister Butcher investigation?"

Powell refused to answer. He threw Pelotas a scowl, then took Curt's arm and moved him to the side, trying to outskirt the group of newspeople who were quickly gathering around the grave.

"No comment," he barked, trying to find an opening in the crowd. He was aware that the media were pushing in closer, circling around for position. People were shouting questions and thrusting microphones at them. He and Curt had their backs to the grave and were only a few feet from the hole.

"There'll be a statement released later," said Powell, moving to his left, spotting what he thought was an opening in the crowd.

"What about the Monroe Davis beating?" yelled a reporter from the back of the crowd.

The group seemed to have closed ranks, pressing closer to the grave. Powell had his hand at Curt's elbow and could feel Curt's arm shaking. He glanced at Curt and noticed his lower lip quivering, and tears streaming down his face from behind his sunglasses.

"I have no comment about that either," said Powell, referring to the recent allegations of police brutality. He had received his second briefing on the incident just that morning. The reports were still coming in.

Powell decided it was now or never. He was determined not to succumb to the bullying tactics of the media. He didn't want to give them that satisfaction, and Curt was in no condition to field questions. He was becoming increasingly unsteady on his feet, and Powell felt his friend's weight leaning against him as they tried to find an opening in the crowd.

Powell grabbed Curt and surged between two cameramen, using his free arm to hook the cameraman in order to get by, like a forward working the low-post and spinning toward the basket. He thought he was home free when he heard someone yell, then a thudding sound accompanied by a groan. Then there was more yelling.

When he looked back, he saw a group of cameramen pointing their cameras at the inside of the grave. A soundman was at the edge of the grave extending his hand, pulling out one of his compatriots who had fallen inside.

Powell shook his head, dreading how the incident would play out on the evening news. He grabbed Curt and practically ran back to the waiting car.

"That's great stuff, Crystal."

Crystal flashed Colin Archer a pencil-thin smile.

Archer added, "That shot of the soundman falling into the grave is a bit touchy, though, don't you think?"

"Run it," she said. She handed the microphone to one of the crew and started for her car. Archer ran after her.

"Wait up, Crystal."

She turned, pausing only long enough to let him catch up.

"Some people," he said, "might take that grave business the wrong way. The network suits might not like us showing members of the press pushing each other into graves in order to get a good photo op."

"It wasn't our crew, was it?" Crystal kept walking, but the anger in her voice was obvious.

"No. But—"

"Listen Colin," she said, turning and gesturing with her finger. "If Powell and Denmark hadn't been in such an all-fire hurry to blast out of here, that would've never happened. You saw the way they treated us. Like the

Butcher's latest victim being his investigator's fiancée is not big news? Like the citizens of this city have no stake in whether their police department ever catches this guy?" Crystal shook her head in disgust. "Francis Powell thinks he can say and do just about anything when it comes to protecting his friends."

"Okay, okay," said Archer, holding up a restraining hand. "I'm on your side, remember?"

"Yeah, sorry, Colin. It's not your fault."

The apology was there, but the words sounded unconvincing to Colin Archer. He'd worked with Crystal long enough to know that she kept certain things secret, even from him. She had that look now. The one she got when she was scheming to get even.

"Do me a favor," he said. They had reached Crystal's car and were standing outside the rear passenger door. "Before you use anything on the Butcher, at least run it by me. I promise I won't step on your action, but if the shit hits the fan, it's going to be *my* little ass on the line."

"I'd never do anything," she said, slipping into the backseat of her Mercedes, "that would jeopardize your position, Colin." She smiled that same smile he'd seen before. That same look of revenge that he'd come to dread. "You know that."

With that, Crystal pulled the door closed and the car started slowly for the exit, leaving Colin Archer standing at the curb wondering what mischief Crystal had up her sleeve.

Crystal put her head back against the leather seat of the Mercedes, closed her eyes, and tried to blank everything from her mind. She could almost do it, except for what had happened this morning. But that was her little secret.

It now rested somewhere in her chest, right behind her heart, sending out small pleasurable jolts of excitement. After a few minutes, she opened her eyes, feeling more relaxed, able to think things through.

Francis Powell, she thought, now had a major problem. His lead investigator on the Barrister Butcher investigation could barely function, let alone head up a complex police inquiry designed to capture a serial killer. From what she'd seen of Curt Denmark at the funeral, it was doubtful that he'd be in any shape to carry on with his duties.

Powell, on the other hand, would continue to function like the political animal that he was. The question was, who would Powell choose to replace Denmark, and how would this latest killing play in the media.

That bit with the soundman falling into the grave, she knew, was borderline stuff. Some viewers would take offense to what they might consider an intrusion by the media into a very private and personal moment. But she could overcome that. She'd done it before, and her viewers, her faithful, had believed her. She'd just put on her serious, somewhat hurt expression. The look that said, "I realize some of you might think this behavior is extreme, and truthfully, so do I, but in the journalistic interest of giving you all the news, even the not-so-pleasant variety, we feel obligated to run the tape."

She had no doubt she could pull it off. And the scene in the grave would have people talking for weeks.

As the car sped down the freeway, Crystal found herself outlining the situation in her mind. Francis Powell had stuck by his friend in the past. With his officially sanctioned execution of Travis Jackson, Curt Denmark had come close to falling, and it was only due to Powell's influence that the investigation into Jackson's death was short-circuited.

But this was different. Denmark's lover had been brutally murdered by the very same killer Denmark was assigned to apprehend. With Travis Jackson, Powell hadn't been willing to risk officially putting his friend so close to the investigation. Would this case be any different? Would Francis Powell take the same position and find a replacement for Denmark?

The more she thought about it, the more she questioned whether Powell would try the same approach this time.

It would be interesting, she mused, to have Curt Denmak stay on the case. The revenge motive would make great press. And who could possibly be more vigorous in the quest to capture the Butcher than the victim's lover?

Crystal gazed out the window at the graffiti-covered freeway signs. They were passing near the area where the Butcher's first victim had been found.

She said, "Turn on the radio, would you, Paul?"

Crystal listened to the all-news station, her mind drifting back and forth between the funeral scene and the newscaster's voice. The announcer reported that the L.A.P.D. was conducting an internal investigation into the alleged brutal beating of Monroe Davis by one of its officers. And that Davis had been released from custody without formal charges being filed against him. The radio broadcast concluded with a quote from Davis' attorney, Gerald Isaacs, stating that Mr. Davis intended to fully pursue his legal rights and seek damages from the City of Los Angeles and the L.A.P.D. for the grievous injuries he sustained at the hands of the police.

"Turn it off," said Crystal.

She thought a moment about the broadcast. She could

see that this Monroe Davis story had potential. She'd seen the videotape of the cop pounding on Davis with his baton. She remembered the look on Powell's face at the funeral when the question about Davis had been asked. Like Powell was in no mood to answer any questions, especially not that one.

Crystal made a mental note to contact Gerry Isaacs. Perhaps, she thought, it was time to use what she knew about Isaacs. Trade a favor for a favor. She thought about how curt she'd been with Isaacs the last time they met. She'd have to do something about that. Maybe invite him over one night and whisper in his ear what she'd heard about his dealing nose candy out of his law office.

That thought, and the expression she could imagine on Isaacs' face when she mentioned it, made her smile. She had learned to hold on to such information, little tidbits of painful truth. There was always the right moment, just the perfect time to apply a little pressure to get what she wanted. Like a fine wine, it wouldn't do to pop Gerry Isaacs' cork too soon. She would let the Isaacs vintage mature and ripen on the shelf before she consumed him.

Just like now, with the Butcher.

At least, she *thought* it was the Butcher.

She'd received the phone call late last night. The high-pitched voice on the other end had identified himself as the Butcher. He claimed to be a big fan of hers. She let the guy go on, not sure if he was a crank or not. Then he described exactly how he'd killed Jamie Sills. Step by step, without emotion, as if he were reading a set of instructions. And when he finished, he asked her if she believed him.

Crystal wasn't sure. She'd received more than her share of crank calls, and there was nothing this guy had said that hadn't already been reported in the papers.

"Tell me something I don't already know," she said. She could hear the caller's breathing become heavier.

"You don't believe me," he said, clucking his tongue. "I'm very disappointed, Crystal."

"I get a lot of these calls," she said. "When the Matador contacted me, he proved who he was. He told me things that only he would know."

She could hear him chuckling to himself. Then he sighed, and said, "Well, Crystal, if you insist." There was a silence on the phone. She could hear the rasp of his breath as if he had the receiver pressed against his teeth.

"I'm going to send you a little present, Crystal," he said. And then he hung up.

Crystal suddenly felt cold, the sort of icy chill that starts in the throat and explodes inside.

"It's cold back here, Paul."

She watched the driver press some buttons on the dash, lowering the air conditioning. But the cold persisted, and she knew it had nothing to do with the temperature inside the car. Her fingers were going numb, turning yellow-white at the tips, even though her palms were sweating. It was the same sensation she'd experienced when the Matador had first called her.

Crystal sat on her hands, trying to warm them. She tried closing her eyes again to relax. She told herself that it wasn't yet time to reveal what she knew. It wasn't yet time to tell her audience that she'd been contacted by the Butcher.

And it certainly wasn't the right time to tell anyone that she'd found a package on her doorstep that morning containing a human tongue wrapped in a sandwich baggie.

Fourteen

He was drawn to the bike after her death, and that sur
prised him. Considering all that he and Jamie had beer
through, and the role that the bike had played in thei
relationship, his almost religious resumption of the lon
morning bike rides was unexpected.

After two weeks, the memories of finding her body ha
begun to haze over—except in his dreams. During th
day, he found himself moving from one room to the next
viewing with painful precision the photographs of the tw
of them, notes in Jamie's handwriting tacked to th
kitchen cabinets, the quilt she'd selected draped over th
sofa, or the various other small touches that were Jamie's

He had come to believe that he needed the long bik
rides to pull himself away from those memories. He wa:
confused, wanting to be inside the house near those thing:
that reminded him of Jamie, and at the same time, findin
the memories too painful to bear.

When the darkness poured in, though, he had n
choice. Each night since the funeral, he'd dreamed of her
Sometimes he'd be lucky and awake in the early morning
ripped from the terror of his dreams, drenched in sweat
his pulse racing, his body still shaking.

But at least he was awake. At least he had escaped, momentarily, from the nightmare.

The rides through the canyon became earlier and longer. Trying to fall back to sleep was useless, and there was always the fear that he'd drop back into the dreams.

Curt found himself often setting out on the roads in the darkness. He'd worked into a sort of routine, forcing himself from his bed the moment he awoke, fighting the lifelong habit of closing his eyes in an effort to get those few extra minutes of precious sleep. Sleep was no longer precious for him. The time he spent away from the nightmares was now what he valued.

Jamie was with him on the bike, when his mind drifted from the road to her face and her gentle ways. While riding, he didn't see her in death, and he was grateful for that. The damp cool morning air, the swirling mists of fog slapping wet against his face as he raced down the hill, reminded him of their rides together, of the jokes she made whispering in his ear. At times he could still feel her seated behind him. He could feel her breath on the back of his neck, and smell her scent as they moved together on the bike.

He had decided to quit the Butcher investigation, to take some time off from the cops, from his practice—from everything. He wasn't sure what he would do, but he knew he couldn't go on doing what he had, acting like he'd gotten over her death and that life had to go on.

He'd been down that steep and winding trail before and was familiar with its dangers. He'd tried to come back too soon after Darren's death, and had tasted what it was like to act the lie. It had almost killed him.

Not this time, not again. No more masks for him. If people thought him pathetic, if they pitied him, then so be it.

Curt sped north down Laurel Canyon, toward Ventura Boulevard. Each corner, even at speed, held memories, images that clicked in his mind like signposts on the interstate.

The Bistro at Coldwater, where he and Jamie had had dinner that summer evening with the French windows open and the hiss of bougainvillea rustling in the warm breeze.

Then there was Dutton's, where they had spent many a lazy Sunday afternoon browsing the nooks and crannies of the old bookstore, buying novels to add to the pile of unread books they already had.

At Valley College, Curt headed back, completing the loop. The morning traffic on Ventura was starting to back up. He maneuvered the bike carefully between the cars as he passed Art's Deli. Through the window, he spotted the same group of old men chatting at their table. He thought of his meeting with Francis Powell, of his agreeing to take on the Butcher investigation. An easy decision, Powell had said. And so Curt had thought at the time.

But none of them are easy, are they?

He braked suddenly, within inches of the rear bumper of a BMW. His mind had wandered to that conversation with Powell, to the research and investigation that had followed. And finally, to Jamie's inanimate form sprawled on the oily gray concrete, her lifeblood draining away forever.

Curt pushed the images of death from his mind, forcing them away by sheer mental effort. He focused on the road and on his aching muscles as he pounded the pedals up Laurel Canyon, consciously not reducing his speed even as the canyon road grew steeper.

Once home, he leaned the bike against the side of the garage and entered the house on unsteady legs. He felt the muscles in his legs throbbing, ready to explode. His knees were numb. He grabbed a quart of orange juice from the refrigerator and drained what was left, gasping for air once he'd finished. He then pulled the sweat-soaked jersey over his head and headed for the shower, flicking on the radio along the way.

The jets of hot water from the shower soothed his now pulsating calves and thighs. He'd overdone that last uphill stretch and he knew it. But he'd had no choice. It was the only thing that worked, pure physical exertion to the point of explosion, to rid himself of the demons of memory.

In the background, just the other side of the steamy hiss, Curt could hear voices coming from the radio. He was barely paying attention, though. He grasped the base of the showerhead with both hands and hung there, letting the spray wash over his hair and face as he dropped his chin to his chest, concentrating on the myriad streams of sheening water cascading over his chest and genitals. The water-blurred image of his own body was like looking through a misty camera lens, and was not unlike the way he saw her now, his Jamie, when he thought of her that last time.

He toweled himself dry and got dressed in the Levis and T-shirt that had become his uniform since Jamie's death.

There were messages on his tape. He could see the blinking red light, and that the number had increased from the last time he'd looked.

He made coffee for himself in the kitchen, then took the cup out onto the deck. The morning fog had disappeared, leaving droplets of mist on the wood railing and patio chair as a reminder of its return.

Curt wiped the chair and sat near the railing, placing his feet on the lower rail. He took a slow sip of the steaming coffee, keeping the cup near his lips, letting the steam rise in his nostrils, cloud his vision, momentarily bringing back the fog.

Francis had called. Curt had caught the tail end of one of the messages inquiring, albeit gently, if he was all right and if he needed anything. Curt knew that Powell was concerned about his well-being, but also, that Jamie's death hadn't signaled a halt in the day-to-day business at Parker Center. Powell wanted to know how he was, but what he really wanted to know was whether he could count on Curt to continue with the Butcher investigation.

Curt thrust thoughts of the Butcher and Francis Powell from his mind and started to plan out what he'd do for the rest of the day.

He'd taken to going to movies in the afternoon, sitting in dark empty theaters, getting lost in the larger-than-life celluloid images on the screen. Action movies. The kind where they blasted the soundtrack, jumping from one chase to the next, not giving him time to think about what the night had in store.

If he were lucky, after the movie the day would be well on its way to being over. He'd leave the theater and head straight for a restaurant. One he and Jamie had not gone to together. He'd find a seat at the bar, somewhere in the shadows, and nurse his vodka. He'd drink until closing.

This day, like the others since Jamie's death, eventually passed. And in the end, Curt found himself gazing at four slick cubes of ice resting at the bottom of clear liquid. He slowly twisted the glass in quarter-turns on the bar, occasionally glancing at the color television overhead, trying to avoid making small talk with the bartender. He'd forgotten where he was, but that didn't matter. In fact, he thought, it was a blessing. Now if he could just forget where he'd been.

The bartender pointed at his glass from the other end of the bar, raising his eyebrows. Curt nodded, then turned his attention to the television. ESPN was broadcasting the Yankee–White Sox game. It was two out in the ninth.

Curt took a look around the bar at the couples who had stopped in for a drink before dinner, and the businessmen in suits slurping down a drink or two, or more, before heading home.

The place, he thought, looked the same as the bar he'd been in the previous night. All the bars were starting to blur in his mind. The smell of stale cigarettes, his forearms resting on hardwood, the puddle of liquid underneath his glass, the mind-numbing relief of the vodka coursing down his throat then shooting to his brain. He tried to remember the last few nights, the places he had gone to drink, and found that he couldn't recall the names. He gave some thought to the possibility that he was becoming an alcoholic. That the vodka was slowly burning away his brain cells and that entire evenings, in fact entire days, were now missing from his memory.

What did it matter, though? Isn't that what he wanted?

Memory had become a viscious armed heckler, humiliating and raping him of his self-esteem. The vodka helped him fight back against his attacker, cutting a wide memory-obliterating swathe through his mind, wiping out the hecklers, the devils of recollection.

Then in the fog of alcohol and melancholy he heard something that grabbed at his heart. On the television was a familiar voice, then the face. Crystal Pelotas. The televised image brought back the parade of demons, each now flashing an evil jagged-tooth smile as if to say, *"You didn't really think you could escape, did you?"*

Curt's eyes locked on the screen. Crystal Pelotas was doing a live promo for her show that would be broadcast later that evening. She said that the Reverend Lamont Poindexter would be interviewed, along with Monroe Davis' lawyer, Gerald Isaacs.

And then she paused. Curt had begun to turn away from the TV, back toward his vodka, when he heard her mention the name.

The Butcher.

Curt squinted at the screen, closing one eye, trying to bring the picture into focus. The images of the Butcher's victims, of Jamie, of the press conference with Powell and Durning flashed behind his eyes. A voice inside told him not to listen, to pull himself away from the image, from the bar, from the fleeting comfort of his vodka.

"I will also be revealing," Pelotas said, "that I have received a communication from someone identifying himself as the Barrister Butcher. A phone call, which, I might add, I am chillingly convinced is authentic."

Curt wasn't sure he'd heard her right. For a split-second he thought Crystal Pelotas had said that the Butcher had called her. Then he told himself that that was impossible. Powell had mentioned nothing about this in his phone message. Had Pelotas received any communication from the Butcher, she certainly would have alerted the police . . . *Wouldn't she?*

Curt felt something rising in his chest, something he hadn't felt in the two weeks since Jamie's death. He knew what he'd heard. The more he thought about it, the more he was certain that his first impression was correct. Pelotas had done it again. Just like with the Matador, but this time it was *his* case. It was something personal.

Curt wondered how long Crystal Pelotas had held on to this tidbit of information. Had the Butcher called her that night? Had he confessed to killing Jamie, described to

Pelotas the way he'd done it? Had he told her that there would be other victims?

The pressure in his chest increased. He recognized it as anger, bubbling up to his throat, filling the space through which he breathed.

How could she do this?

He tried to think it through one more time, what Pelotas had said. How many days had elapsed without the police knowing? Perhaps the Butcher had contacted her more than once? Perhaps he'd said something that would have aided the police in his apprehension?

Perhaps . . .

They'd never know, Curt thought, since Crystal Pelotas had decided that it was more important that she scoop the other networks with this story than catch the maniac that was out murdering innocent people.

The one who had butchered his Jamie.

Curt threw two twenties on the bar, not waiting for change. He headed outside to the parking lot.

Later, when he looked back on this moment, he would have no recollection of where he had been when he saw the Pelotas report. He wouldn't recall the name of the restaurant, or what the bartender looked like, or what route he had taken to the television studio.

But this loss of memory wouldn't be due to the vodka. The blind rage he felt was not the product of alcohol dulling the brain. Something inside that he thought had been lost forever had ignited. Words would not come to him, as he visualized what he intended to do. Only action, like the characters in the movie he'd watched that afternoon.

Anger and resentment had taken hold and, like a hand planted firmly atop his head, were directing Curt in one single-minded direction, refusing to let him pause, refusing to let him look to the side to gain perspective.

"The Los Angeles Police Department, like police departments across the country, has got to learn that it cannot, and I repeat, *cannot*, brutalize its black citizens without serious repercussions."

The Reverend Lamont Poindexter removed his glasses, a gesture he believed focused attention on his forthcoming comments.

"Mr. Davis has been savagely beaten by the police. We've all seen the tapes. They speak for themselves." He gestured with the glasses, then replaced them on his face.

"Well, that is true, Reverend," said Crystal Pelotas. "But what our viewers, and I'm sure the citizens of this city wish to learn is what you hope to achieve by your presence here."

"I view myself as a catalyst, Ms. Pelotas. A rallying point, a center for the black community. I will lead my black brethren in their efforts to rid this city of the racist thugs and bullies hiding behind the badges of the Los Angeles Police Department."

Gerry Isaacs sat at Lamont Poindexter's side. Both men faced Crystal Pelotas, at a slight angle to the camera. They were taping the show that would run later that evening.

Crystal thought Gerry Isaacs seemed unusually quiet, apparently satisfied to let Poindexter do most of the talking. She wondered if Isaacs was high.

"Have you, Reverend Poindexter, experienced any backlash from the black community. I mean, you are a citizen of New York. Until recently, your voice has been a quiet, I might even say, totally silent one in this city.

Now, with the national publicity that the Monroe Davis beating has brought, we suddenly find you in Los Angeles, speaking, according to you, on behalf of a black community that until now has not seemed to garner much of your interest."

She paused, flashing a small smile, showing the camera that she had no personal animosity toward the minister, but as a reporter felt it her obligation to question his motives.

"Let me answer that," said Isaacs, coming to life. He was dressed casually for him, in a double-breasted camel hair blazer over a pinstriped dress shirt with French cuffs, highlighted with initialed gold cuff links. Completing the outfit were an English paisley tie and matching pocket square, a pair of wool plaid trousers, and whiskey-colored suede slip-ons with kiltie. His legs were crossed, and it was the kiltie that he had been silently playing with, fingering the soft leather, during most of the interview. He leaned forward to make his point.

"I requested Reverend Poindexter's assistance to help calm what I saw as an increasingly violent community reaction to these police atrocities. Monroe Davis is only the latest victim of L.A.P.D. brutality. Unless something is done, starting at the top, the brutality toward blacks and other minorities is going to increase. The people of this city are no longer willing to quietly sit by as their fellow citizens are victimized by a police department that, well, for want of a better word, has racist bullies in positions of authority. The slogan on the patrol cars says, 'To Protect and to Serve.' I doubt very much whether Mr. Monroe Davis feels he's been protected or served very well.

"Reverend Poindexter," said Isaacs, "has a keen and experienced insight into community dynamics. He is a respected leader not only in the black community but nationwide. It was my intention by asking him here, to have him help focus the attention of the nation on this problem. Reverend Poindexter and I will be working very closely together to see that this latest incident is not quickly forgotten."

"That means," said Crystal, "that the reverend will be with us for a while, at least until the planned rally next week?"

"That's correct," said Poindexter.

He was growing tired of the interview, and the interviewer. He could tell the Latina was suspicious. He was used to that, other minorities reaching and grabbing for a piece of the pie. *His* pie. Still, he thought the exposure was good, as long as the Latina didn't get too sharp with her questions.

Poindexter was about to mention the time and location of the rally when he heard a commotion coming from the other side of the stage, behind Crystal Pelotas. She then swiveled her head at the noise, which had now been elevated to shouting, someone yelling, "Hey, you can't do that," then a bank of lights crashing, and the glass making a shattering sound.

Poindexter didn't immediately recognize the man striding toward the set with a half-dozen stage hands in his wake. The man took a position opposite Crystal Pelotas, who remained seated. As the man addressed her, Crystal made an almost imperceptible gesture to the stage crew and the director telling them to back off and to keep the camera running.

"Why, Mr. Denmark," she said, forcing a smile. She tried to appear relaxed, while at the same time wondering if the man standing opposite her with his fists balled at his side was about to pounce on her.

"This is an unexpected surprise," she said. "I'm sure

Reverend Poindexter and Mr. Isaacs wouldn't mind if you joined the discussion." She gestured with an outstretched hand at her two guests.

"Cut the crap," said Curt. He knew she was patronizing him, almost as if she had planned the whole thing to happen just this way.

"Don't you think you have any moral obligations at all? Did it ever cross that publicity-hungry mind of yours that by holding back information on the Butcher you could be jeopardizing the lives of future victims?"

"Well, uh . . ." Crystal paused as if searching for words. In fact, she wanted Denmark to go on, to plunge forward without having time to think it through.

"Three people have been killed already. Now, this maniac, this killer, contacts you, how many times?"

She didn't answer.

"And you keep it to yourself. You hold back this crucial information. And why? Because it makes for a better story. Screw the fact that what you know might help us find the killer. Forget all about the innocent people who might lose their lives because of you. All that's important to you is that Crystal Pelotas gets ratings, right? The God-Almighty news story."

She glanced at the director, who by this time had taken up a position behind the cameraman, making sure that the entire confrontation was on tape.

Curt had caught her glance. For the first time since he'd barged onto the set, his mind took control over his emotions. His better judgment sounded an alarm that told him he'd gone way overboard. But the anger he'd felt watching Pelotas in the bar still seethed inside, blinding him to what he knew was right.

He pointed an admonishing finger, wagging it within inches of her face. "I promise you this, lady. If somebody dies because of your damn ego, you're going to have a lot more to worry about than ratings."

With that, Curt gave both Poindexter and Isaacs a look, then turned and stomped off the set.

For a moment the three people on stage were silent, looking to one another, then embarrassingly at the camera, then away again.

Finally, Crystal said, "Are we still rolling?" She waited, seeing Colin Archer anxiously nodding his head.

"Well, ladies and gentlemen. You saw the entire incident here, live. First"—and she gave Poindexter and Isaacs her best sympathetic, well-meaning expression—"let me extend my apologies to Reverend Poindexter and Mr. Isaacs for this very unexpected intrustion."

She turned from her two guests back to the camera.

"One has to wonder," she said, "after such an exhibition, just who's running the ship at the L.A.P.D. If people like Mr. Curt Denmark are placed in charge of important and sensitive investigations, well, you saw what happened, ladies and gentlemen." She waved her hand in the air. "One has to question the wisdom and leadership of our chief of police in appointing Mr. Denmark in the first place, and especially in allowing him to remain in his post given his obvious unstable emotional condition."

Again she paused, flashing her knowing, sensitive look. She needed to balance the excitement and resentment that she felt might be creeping into her delivery.

"We all know that Mr. Denmark has been through a lot," she said, lowering her voice. "What with the tragic death of his fiancée at the hands of the Butcher . . . God knows if any of us would have the strength to maintain our sanity, our emotional stability under such circumstances. I'm sure our hearts go out to Mr. Denmark for the loss he has suffered.

"Still, hasn't the time arrived for Mr. Denmark to step down? Shouldn't somebody at Parker Center take charge of what is obviously a law enforcement ship that is substantially off course and in danger of sinking?

"I'm sure," she said, nodding to Poindexter, "that Reverend Poindexter has something to say about that issue and others, and perhaps we can ask him back sometime in the very near future." The camera quickly flashed to a smiling, nodding Lamont Poindexter, then back to Crystal. "But for now, we've run out of time. This is Crystal Pelotas, *Real News for Real People*, saying goodnight."

There was total silence on the set. It lasted for nearly twenty seconds, then Colin Archer started to clap his hands, slowly at first, then picking up the pace as the others joined in.

Crystal smiled at the applause, going into a mock bow as she removed her microphone.

"Incredible," said Archer. He was walking about the set, back and forth, wringing his hands as if unsure what to do next. Poindexter and Isaacs had gotten up and were huddled together in conference at the edge of the stage.

"I want to see that tape," said Crystal. She started for her dressing room, not acknowledging the fact that her two guests seemed somewhat lost.

"I want," she yelled back, "to see that tape right away, Colin."

Archer chased after her, saying "But we can't show this, Crystal. Come on. Not without the network checking it first. Crystal, wait!"

He sat with his hand on the phone, replaying the incident at the television studio. It made him wince. He thought of what Powell would say once they showed it. And they *would* show it, he knew that. Crystal Pelotas wouldn't pass up an opportunity like this.

They'd be after his head now, saying he was too close, too emotionally tied to the investigation to be any good.

And, he thought, maybe they were right? Maybe he should step down as he'd decided, and let someone else head up the investigation. Every time he thought of the Butcher, every time the name was mentioned on the TV or in the newspaper, he saw Jamie. Not the other victims. Not the fear of the killer striking again. Not his professed anger at Crystal Pelotas for withholding information. It was Jamie whose face he envisioned. It was his anger at her death that he felt controlling his every thought.

Revenge was what was keeping him going now. A desire to personally do to the Butcher exactly what he'd done to Jamie.

But he knew that wouldn't work. If he didn't calm down, get himself under control, even Francis Powell would feel obligated to relieve him. He was too much of a loose canon now. Francis would tolerate a lot from him, but this last incident would surely test his patience and their friendship.

Curt lifted the receiver. He'd decided on what he would tell Powell. He'd admit that he'd blown it, that when he'd heard the news of Pelotas' conversation with the Butcher he had exploded. Totally out of control.

But he was over that now, he'd say. He'd gotten it out of his system. In fact, he'd tell Powell—showing him how he'd calmed down, how he had gained insight into himself—that Crystal Pelotas had provided a service by withholding her information. The anger it had caused had yanked him from his depression, had shown him that with each day, each hour that the Butcher remained on the loose, Jamie's death remained meaningless. Only after

Jamie's killer had been caught and brought to justice would her dying not have been in vain.

He'd tell Powell all of this, and would apologize for flying off the handle. He formulated the words as he dialed Powell's number. He would apologize for the last two weeks. It was behind him, he'd say.

He waited, listening to the phone rings: three . . . four . . . five.

Yes, he'd tell Francis that he was okay, that the anger would no longer control him.

He'd tell Francis Powell whatever lies he had to in order to stay on the Butcher's bloody trail.

Fifteen

Ernie Foley poked his index finger over the edge of the cup and stirred his coffee.

"Handy little gadget you have there," said Jake Barnes, using a plastic spoon stained brown with white goop caked along the edge to stir his.

Foley held up his hand, looking at his palm. He pointed his index finger upward, casually inspecting the topic of conversation. The nerve in the finger had been deadened during a pursuit of a burglary suspect. The suspect had jumped from a window, landing on the finger as Foley crouched below. A narrow sliver of broken bone had severed the nerve.

Unable, in the opinion of the department's doctors, to effectively pull the trigger of his Smith and Wesson, Foley had been transferred from Detectives to a cushy desk job in Internal Affairs. This despite the fact that he could still shoot circles around the top qualifiers on the range.

Shortly after his arrival, Foley was partnered with Jake Barnes, who had opted for a transfer to Internal Affairs instead of entering into lengthy litigation with the department over a claimed stress disability.

Barnes, as his doctor had testified at the civil service

hearing, suffered from an irregular heartbeat which was exacerbated by the stress of police work. When it was discovered that Jakes' doctor was licensed to practice medicine in Mexico but not in the United States, Barnes chose the better part of valor and agreed to take the investigator position alongside Ernie Foley in Internal Affairs.

Both men stood near the coffeemaker, sipping on their coffee and trying to catch a glimpse down the new secretary's blouse. They'd been working on it for weeks, refining their technique, fine-tuning their approach.

"You get the paperwork on Lampley?"

Foley nodded, resting his lips on the edge of his cup, shifting his eyes over the secretary's shoulders as she banged away at her typewriter.

"Nasty case," said Barnes. "I'd hate to be in that kid's shoes."

Foley nodded again. "You wanna be the good guy this time?"

"You take it. It don't suit my disposition this morning."

Foley smiled, taking one last glance at the secretary's cleavage before heading back to the closet-sized room they called their office.

Once inside, Foley placed his coffee on one of the two battered wooden desks and lifted the phone.

"Has Lampley checked in yet?"

Barnes stood at the open door, leaning against the frame, blowing over the rim of his cup.

"Good," said Foley. "We're on our way." He placed the receiver back on the hook, grabbed a manila file folder, and headed out the door with Barnes following right behind.

"He's in number three," said Foley. "We'll go in together. You take it first. I'll jump in when I think he's ripe."

"We aren't the first, are we?"

"Nah. The D.A.'s Office questioned the kid, and Jackson did a preliminary workup the night it happened."

"He got a lawyer yet?"

"Not that I know of," said Foley.

They stood a few feet from the interview room. Through the window, they could see the subject seated behind a small metal desk in the middle of the room. There was a Styrofoam cup of coffee in front of him.

Barnes went in first.

"Officer Lampley," said Barnes, striding into the room and taking a position opposite the subject, standing at the edge of the desk. "I'm Investigator Barnes, and this is Investigator Foley."

Barnes gestured toward Foley, who was leaning against the wall behind Lampley. Foley gave Lampley a nod of the head and a slight wave.

"Let's cut through all the bullshit," said Barnes, using his no-nonsense command voice. He took the file from Foley and began slapping at it with the back of his hand as he paced around the room.

"You're in some deep shit, Officer Lampley. I suppose you know that? We're here to help, if we can. But from what I've read in this file, your dick is on the block."

Lampley remained silent. The cup of coffee remained on the desk in front of him, untouched.

"If we're going to help you save your ass on this, you're going to have to level with us."

"I already gave my statement," said Lampley. "To the D.A."

"We know all about that," said Barnes. "Ya see, this has got nothing to do with the D.A. This is the department talking now. That's why Investigator Foley and I are here. We're talking about your career, son."

Barnes took a deep breath, letting his last comment sink in before continuing.

"The D.A. is gonna do what he wants. They might investigate the whole thing and end up doing nothing. That happens sometimes. 'Cept, I wouldn't count on it if I was you. Word is that they're gonna ask the grand jury for an indictment."

Lampley's head swiveled.

"That's right," said Barnes. "Assault with a deadly weapon, felony battery, maybe even attempted murder."

Foley held back a smile. He knew there was no way the D.A. would charge attempted murder. The talk was that they were considering assault and battery charges. Maybe even a misdemeanor. The D.A. was biding his time, waiting to see what developed politically before taking a position. Normally, the D.A. investigators would take a few weeks investigating allegations of police brutality, then, when the public uproar over the incident had died down, a spokesman for the prosecutor's office would announce that they'd found insufficient grounds to warrant a criminal prosecution. The officers would be suspended without pay for a couple of weeks and everyone would be happy, except the poor slob that got hammered.

In Lampley's case, however, nothing was a sure bet. The community reaction over the beating of Monroe Davis continued to remain front-page news. You could still turn on Dan Rather or Peter Jennings and catch the video of Lampley beating Monroe Davis repeatedly over the head, even as Davis lay curled up on the ground.

Foley and Barnes had received word from the brass that Lampley was expendable. If it would take the pressure off Francis Powell and the department to make Terry

Lampley the sacrificial lamb, then that's exactly what they were to do.

Barnes placed his palms on the desk and leaned close to Lampley's face.

"Tell me what happened, son," he whispered "Did you lose it out there? Did you see that big black motherfucker about to go after Cheryl Kent and just lose it, flip out? You and Kent had a thing going, didn't you?"

Lampley started to shake his head, then saw the snide smirk on Barnes' face.

"She's a cute little thing, isn't she? I wouldn't blame you for wanting to get a piece of that. Especially a guy in your position, your wife leaving and all."

Lampley blurted, "How did you . . . ?"

"It's our business to know," said Barnes. "Come on, son. That's how it went down, right? Kent's driving a U-boat. All by herself. She's supposed to be just writing reports, nothing hairy. Then she's unlucky enough to spot Davis, who she recognizes from the warrant photo as being a felony parole violator. She calls for backup, broadcasts a Code-6-Charles, Armed-and-Dangerous. But before it gets there, Davis stops the car and gets out. Kent's got no choice but to get out herself and put him in a felony prone position. Then Davis makes his move.

"By the time you arrive, Kent and Davis are struggling over her gun. Or at least that's how it looks to you. You order Davis to hit the ground, and he yells something back, still moving towards Kent's service revolver.

"Fuck you, honkie," whispered Lampley.

"What did you say?"

"It's what he said," said Lampley. His eyes drifted away from Barnes, back to the incident in the street. "He said, 'Fuck you, honkie.' "

"Right," said Barnes. "And you got pissed and said

something back, then started to beat the holy hell outta the guy with your baton. Which, I gotta admit, just between us girls, is exactly what I woulda done, maybe even shot the black bastard."

"The problem is that you got a little carried away, didn't you? You had the asshole on the ground and kept clubbing his thick black skull. And then there's the fucking video tape, Terry. Piece of bad fucking luck there. Kent's trying to pull you off the guy, and you're still swinging away like Darryl Strawberry with a fungo. It's all on tape, man."

"She'll back me up," said Lampley. "Cheryl saw how it happened. I had no choice."

Terry went over the series of events in his mind, aware that Barnes and Foley knew he was thinking, knew he was trying to catch up.

He'd heard Cheryl Kent's request for backup, then her Officer-Needs-Assistance call. He was in the area, no more than three or four blocks away. He had planned for an uneventful night, but this was serious—and it was Cheryl.

When he arrived at the scene, Cheryl was out of the patrol car, leveling her service revolver at Monroe Davis, who was in a sort of crouch on the ground a few feet away.

He could tell she was scared, saw it in her eyes, the way the gun was shaking along with her voice. Then Davis started to get up. His hands were raised, palms forward, as if he were giving up, but he wasn't listening. She was yelling for him to stay down, and he wasn't listening, kept inching his way toward her, his hands still raised.

Davis was smiling, or at least baring his teeth. Lampley remembered seeing that. Then Davis got up on his knees, practically walking on his knees toward her. And still she yelled for him to get down.

He just wouldn't go down, wouldn't listen . . .

Lampley remembered ripping himself from the patrol car, trying to make sense of what he'd seen, trying to shake the whiskey and the depression from his head.

It had all happened so fast.

Before he knew it, he was hovering over Davis, swinging his baton back and forth, like he was harvesting grain growing from the back of the black man's head.

He didn't remember anything after that. Not until the other units arrived. He remembered seeing Monroe Davis laying on a stretcher being shoved into the back of an ambulance.

And he remembered the tight feeling he had in his chest, like a foot pressing down, as he watched his fellow officers trying very hard not to make eye contact with him.

Lampley blinked, and realized he'd been gone. How long, he didn't know. Barnes' face was still there, no more than a foot away, flashing a knowing smile.

"Think again, son," said Barnes. "Kent's got her own ass to watch out for on this one. Shit, putting women in U-cars all by themselves is a damn stupid idea. You don't gotta be a mental giant to see the problems. But that's ancient history, and far be it from me to risk a fucking sex discrimination suit by bringing the idea up with the captain. Hell, she shoulda shot the fucker as soon as he made a move. Woulda saved us all a whole lotta trouble."

Lampley drifted back. He wasn't sure exactly what Cheryl Kent had told the investigators. He wasn't sure what Monroe Davis had said. He remembered sitting in the parking lot, tugging on the end of a bottle and feeling sorry for himself. He remembered telling himself that he'd get even with Susan. He remembered making plans to get Jeff back.

Jeff . . .

He'd almost forgotten about his son. How would the boy take all this? What would Susan and her parents tell him about the pictures of his dad on TV? Would the kids tease him at school? Would Jeff ever want to talk to him again?

"She said you smelled like you'd been hitting the sauce," said Barnes. He stood with his arms crossed, shaking his head slowly back and forth, the parent having caught the child with his hand in the cookie jar.

Barnes said, "That don't help matters, son. Drinking on the job looks real bad."

Lampley's head began to spin. He could no longer clearly focus. The walls seemed to have shadows, double images that made him dizzy.

Ernie Foley stepped forward, motioning for Barnes to step back.

"We've kept the booze thing under wraps for now, son," said Foley, taking a seat at the table.

"Listen, Terry." Foley waited until he'd made eye contact, then continued in a soothing, fatherly voice. "We're on your side here. We don't want to see you get hurt. You're a good cop, with a good record. We all know what it's like out there, heat of battle, that sort of thing. You were perfectly in the right using any force necessary, even deadly force, in the protection of a fellow officer."

Lampley nodded in agreement. He hadn't been listening to Foley's initial comments, but was now paying closer attention.

"I think my partner is right," said Foley. "You just got a little carried away. I don't blame you one bit. But ya see, we gotta job to do. We gotta get a statement from you about exactly what happened out there. Truth. It's gotta be the truth.

"Ya know," he said, moving his chair closer and patting Lampley on his shoulder, as if they were teammates and Lampley had just made a great basket or scored the winning touchdown, "there's an old saying. 'The truth shall set you free.' You ever hear that one?"

Lampley didn't respond. He was listening to Foley, but still thinking about his son, about how his being involved in this might affect their relationship.

"Tell the truth, Terry. We'll do what we can to see that you come out of this thing okay. We can probably even make sure that stuff about the booze never gets reduced to writing."

Lampley slowly turned to face Foley. Foley had that look about him, like a kindly priest hearing confession. Lampley knew what the two investigators were doing, whipsawing him back and forth; Barnes, the bad guy, and Foley playing his friend.

He knew that, and yet, he wanted to tell Foley what had happened. He wanted to tell him about Susan, and Jeff, and about how things hadn't turned out the way he'd planned. He wanted to tell him that he was still a good cop, that if they just gave him one more chance he would make everything all right.

"Where do you want me to start?" he said.

The stenographer was packing up her equipment. A half-dozen empty coffee cups cluttered the table. Terry Lampley had started chipping away the Styrofoam, leaving a pile of white chips, like department-store snowflakes, littering the tabletop.

"You did good, kid," said Barnes, gathering up the loose paperwork and stuffing it into the folder. He held the door open for the stenographer.

"What's going to happen now?"

Foley said, "It's out of our hands, Terry. Your statement along with the rest of Internal Affairs' investigation will be reviewed by the brass, the D.A."

"Will they fire me?"

Foley hesitated. He felt a twinge of sympathy for the young cop. "Don't know," he said, lying.

"Maybe," murmured Lampley, "I should get a lawyer."

"That might not be such a bad idea, kid." Foley got up and headed for the door. "You okay, kid?"

Lampley didn't answer immediately, then after a few seconds he nodded.

"They still got you suspended with pay, don't they?"

Lampley nodded again.

"Good. Save your money, kid. You might need it. Lawyers are expensive these days."

With that, Foley exited the interview cubicle, leaving Terry Lampley seated inside, staring into an empty coffee cup.

Jake Barnes stood at the other end of the hallway, sweet-talking the stenographer. When he saw Foley, he looked up and yelled.

"Hey, Ernie. Didya hear the latest one?"

Foley paused, waiting for the punch line.

"The department's developed this new high-tech weapon. It's called the Stealth Baton. It's invisible to video cameras. You can whack away at some sleazeball's head, and all that shows up on the film is you waving your arms." Barnes began moving up and down on his toes, flapping his arms. "It looks like you're just dancing. Get it?"

Foley smiled. A Stealth Baton . . . It was funny. Though he doubted whether Terry Lampley would see the humor in it.

Sixteen

He had his back to the others, sitting on the stool at his workbench in the corner of the lab. He could hear the women cackling among themselves, not paying much attention to their work, as if it were secondary to where they were going out that night or what their boyfriend had bought them the day before.

Nestor put his mind to his work as he always did, carefully forming the porcelain crown to fit the plaster impression. He placed the crown in its position and inspected it, slowly turning the impression to one side then the other, checking the fit. Then the crown came off, to be further sanded and filed and fitted until he was satisfied that it was a perfect replacement for the patient's natural tooth.

People were still talking about the Butcher's latest victim. Two weeks had passed and the killing was still a prime topic of conversation, not just among the women working in the lab with Nestor, but in the newspapers and on television.

Nestor had seen the funeral on TV. His beautiful Crystal, looking gorgeous and sexy, but mournful in that black silk-like sheath. The camera had followed her as she climbed with the other journalists up the hill to the grave site, the black sheath clinging to her rear, accentuating her thighs, her long muscular legs.

Nestor had watched the tape of the funeral every night, laying in bed with Eleanor and Gracie, letting his Crystal make him hard. He remembered the pleasure, gripping himself firmly, his body on the edge of explosion, then placing the call to her, letting her voice pour down into his chest, filling his loins until, as he whispered his promise, he exploded.

He wanted to do it again.

As he sat at his bench, staring at the set of white chalky teeth in front of him, the tingling sensation between his legs returned. He started to place his hand down there, then stopped.

He couldn't do that here.

He forced himself to concentrate on the teeth, slowly tracing the outline of the impression, the surface of the chalky plaster where it contacted with the smooth glassy porcelain. He forced himself from his thoughts of Crystal, his desire to call her that very moment.

Nestor thought that Crystal had been treated badly at the funeral. As if Francis Powell felt he was better than her. Nestor had seen it on Crystal's face, that look of resentment. Such a beautiful face to be marred by something so small, so common. Nestor had felt like reaching through the TV screen and stroking her soft skin. He wanted to tell her that everything would be as she desired, that he, Nestor Stokes, the Barrister Butcher, would do all that and more for his beloved Crystal.

He'd had no idea that the woman in the garage was Denmark's woman. When he heard about it the next day he was alarmed, fearful that he'd finally done something that would lead to his capture. The police would think it was intentional, he thought. That he'd gone after his hunter's friend out of some vicious sense of revenge.

But he'd had no idea.

Not until he read the story in the newspaper. And even then, he wished he could take it back, reverse time. He held no grudge against Denmark, or for that matter against the woman, personally. She was a symbol, that was all. In the right place at the perfect time. Nothing personal. Not like with the others.

After the first few days, Nestor got over his concerns. He still felt mildly sorry for Denmark, but that's as far as it had gone. He stopped worrying about the woman and being caught. After all, she'd been treated like the others. Nothing special. Nothing to identify him as her killer.

Except . . . ?

Nestor's mind flashed to the videotape of Denmark charging onto the television set and pointing his accusing finger at Crystal. The shocked faces of the two guests clicked in his memory, Poindexter and that greasy attorney, Isaacs. Nestor had taped the incident, but he didn't like to watch it. He didn't like to see anyone talking to his Crystal the way Denmark had.

But Denmark's anger was understandable. Nestor thought: If anyone had harmed his Crystal, he would have done more than just point his finger.

Nestor's thoughts drifted back to the garage, to the last thing he'd done that night.

Perhaps he shouldn't have taken it?

Nestor looked around, making sure he was unobserved. He reached into the pocket of his lab coat and carefully removed the gold pin, holding it closely against his stomach so that none of the others could see it.

A delicate presentation, he thought. Handmade. The artisan obviously knew about cats, even loved them. You could see it in the facial features, the eyes. Like his Eleanor's eyes.

The brooch he had bought for his mother . . .

The pin had called to him that night, reflecting the dim overhead garage light, catching his eye just as he was readying to leave. He remembered standing over the woman, gazing down at the pin, mesmerized by the dark sapphire eyes.

He'd told himself to leave, that taking the pin was not part of the plan. It was the sort of mistake that could only lead to trouble—and almost had.

If he had not delayed his escape to take the pin, he would have been on a different block at a different time. He would have gone unnoticed.

But it had been too late. Once the golden cat had cast its spell over him, there was no getting away.

Nestor pushed the events of that night from his mind. Sufficient time had passed and he still had not been caught. He told himself that he was worrying needlessly. Everything would be all right.

As he did with the porcelain crown, Nestor held the brooch in his fingertips, letting it catch the light, the gossamer reflection of the stones like delicate spiderwebs at the bottom of a dark pool; the soft, fluid, graceful design of the gilded feline.

He slowly turned it over, reading again the one-line inscription on the back: *For Jamie, With All My Love, Curt.*

The Irish Castle Bar stood on the edge of Chinatown, a few blocks northeast of Parker Center. On one side was a Chinese market with ducks by the dozen hanging in the front window. On the other, Dr. Choi Kim sat behind a

large storefront window, administering acupuncture to
his patients in full view of passersby.

The bar was covered with a thick coat of emerald
green, even extending to the iron security bars over the
windows and doors. There was a shamrock painted over
the front entrance, which on this Friday afternoon Francis
Powell touched for good luck as he entered.

The change from blazing noonday sun to the darkness
of the bar momentarily blinded Powell. He stood a few
feet inside, waiting for his eyes to adjust. A damp, stale
beer and cigarette smell rushed at him. He sniffed, trying
to clear his head of the slightly nauseous feeling that came
over him.

The bartender, an overweight fair-skinned redhead
with a naval tattoo on his forearm, stood behind the bar,
polishing a shot glass with a stained white towel. He gave
Powell a quick once-over, then continued his polishing.

Two elderly Chinese men sat at the far end of the bar,
their heads bowed as if in prayer over partially empty shot
glasses. Powell spotted Georgie Fong seated in a booth in
the corner, the phone pressed to his ear, busy making
book. In the booth next to him were two white women
dressed in long silk pastel-colored sheaths, like oversized
Chinese dolls. Their faces had been painted pasty white,
except for the heavy black eyeliner and blue rouge around
the eyes, and the Betty Boop red lips. They took one look
at Powell, grabbed their purses, and left through the rear
exit.

Powell followed the women, walking toward the rear of
the bar. He watched them leave, then shifted a curtain
that separated the small hallway from a private room in
back.

In a corner of the room, Curt Denmark sat drinking

vodka from a tall glass at a table off to the side, almost out of view.

"Breakfast of Champions, eh?"

Curt looked up from his vodka, expressionless, then went back to drinking. On the table in front of him was an empty highball glass, and one half-full.

"Mind if I join you?"

Curt didn't answer, just stared into the vodka, slowly turning the glass on the table, as if he were focusing the lens of a camera.

A waitress, a Chinese girl with bad teeth who Powell figured couldn't be much older than eighteen, if that, came to take their order. She was dressed in a green miniskirt and a low-cut blouse trimmed in white, with green shamrocks along the edge. She wobbled on a pair of battered green metal-flake spiked heels, and yanked at her black fishnet hose as she waited.

"Just coffee," said Powell.

The waitress looked at Curt. He didn't respond, except to point at his empty glass, toss down the rest of his vodka, and nod his head.

Powell leaned back in the booth, resting his arms on the back of the worn vinyl. On the wall behind them hung a faded brown photo of a Dublin street scene. The plastic covering the picture was torn and scarred. The photo was framed in unfinished wood, which over the years had taken on a stained look from the dirt and grime, the spilled beers, the wasted lives. It was attached to the wall by four heavy metal screws.

Powell focused on Curt, watching his friend pinch pieces from a wet cocktail napkin, roll them into little balls, then flick them across the room.

"You gonna talk to me," said Powell. "Or do I gotta beat it outta you?"

Curt shrugged, then glanced at Powell, twitching the corner of his mouth in a false smile. "Just what might you want to talk about, Francis?"

"Oh, shit," said Powell, feigning nonchalance. "I don't know. Maybe the fucking weather, something important like that. Jesus, Curt . . . Whadya want me to say?"

"You're the one wanted to talk."

"Okay, okay. Let's get a few things straight . . ." Powell paused until after the waitress had placed his coffee and Curt's vodka on the table.

After she left, Powell said, "You comin' back, or are you just gonna sit here and drink yourself to death?"

Curt's eyebrows came together, and Powell could see that he'd struck a nerve. The anger quickly subsided, though, and was replaced by a look of melancholy sadness.

Curt started slowly: "I can't handle it any longer, Francis. I thought I could, but I can't. Do you understand that? It's starting again. The faces. Darren, Jamie . . . I know what's next, Francis." He finished off the vodka, unintentionally slamming the glass on the table. "It scares the shit outta me."

Powell waited for Curt to continue.

"Jamie and I used to talk about it. My moodiness, she called it." Curt sighed, and a half-smile flashed across his face, then quickly disappeared. Powell could tell Curt was holding back, but knew his questions would do little good. It had to come from Curt. The time had to be right for him.

"Ya know what that's like, Francis? You wake up one day and feel pretty good, at least you have hope that you can make it through to dinner without falling apart. Then you're on your way to work, on the freeway or at lunch at a table by yourself, and it hits you." Curt angrily slammed his fist into his hand. "Like some invisible wave washing over, pounding you senseless. And you go down gasping for air, grasping for something to hold on to, but there isn't anything. Just darkness. And motion, always the swirling tugging motion downward.

"And there's not a damn thing you can do about it, Francis. You tell yourself it's happening again, you know it's changing you, and there's nothing you can do. The helplessness just fuels the whole thing, makes you want to end it any way possible. And I mean *any way*.

"I used to tell Jamie that I just felt like crying sometimes. No particular reason, at least nothing that I could point to and say, that's the thing, that's the reason this shaft's being driven through my heart."

Curt continued, "Jamie knew. Maybe better than I . . ." He brushed at a tear with the back of his hand, took a deep breath, and tried to gather himself.

"She had incredible patience. Even when I'd take it out on her, she knew it would eventually pass. I don't know what I'll do without her, Francis. I don't know if I can."

"Maybe you should take a leave," said Powell. "As long as you want. Get away from all this shit for a while. I'll put someone else on the case. Hell, with that goddam Poindexter and his group shouting for my hide, I'd be tempted to go with you."

"I guess I didn't help matters much with that Pelotas stunt?"

"Buddy, that's the least of my worries. Isaacs and Poindexter are making this thing into a circus. They want me to step down as chief. They say the department has a history of condoning brutality, especially when it comes to minorities." Powell shook his head in exasperation. "Fuckers don't know what they've bit off, if they think I'm gonna just walk off into the sunset. Tooth-and-nail, Curt.

They're gonna have to fight me tooth-and-nail to get me outta here."

"What about the kid?"

"Lampley? Hell, he screwed up. If it wasn't for the video, we could probably stonewall the whole thing, say it never happened, that Monroe Davis is a fucking ex-con, parole-violating, lying sonofabitch.

"But that video changes everything. Far as I can see, Lampley's dead meat. He's gotta go. The D.A.'s gonna indict him. Hell, the kid'll be lucky if he doesn't end up doing time behind all this."

Both men were silent for a few moments. Powell took a sip of coffee, then winced.

"Cold!" he muttered, pushing the coffee away. The waitress came through the curtained entry, but Powell waved her off.

"It's been three weeks, Curt. The bastard hasn't struck in three weeks. Maybe he's finished."

Curt thought about what Powell said. You could never tell with these guys. The serial psychos. Sometimes they just kept killing until they were caught. Sometimes they suddenly stopped, faded into the woodwork, their crimes never solved. Perhaps the Butcher had had enough?

But why Jamie? Why couldn't he have chosen someone else as his last victim?

Powell looked at his watch.

"Curt, I gotta get back." He slipped out of the booth and stood at the edge of the table, hands in his pockets.

"It's up to you, buddy," he said. "You said that you had things under control and I believed you. If things have changed, well . . ." Powell looked down at the floor, shuffling his feet. When he looked up again, he said, "You do what you have to, Curt, but I gotta know by next week."

Curt didn't answer. He pursed his lips and nodded his head. He heard Powell cluck, then sigh, before patting him lightly on the shoulder as he left the room.

Curt waited a few seconds, then looked up. His Chinese shamrock was there, standing at the edge of the table, grinning her snaggletoothed grin, and replacing his drink with a fresh one.

Terry Lampley sat in the lawyer's waiting room, absent-mindedly leafing through a copy of *The National Review*, which, along with the lawyer's promotional brochures, was the only reading material available.

"Mr. Lee will see you now," the receptionist said, pointing to her right. "Just go through the door."

Terry placed the magazine back on the coffee table and got up. The phone call he'd received from the attorney that morning kept replaying in his mind. He wasn't sure what to expect.

He opened the door, glancing around for a moment, then headed to his left, down a short hallway. A tall, lanky young man, Terry guessed only a few years older than he, came striding from one of the doorways to meet him, his hand extended.

"Robert D. Lee," said the man, smiling and pumping Terry's hand. "Glad to meet you in person."

Lee had on a pair of pleated gray slacks with cuffs, black wing-tips, a long-sleeved white shirt, burgundy suspenders, and a burgundy and black bow tie. His hair was sandy brown and trimmed neatly around the ears and neck. A pair of gold wire-rim and tortoiseshell glasses were perched on the end of his nose, making his face look older.

Lee gestured for Terry to enter one of the offices, then closed the door behind him.

"I thought it was 'E' Lee," Terry said, looking for a place to sit. "You know, like the general."

"Nope," said the attorney. "It's 'D,' like the congressman from Orange County, Robert Dornan. My mom's a big fan."

Terry smiled, trying to fix the attorney's exact age, and wondering why anyone would name their child after a right-wing congressman from California.

"I want you to know," said Lee, "that I admire you very much." He was seated atop his desk, not in the leather high-backed chair. Terry sat in one of two club chairs that were opposite the desk.

Lee reached for a pipe from a rack that held a half-dozen. He dipped the pipe into a clear glass humidor.

"What they're doing to you is scandalous," he said as he put the pipe between his lips and continued to talk, tamping the bowl with his finger.

"The liberal establishment in this city doesn't have the slightest idea what it's like out there in the trenches. But I do, Terry, believe me, I certainly do."

Lee picked a silver lighter from the desk, aimed it at the top of the bowl, and released the flame. Terry watched the attorney's chest heave in and out, sucking at the end of the pipe, blowing clouds of fine white smoke into the air.

Between puffs, Lee said, "You've come to the right place, Terry. The Negro—and I hope you don't take offense at this, because I mean it only in the most clinical sense—has throughout modern history found himself cast in the role of society's villain. Sometimes, I'll grant you, unfairly and without basis in fact. But, for the most part, for good reason."

Terry heard the faint whistling noise of Lee sucking air through the pipe as he spoke.

"I'm sure that Monroe Davis is no exception. A convicted felon . . . In violation of his state prison parole . . . No, Terry, I believe you did a service for all the good, law-abiding, moral people of this city, the silent majority, when you took Monroe Davis out of commission."

Lee smiled quickly, as if he were in a hurry to get on with the next course of business.

"Now what we've got to do first," he said, "is get organized."

He took a seat behind the desk and removed a yellow legal pad from one of the drawers. He then took out four number two pencils, already sharpened, and placed them alongside the pad.

"They've charged you with one count of assault with a deadly weapon, and an additional count of felony battery." He scribbled some notes on the top of the legal pad as he spoke.

"You've given a statement to the D.A. and to Internal Affairs. We'll have to get copies of those. Were either of them taped?"

Terry shook his head. He watched as the attorney furiously jotted on the pad, clamping and reclamping his teeth around the stem of the pipe.

"There was a reporter, a stenographer," Terry said. "During the Internal Affairs interview."

Lee paused and looked up. He grinned with his teeth together, still clamped on the pipe. "That's good," he said.

Terry wondered what was so good about it. He'd told Foley and Barnes the whole story, but when he finished, he had the sinking feeling that it hadn't come out the way he'd intended. Maybe it was the time that had elapsed since the incident. Or maybe, he thought, it was the expression of pity on their faces when he'd finished telling his story.

"I want you to tell me the whole thing," said Lee. He removed a microcassette recorder from the drawer and placed it atop the desk. "From the beginning," he added, still taking notes. "Don't leave out anything."

Terry took a deep breath. He focused on a photograph in a frame on the wall behind Lee's desk. It was a picture of Lee shaking the hand of a man with a bushy black moustache. There was handwriting on the photo and a signature that Terry couldn't make out. It took him a second or two to identify the man with the moustache as G. Gordon Liddy, the convicted Watergate burglar.

Terry went on to repeat essentially the same story he'd already told the D.A., Barnes, and Foley. When he finished, he slipped down in his seat, threw his head back, and took two deep breaths, trying to slow his heartbeat.

Lee kept jotting notes, having filled the first yellow legal pad and half of a second. After a few minutes, Lee broke the silence.

"So it was your intention that night to just take it easy. You didn't want to get involved in anything. You were too caught up in your wife and son leaving?"

Terry nodded.

"And then you get this distress call from Officer Kent, whom you'd known since the academy."

Lee flashed a quick, almost embarrassed smile, not waiting for an answer. He tapped the tip of his pen against the legal pad as he thought.

"Mm. Do you remember exactly where you were when you got Kent's call?"

Terry shrugged. "A few blocks away, maybe five or six.

I'm not sure. I'd just stopped a guy who had run a red light, almost hit the side of my patrol car."

Lee's eyebrows raised.

Terry said, "I guess I'd forgotten about that," dismissing the omission with a wave of his hand. "It isn't important."

"Let me be the judge of that," said Lee. "Did you mention anything about this driver in your other interviews?"

"No. Like I said, it didn't seem important. I didn't want to issue the ticket in the first place. It's just that the guy practically killed me, running the red. I was more mad at him than anything else."

"So you get out and approach the guy's car. What does he look like?"

Terry shrugged again. "I don't know. Average, I guess. I really wasn't paying close attention. And I was only there for a couple minutes before Cheryl's call came over the radio."

"Old, young? Short, fat?"

"Middle-aged. Not fat. Average height. Maybe around five ten, no taller than six feet."

"Hair. What about hair?"

"Brownish, I think. Thin on top, like he was losing it."

"What else?"

"Compact car. Japanese."

"You wouldn't recall the plate, would you?"

"No way. I remember it being a compact, though. The guy was alone in the car. He looked nervous, but then most people do when I stop them."

"Yes," said Lee, now tapping the metal end of the pen against his teeth. To his right on the desk, his pipe rested in a walnut cradle designed specifically for that purpose.

The room was filled with the warm woodsy aroma of tobacco.

"I want you to think, Terry. I want you to try and remember everything about this man that you stopped." He held up a restraining hand. "I know it might not seem important to you, but we can't be sure at this point what might and might not turn out to be important. Besides, if he was the last person to see you before the incident, he might be able to tell us something about your demeanor, your state of mind at the time."

Terry closed his eyes, throwing his memory in reverse. He hadn't given any thought to the man until now. In fact, when he made his previous statement to Foley and Barnes, he'd totally forgotten the incident with the compact car. Now that some time had passed, he found himself remembering with greater clarity having stopped the man moments before receiving Cheryl Kent's call for help.

"I asked for his license," Terry said, speaking slowly, not focusing on Lee, his attention momentarily transfixed on the photograph that hung on the wall behind him.

"He did seem nervous, worried. I asked him if he'd been drinking, and he said no. I didn't smell anything, booze, I mean. He said he'd been in a hurry to get home, and was sorry about almost clipping me. I had my citation book out, but hadn't started to write." Terry refocused on Lee. "That's when the call from Kent came in."

"And you just left the man there?"

"Had to. She needed help, and I was only a few seconds away."

Terry could see the driver's face now. Middle-aged, skin sagging under the chin and jowels. Head balding on top, with wiry brown and gray hair at the sides. Wearing a jacket, a light windbreaker.

Then Terry remembered something else. He wasn't sure if he was mixing up two different incidents, or if he had confused the driver with someone else.

"What?" said Lee.

"There was something about the guy," Terry said, straining to remember. "It's all pretty vague, and I might be mixing him up with someone else, some other arrest or something."

"About this guy? The one that almost hit you?"

"Yeah. I remember something on the seat, between the driver's legs." Terry shook his head. "I wanna say it was a trinket of some sort. Looked like an animal, maybe a lion or a tiger. With dark stones for the eyes. I barely had time to notice it."

He put his elbows on the desk and supported his head with his fingertips. There was something about that trinket, he thought, something that had just caught in his mind. He tried to force himself to think harder.

"I don't know," he finally said, massaging the corners of his eyes with his thumb and forefinger. He felt fatigued, worn out.

"Okay, don't worry about it now," said Lee. "Maybe it'll come to you later." He reached across the desk and turned off the tape.

"In a way," he said, removing the cassette and placing it in his desk drawer, "we're lucky. This incident with Monroe Davis happened on a big news night, the same evening that the Butcher's last victim was killed. The media has been torn between the Poindexter-Isaacs circus and their coverage of the Jamie Sills killing. Now with Curt Denmark about to get the shaft from Powell, the rumors of his replacement are spreading like wildfire." Lee reached for his pipe, relighting it as he spoke.

"The guy's got balls, I'll give him that," said Lee.

"Killing his own damn investigator's fiancée." He shook his head, blowing a plume of smoke toward the ceiling. "Crazier than hell, but the guy's got balls."

Something popped in Terry's mind at the mention of the name. Curt Denmark. It was coming clear very slowly. Too slowly, because he could feel the importance of this memory, like a dull ache in his subconscious.

When it finally came to him, he looked down to see his hands white-knuckling the arms of the chair. He felt his genitals warm and moist between his legs and his forehead wet with perspiration.

The attorney was still there, behind the desk, just staring at him. Terry realized he'd been gone for a few moments, and that the attorney was probably wondering whether his latest client had, in fact, flipped out, gone over the edge.

"The trinket," Terry whispered, locking his eyes on Lee's. He saw himself seated inside the juvenile courtroom. He saw the face of the attorney arguing to the court, and the woman—*his friend?*—looking on, watching the attorney's every move. Those faces began to merge with the same faces he'd seen in the newspapers and on TV. Curt Denmark and the woman. Together. They were the same.

And he saw the trinket, a golden brooch, the same as that day in court. It was fastened to the woman's lapel— Denmark's friend—glittering in the light of the courtroom.

And then it was on the car seat between the balding man's legs.

"A cat," Terry whispered. "A golden cat."

Seventeen

"You're gonna love this place, Lamont. It's okay that I call you Lamont?"

Poindexter didn't answer. He turned and smiled at Isaacs, then turned back. He wasn't crazy about the attorney's familiarity, but it was something he could tolerate. He'd have to. Like now, cruising through West Hollywood in Isaacs' Mercedes convertible, the top down, all those people staring at the two of them. It was good for business to be seen, but not with the wrong people in the wrong places. He wondered what the brothers and sisters would say if they could see him now.

"All the big-time celebs come here," said Isaacs.

Poindexter realized the attorney had been talking, and that he'd missed the first part of the conversation.

"Madonna, Michael . . . You name 'em, they've been here."

They were passing Cedars Sinai Hospital. Monroe Davis had been transferred there for some tests. Davis had experienced dizziness and headaches after the beating, and the symptoms had not abated.

"It's too bad Mr. Davis couldn't join us," said Poindexter, gazing up at the giant hospital complex.

"Uh, yeah. Too bad."

Isaacs maneuvered the Mercedes to the curb, where they were met by a phalanx of red-jacketed parking attendants.

"Keep it close, and don't ding the paint," said Isaacs, tossing the keys to the attendant.

The two men stood for a moment in front of The Ivy. An elevated brick patio framed with a white picket fence fronted the restaurant. Tables and chairs, wicker settees, and gas heaters were crammed close together, leaving a narrow path to the back, where the maître d' stood behind his podium, the phone cradled between cheek and ear, talking and gesturing to the line of disgruntled people waiting for a table. He continually scribbled, then erased, in a reservation book that lay open on the podium.

Poindexter said, "Looks crowded. Maybe we should try someplace else."

He was having that feeling again, like in the Mercedes. He liked good food and fine restaurants as much as the next person, but this place was definitely not low-profile. He kept thinking that if he was going to get his picture in the papers, it would be better if he were at a rib joint in South-Central Los Angeles then some trendy boutique eatery on the West Side.

"Don't worry," said Isaacs, placing his hand on Poindexter's back and gently nudging him to the head of the line. Poindexter could feel the looks of disdain from the people waiting.

"Maurice," said Isaacs, holding his arms out at his side and moving toward the maître d' as if he were about to embrace the man. The hug turned into a tentative handshake when the maître d' started to back away. Poindexter noticed the folded hundred in Isaacs' palm as the two men shook hands. The handshake turned from something tentative and mildly unpleasant to the vigorous greeting of two old friends who haven't seen each other in a long time. It seemed to go on forever, as if, by touch alone, the maître d' were attempting to determine the denomination of the bill that Isaacs had placed in his palm.

Isaacs whispered, "Isaacs, Gerry Isaacs." He pointed to the reservation book. "Party of two."

"Ah yes," said Maurice, shoving his hand and the hundred dollar bill into his pocket. "Right this way, Mr. Isaacs. We have a nice table near the fireplace. The best."

Isaacs turned and winked at Poindexter as the two men followed the maître d' inside.

The restaurant looked like it had once been a small home. There were three rooms that opened onto each other, and a fourth room with only a few tables adjacent to the bar. Like the patio, the tables were squeezed into each of the rooms, allowing only enough space for a very slender waiter to scoot through, holding plates and dishes overhead.

Baskets and woven mats hung on the walls, and the inside dining rooms had a sort of adobe whitewashed look. Casual, but uncertain. Like the decorator had attempted to create a country inn, then changed his mind to Santa Fe midway through.

They were seated at the center table in the main room, right off the entrance, just in front of the fireplace. Anyone entering the restaurant had to pass right by their table. Poindexter figured this was the premier spot in the place, and the look of self-satisfaction on Gerry Isaacs' face merely confirmed his suspicions.

Isaacs excused himself to use the bathroom, giving Poindexter an opportunity to take in the interior of the restaurant.

The room was filled with the sounds of voices and

laughter, clanking plates, and every so often a car horn or ambulance siren from the street outside.

Almost immediately after Isaacs returned, Maurice gestured to a young man standing at the entrance, who approached and handed each of them a menu.

"Can I get you something from the bar, gentlemen?"

The waiter looked to be in his early twenties, handsome, with somewhat feminine features. His sandy blond hair was pulled back in a ponytail, accentuating his deepset eyes and strong cheekbones. He walked and held himself with the grace of a dancer.

Isaacs looked to his guest, then said, "We'll see a wine list. That okay with you, Lamont?"

Poindexter nodded his approval, grating internally at the use of his first name. He'd noticed Isaacs continually sniffing and wiping at his nose. The symptoms were all too familiar. The reason, he guessed, for the bathroom visit; a little snort while sitting on the can. Poindexter figured that Isaacs probably didn't even close the stall door in a place like this. People were that way in L.A. Laid back, they called it.

"Isn't this place great?" said Isaacs, placing his elbows on the table and leaning forward. "I come here a lot." He sipped on a glass of ice water. "Business, you know."

"Of course."

Poindexter wanted to eat and leave. It was a pity, he thought, that he was with the attorney. He'd heard of the restaurant, and wouldn't have minded at all having a leisurely meal. But not with the lawyer. And not now, when the media and the community were so carefully attuned to his every move. Now was the time to show them that he was one of them. A man of the people. He opened his menu, holding it in front of his face.

"Jesus," he muttered, then lowered the menu to see Isaacs seriously studying the wine list.

"They want twenty bucks for meat loaf! A la carte. No salad, no soup, nothing. Just meat loaf. You mean to say they get twenty bucks for meat loaf here?"

Isaacs looked up from the wine list and smiled.

"It's good," he said, then returned to the list.

Poindexter clucked in disbelief, smiling and shaking his head.

"My moma used to make the best meat loaf in the world. No way you're gonna tell me this meat loaf is better than hers. And even my momma's meat loaf ain't worth no twenty dollars."

The waiter returned, stroking at his ponytail with his hand.

"Have you selected a wine, sir?"

"How's this 1982 Beaulieu Cabernet?"

"Very nice, sir."

Poindexter would have bet that the ponytailed waiter had never tried the wine. He looked to be more the mineral-water-and-lemon type.

"For forty bucks a crack," said Isaacs, "I hope you're right, kid." He handed the wine list to the waiter. "We'll have a bottle of that."

Poindexter watched the waiter disappear into the kitchen.

"You got everything set for the march?"

Isaacs had been silently flirting with two women at a nearby table and had only partially heard the question.

"March? Oh, yeah. Right. No problem, Lamont. I notified the media. The place will be crawling with camera crews. You've got your people ready to go. I expect a big turnout. The press is all over Parker Center these days, what with this latest business about Curt Denmark and the Butcher investigation."

"Whadya think Powell's going to do?"

"Dump him," said Isaacs, matter of fact. "He's got no choice. It'd be political suicide to keep Denmark on board. And Francis Powell's not the type to take chances when it comes to his public image."

Poindexter nodded, at last agreeing with something the attorney said.

The waiter returned with their wine, opened the bottle, and poured a small amount in Isaacs' glass. After the tasting ritual had been completed, both men ordered the meat loaf.

Poindexter took a sip of his wine, then placed the glass on the table, slowly twirling the stem, gazing into the sanguine liquid.

"Who do you think they'll pick to replace Denmark?"

"Don't know," said Isaacs. "Does it really matter?"

"I guess not. It's got nothing to do with what happens to Lampley."

"Listen, once the D.A. went for an indictment on Lampley, the die was cast. They can't back down now, even if they wanted. Lampley's going to go down in flames, that's for sure. What we have to watch out for is a rail job. You know, Powell and Durning pushing this case through the courts as fast as possible, working some deal with Lampley and his lawyer on the back end."

"Keep it in the public eye for as long as possible."

"That's right," said Isaacs, tossing down the rest of his wine. He looked around for the waiter, then reached over and poured himself another glass. "That's why this march is so important. We get national coverage, keep the fires stoked. We don't just want Lampley's head. It's Powell and the rest of 'em that we're after. That way, even if they

slide Lampley through on the express, we still have something to talk about."

"You're learning, Mr. Isaacs." Poindexter allowed
himself to smile, realizing that he may have underestimated the lawyer.

"And at the same time," said Poindexter, "you've got
the civil case against the city."

"That's right. We'll get 'em from both ends. They
won't know what hit'm."

The waiter arrived with their meal, two plates of
mashed potatoes and gravy, with a large slab of what
Poindexter had to admit looked like great meat loaf. He
poked his fork at the meat, then swirled it in the gravy
before bringing it to his mouth.

"Mm." His eyes closed, savoring the flavor. "I gotta
admit, this is good." He looked up at the ceiling and said,
"Momma, I'm sorry, but this is damn good meat loaf."
He laughed and started to cut himself another piece. "But
it still ain't worth no twenty bucks," he muttered.

The two men finished their meal, then had dessert from
the pastry tray, washed down with coffee. When they'd
had refills on the coffee, the waiter brought the bill and
placed it in a tray on the table. Poindexter glanced at the
bill, noticing that it totaled just under a hundred dollars.

Isaacs grabbed the bill and got up to leave.

"You ain't gonna pay?" said Poindexter, looking confused, and wondering if Isaacs intended to stick him with
the bill.

"No problem, Lamont."

Isaacs made his way toward the exit, holding the check
in his right hand. As he passed the waiter, he handed the
check to the young man.

"Thanks for the great service," he said. "I left a hundred with Maurice, that should take care of it."

With that, Isaacs quickly herded Poindexter out of the restaurant to the curb, where the Mercedes was already waiting.

From where he sat, on his deck at the back of the house, Curt felt he could see things more clearly now. His choices, the memories . . . All that had happened to bring him to this point.

The place where it had happened, a shallow ravine just partially in view, was now covered with brush and wild-flowers, the evil camouflaged by poppies splashing the hillside with dabs of bright orange.

But he wasn't fooled by the passage of time. If he looked hard, he could still see the blood. That look of terror on Jackson's face. His own fear screaming inside his head, pressing to be released.

He had killed a man there. And, he told himself, saved another.

But for what? For this?

His mind drifted over the events that had taken place just a few yards away: Travis Jackson, that one moment when he was sure that Jackson could not be stopped, the glint of the blade raised in his hand. It was a knife, at least that's what he told the first cops on the scene. Jackson had it, in his hand. Like this, he'd shown them. But they never found a weapon. Nothing that even came close. Maybe it was a reflection, the detective had suggested, with a look that said he wanted Curt to go along with the story, that it would be easier for everyone. In the end he went with the reflection, taking some comfort in the detective's nod and knowing look. It was all written down, nice and neat. Perfect. Everything slipped right through. Everything except for the knife that he knew . . . *thought?* . . . he had seen.

The knife was never mentioned. Except in his dream, the one he regularly had. Just before shooting Jackson, he always saw the knife. He looked for it. It was there, verifying his act of violence. He was not an animal like Jackson, with simple revenge as a motive. Curt told himself he was better than that.

Then he jumped forward in time. A familiar scene, he and Jamie only a few weeks ago, out on the rocks, holding each other and trying to make sense of the past.

As if mere love would be enough.

As if anything he gave his heart to could overcome the forces he didn't understand. He felt naive. Naive and embarrassed that he had weakened himself by loving.

He should have known better.

He had come through so much. They had come through the worst of it together. Was this now how it was supposed to end?

Curt wanted to believe there was a reason for what had happened. An explanation, something logical and orderly, for the emotional beating he'd sustained at the hands of time. He thought, if only he could sharpen his insight, look deeper inside himself, he would be able to see it.

Perhaps he was too close?

Step outside, he told himself. Get the big picture.

But in the end it always came down to violence and confusion. Maniacs presiding over the universe, cutting and slashing and gouging their way. Nothing rational. Unless the rational order to this life was the lack of order. Unless nothing made sense, except the preservation of self above all else.

He couldn't live that way. There had to be some standard, something against which he could measure himself. Some gauge or criterion, be it religious or secular, no matter how ambiguous, that defines the way we live our lives.

So he told himself that there was a hierarchy of values, and that the longer he hung around, the clearer those values would become.

It was something. It provided a reason for persevering.

He convinced himself that what he was here for now was to achieve some small sense of resolution by finding Jamie's killer. It didn't matter that deep down he knew that the Butcher would only be replaced by some other psychotic murderer, and he by someone else. Over and over again. The deadly process never ending.

It didn't matter that this act of resolve on his part amounted to no more than an insignificant bleep in a universe gone mad, where lunacy reigned supreme and maniacal madmen became instant media celebrities.

The alternative was too bleak. The alternative was closing his eyes and letting the wave of sorrow wash over him. Tumbling head over heels into obscurity. Taking a deep breath and letting the water fill his lungs until all was darkness.

Yet, still, it was tempting.

Eighteen

From Francis Powell's top-floor office, they could see the throngs of marchers gathering a few blocks away.

"Ya know," said Powell, gazing out the window, "the only good thing about all this is that it's taken some of the pressure off finding the Butcher." He looked at Curt, then scolded himself for making the comment.

"It's okay, Francis. I know what you meant."

Powell nodded, returning his gaze to the street below. Both men stood side by side, staring out the window at the thousands of people milling about in the street. The march was set to begin in a few minutes. A half-dozen television vans were parked along Temple Street, and camera crews were busy taking up positions along the route. The marchers were to walk from the other side of the Hall of Administration to the front of Parker Center, a distance of approximately five blocks.

"Turn on the TV, would you, Curt?"

Curt removed the remote control from atop an oval maple coffee table that stood in the center of a small sofa and two matching chairs. On the opposite wall, set on one of the floor-to-ceiling bookshelves, was a portable television. He pointed the remote at the TV and clicked through the channels until he found the coverage of the march.

"Pelotas is covering this thing live," said Powell, turning away from the window and joining Curt. They stood a few feet away from the TV, their arms crossed, waiting and watching.

Crystal Pelotas' face appeared on the screen. She was talking to one of the crew, apparently unaware that she was on the air. Within a moment, she found the camera, held her head high and addressed her audience.

"Crystal Pelotas reporting from downtown Los Angeles. We're here today for the march sponsored by the Citizens Committee Against Police Brutality. As you can see, there are hundreds if not thousands of people who have gathered here this morning to participate in this demonstration. We've been told by march organizers that the marchers are to proceed down Temple Street to the front of Parker Center. There, Rev. Lamont Poindexter will demand an audience with Chief of Police Francis Powell."

"Fat chance," muttered Powell.

"Let's see," said Pelotas, "if we can get Rev. Poindexter to make a few comments before the march begins."

The camera panned along the sidewalk, following Crystal as she approached a small group of people. Lamont Poindexter was in the group.

"Rev. Poindexter," she said, coming alongside him and thrusting a microphone in his face. "Would you care to make any comments to our audience concerning today's march?"

"Uh, why, yes . . ." Poindexter looked around as if trying to find the right camera. "Today's march," he said, starting slowly and building up speed, "is the culmination of many hours of hard work by the concerned citizens of this community. It is symbolic of the struggle currently going on in cities all across this great nation." Poindexter had found his rhythm, his deep bass voice undulating a cadence that allowed those that had gathered around him to shout their support with each sentence. It reminded Curt of a religious revival meeting.

"The time has come," said Poindexter, "for the little people of this country to rise up and make their voices heard." He turned, acknowledging the cheers of the crowd.

"Reverend, do you actually expect that Francis Powell will consent to talk with you this morning?"

"Well, Crystal. That's up to Chief Powell. We're here. We're ready to talk. The ball, as they say, is in his court."

"Ball, my ass!" muttered Powell. "I'd like to go down there and slamdunk that bastard." He poured himself and Curt a cup of coffee and took a seat on the sofa. Curt sat on the arm of the sofa, balancing the cup on his knee.

"I know exactly how you feel," said Curt. He flashed a mischievous grin.

"Yeah," said Powell, thinking of the incident between Curt and Pelotas on the set of *Real News*. He sipped at his coffee, returning the smile. "I suppose you do."

Both men returned their attention to the screen. Crystal Pelotas and Lamont Poindexter were being gently swept away in a sea of human bodies.

"Well," said Pelotas, stepping away from the group of marchers, "it appears the march has started. March organizers have set up an area in front of Parker Center where, we've been informed, certain speakers will address the crowd. I'm sure Rev. Poindexter will be amongst them. You might recall that Rev. Poindexter was recently a guest of ours on *Real News*, the same evening that former Butcher investigator, or perhaps I should say soon-to-be-former Butcher investigator Curt Denmark made an *unexpected* guest appearance."

Powell looked at Curt, who winced at the mention of the incident.

"Ballsy bitch," said Powell. "She's got your ass fired already, Benny."

Pelotas continued, "Chief Powell has yet to announce a replacement for Denmark, but it is expected that such an announcement will be made in the very near future. Both Chief Powell and Curt Denmark were unavailable for comment when contacted earlier by members of our staff."

Powell looked at Curt. "Did they call you?"

"Nope."

"Shit. That's typical." Powell shook his head, then gulped down some coffee. "Not that I would've talked to those assholes anyway."

"She knows that, Francis. She's got nothing to lose by saying she tried to contact us, because she knows there's no way you're going to give her a statement, especially after that bullshit of hers in not telling us about the Butcher's phone call."

"Butcher's phone call, my ass!" said Powell. "Buddy, I'm beginning to think this broad is making all this shit up. You ever notice she's got no tapes of any of these alleged conversations? What's to stop her from just claiming she's received the calls in order to boost her ratings?"

"She had the description on the Matador."

"Yeah, so what? Maybe she got lucky. We already had most of that information already. Maybe she figures she's found a good thing. She gets on the tube and claims that the Butcher trusts her, that he calls all the time and tells her his deepest secrets. There's no way we can contest that, except to ask, 'Where's the tape?' "

"And she claims," said Curt, "that she didn't have time to set up the tape—that it's a misdemeanor anyway to secretly tape telephone conversations."

"Bullshit," said Powell. "Nobody's going to prosecute her for taping those conversations and she knows it. It's just a way out. If you ask me, I don't think the bitch ever talked to the guy."

Curt continued to watch the television. They were showing the march from overhead, taped by a cameraman inside a helicopter hovering over the crowd.

Curt thought about Pelotas' most recent reports. She'd already announced that she'd received a second phone message from the Butcher. That he told her he'd picked his next victim and would be striking again very soon. Pelotas claimed to have tried, to no avail, to get the Butcher to talk more about himself, to unintentionally reveal something that would aid in his capture.

Over the last few weeks, Curt's emotions had rollercoastered from the depths of sorrow and grief over Jamie's death to the heights of anger and rage. Right now, he was poised at the top of the tracks, craving revenge, motivated almost entirely by his desire for vengeance. It filled him with a sense of power. And it worried him.

He'd received the okay from Powell to continue on the Butcher investigation, though he knew Francis would be keeping a very close eye on him. He had guaranteed Powell that the worst was over, that he was okay.

Only Curt knew that he wasn't.

He was still hitting the vodka pretty hard, but he thought he could handle that. He'd become an expert at camouflaging his true feelings. In the years since Darren's death, he'd collected a closet full of masks behind which he could hide.

From where he sat, perched high on the tracks, waiting

for the car to roll forward or back, Curt felt precariously balanced between where he'd come from and where he was about to go. Behind him was the steep uphill climb he'd made since that night in the parking garage. Immediately in front, the terrifying plunge into new and unknown depression and sorrow.

But it wasn't as if he had a choice. He'd paid his money. He was strapped into the car for the duration. There was no getting off until the wild ride had finally run its course.

He was wearing his white suit, the one he always wore. And the bushy white goatee that tickled his upper lip.

"Hon, you look like that chicken guy, what'sisname? The old guy with the beard. The colonel, that's it. Colonel Sanders, that guy useta' sell fried chicken." She started to giggle.

"Here," he said, tossing the cheap calico skirt and blouse to the woman. "Put these on."

She inspected the clothes, then smiled a knowing smile as if she'd been through this before.

"Whatever you say, hon."

She sat on the edge of the bed, pulling off her skin-tight black latex pants. When she'd peeled one leg down to the ankle, she kicked one of her red spiked heels into the air, then repeated the process with the other leg. She removed her nylon see-through halter top, twirled it in the air on one finger, then let it fall to the ground.

"You want I should keep these on, hon?"

She stood before him, her hands behind her head, slowly moving her hips from side to side, wearing only a white lace bra and a skimpy pair of white lace panties. She pulled at the crotch of the panties, giving him her pouting look.

"Yes," he said, feeling himself get hard at seeing the contrast of white lace against chocolate brown skin.

He was on his back, laying on the bed, watching her get into the skirt and blouse. He had a riding crop in his hand, and was gently slapping it against the mattress.

"You ain't gonna hurt me with that thing, are ya, hon?"

He didn't answer.

"Like last time," she said. "Right?"

She was dressed in the skirt and blouse, barefoot, standing at the end of the bed.

"Like last time" he said, still beating a slow rhythm with the riding crop. "You're Missy. And I'm Master Robert."

"Whatever you say, hon."

"Master Robert!" he corrected.

"*Massuh* Robert," she said, emphasizing the first word. She came closer.

He said, "Undo my pants, girl."

She bent over, watching him watching her. Slowly, she undid his belt, then unzipped his pants.

"Yes, massuh," she said, reaching inside his pants and grasping his penis. She raised her eyebrows and made herself swallow hard, acting the part.

"Why, Massuh Robert," she exclaimed. "You's *so-o-o* big!"

"That's right, Missy. Now you know what makes Massuh Robert feel good, don't you?"

She smiled, thinking about the hundred bucks that the man had already placed on the nightstand.

"I sure does, Massuh Robert."

She leaned over and gently placed her mouth over the tip, slowly moving up and down the shaft.

"Jesus," he moaned, "that feels good. Just like that."

She came up for air, saying, "Missy knows what her massuh likes." She started back on him, harder and faster. "Uh huh," she said. "Missy knows all 'bout her Massuh Robert."

When she had finished, she quickly wiped herself and him with a towel from the motel bathroom.

"I gotta get goin' now, hon," she said, slipping into her pants and top. "You know how to get hold of me when you feel the urge." She smiled, then shoved the hundred dollars into her pocket and headed for the door. "You take care of yourself, *Massuh* Robert." She giggled as she left the room.

Robert Dornan Lee remained on the bed, eyes closed, thinking. He felt relaxed, the pressure dissipated for the time being. His mind drifted away from the girl to the events of the past week. He thought about Terry Lampley, and of what he was about to do to help the troubled police officer. About contacting Curt Denmark. He visualized how it would happen, what he would say, and how Denmark would react.

Francis Powell had made a mistake, Lee thought, letting Denmark remain on the case. But that wasn't his problem. In fact, it worked to his advantage. Denmark was emotionally bound to the case. Denmark would jump at the chance of trading for information that would lead to the Butcher's capture.

Lee opened his eyes, gazing at the water-stained cottage-cheese ceiling. He was taking a chance, he thought. What he was about to do was no doubt unethical, perhaps even obstructing justice.

He would tell Denmark that Lampley had stopped the driver to issue a traffic citation. That was the truth.

That Lampley was called away before the citation could be issued. Again, the truth.

That Lampley remembered seeing a gold stickpin in the shape of a cat with dark blue eyes, on the seat next to the driver. Also the truth.

And that Lampley recalled having seen the same pin being worn by Jamie Sills while they both had been sitting in juvenile court.

So much of it was truth, he thought.

And only one little lie. A minor transgression. Not even that. After all, Terry Lampley now actually believed that he remembered the license plate number. It had been there, in his mind, all the time. It had just taken a little coaxing, a little hypnotic suggestion to bring it to the surface.

Hell, the cops used the technique with their witnesses, so why shouldn't he?

It was a matter of tactics, he thought. If Denmark found out that Lampley's memory had been enhanced through hypnosis, he might question the officer's credibility. It was the sort of thing that had to be disclosed to the ultimate trier of fact, a judge or jury, opposing counsel. Curt Denmark might view that as a problem.

No, Lee thought. He'd conveniently leave out the hypnosis.

The Butcher had already announced to the world that he'd selected his next victim. Denmark and Powell and the others would be chomping at the bit to catch the killer before he struck again. Lee figured he'd just waltz into Parker and lay it on Denmark, watch his eyes pop out at the information.

Sure, that was what he would do. Act like he had nothing to hide.

And who would ever find out?

He'd never mention it, that was for sure.

And Lampley had no choice. The young cop was looking at doing some serious time.

And this was just a little fib, a relatively innocent omission.

Who'd notice?

Who'd care?

Nineteen

Knocking and receiving no answer, Powell unlatched the gate and walked around to the rear deck. Curt was there resting on a chaise, gazing out at the canyon sunset. An ice bucket, a bottle of Absolut, and two glasses—one of them full—were within arm's reach on a small glass-topped table. The charcoal smell of barbecue filled the air. Powell noticed two large steaks slowly cooking on a small hibachi.

"You've got a great security system," he said. "I guess you figure that as long as they're quiet, the damn burglars can take whatever they want."

Curt sat up and swiveled around. "Hey, Francis. Sorry. I've been meaning to install an extension to the front bell. Just never got around to it." He gestured for Powell to have a seat on the chaise near his.

"Fix you a little toddy?"

Powell eyed Curt carefully but quickly. It didn't go unnoticed.

"Don't worry, Francis. I've limited my drinking to nights only, and I put my car keys in a place where I'd have to be sober to find them."

"I didn't say anything."

"You didn't have to."

Curt poured Powell about three fingers of vodka over ice.

"Steaks smell great," said Powell, taking the glass and reclining back on the chaise. "Wish I had a place like this. Sit here evenings and watch the sun go down, listen to the coyotes in the twilight."

Both men were silent for a few minutes, sipping on their drinks, alone with their thoughts. The sun had dipped behind the foothills but the air remained warm, abuzz with the sounds of insects swarming in the canyon.

Curt had decided to get Powell away from Parker Center to tell him about the phone call from Robert Lee. He wasn't quite sure what to make of Lee's information, how much weight to give it. It was like so many other claims made by defense attorneys, including himself. You wanted to make the best bargain possible for your client, exact as much leverage as you could in trying to cut a deal prior to trial.

If what Lee had said were true, if Terry Lampley could deliver what Lee promised, the Butcher would soon be behind bars. Curt could feel it, his hands slowly closing around the killer's throat. The maniac's reign of terror would be over. Jamie's death would be avenged.

But Lee would exact his price. He'd want a deal on the Monroe Davis case. And that presented some major-league problems with Francis.

Powell said, "So what is it that's so important you feel you have to ply me with liquor and dinner? You already catch the Butcher? Got him hooked up in the garage or something?"

Curt laughed. "Not yet, Francis."

Powell sipped from his vodka, then swirled the liquid in the glass, watching the sun reflect off the melting ice.

"I received an interesting phone call this morning," said Curt. He kept his eyes focused away from Powell, looking out over the railing as he spoke. "Robert D. Lee."

"Lampley's lawyer?"

"Right."

Powell turned to his side, facing Curt.

"Lee says Lampley's got some information on the Butcher."

Powell sighed, slugged down the rest of his vodka, and reached for the bottle, saying, "Yeah, and I'm gonna sign a million-dollar bonus to pitch for the Dodgers next year. Jesus, why is it that this doesn't surprise me at all?"

"Listen for a second, Francis. I thought the same thing when he first called. You know, that Lampley was just grabbing for straws, trying to come up with an angle on the Davis case."

"Yeah, so?"

"Lee mentioned something that got my attention. He said that Lampley stopped a car just before the Davis incident, the same night that Jamie was killed. That he saw something inside the car. A pin, a cat made out of gold. He recognized having seen the pin before. In court."

Curt swung his legs over the side of the chaise.

"Francis, that gold pin was Jamie's. I gave it to her."

Powell's brow furrowed. He took a deep swallow of vodka, then another.

"Lampley's got the license number of the car. He places it just a block or so from the parking garage where Jamie was found."

"Shit."

Powell reached for the bottle, then thought better of it. He smelled something burning, looked around, and saw flames rising from the hibachi. Curt got up and adjusted the grill on the barbecue. When he returned, Powell had poured them both another drink. Curt took his and placed it on the railing as he stood peering out into the twilight.

"Do you believe him?" said Powell.

"I don't know. What do you know about Lampley?"

"Whatdya mean?"

"I mean, what kind of cop is he?"

Powell shrugged. "Average, I guess. As far as I know, no complaints in his personnel file. Good promotability ratings. Gets along. A pretty regular guy."

"What I mean, Francis, is Terry Lampley the sort that might make something like this up to save his own neck?"

Powell laughed. "Hell, that's impossible to say. He might. Anybody might, given the situation. Even the lawyer."

"Yeah, that's about how I looked at it."

"But the pin? How'd he know about that?"

"He'd seen Jamie and me in court. Lee said Lampley had noticed the pin, but didn't think much of it until after that night."

"Now wait a minute, Curt. I read the initial reports. And nowhere in those interviews does Lampley say anything about a pin, or even stopping some guy in a car. It sounds a little fishy to me."

"Lee says he forgot. That with all the pressure of the Davis thing, all the interviews and reports, the public attention, Lampley had put it out of his mind."

"And he just conveniently remembers it now, after he's been indicted, when it would do him the most good to have a bargaining chip to deal with."

Curt turned from the railing. "Dinner should be about ready," he said, walking toward the hibachi.

Powell looked confused, wanting to hear more about

Lampley. He followed Curt to the barbecue, watching him fork the steaks onto a large ceramic platter.

"You know he ain't gonna give up what he's got without a promise."

"Yes," said Curt, pulling the hibachi toward the edge of the deck.

"Think about Isaacs and Poindexter. Those two'd be on me faster than flies on shit if they got wind of any deal with Lampley."

Curt had expected this response from Powell. Powell's head was on the block, and despite his tough talk about never stepping down, the political heat had been turned up a few notches. Editorials were already showing up in the papers and on TV, questioning whether it was time that the chief take an early retirement for the good of the community.

"I'm going to talk with them," said Curt. "No guarantees, no promises." He looked into Powell's eyes, trying to decipher his friend's thoughts. What he saw were two dark murky pools, unmoving and nonreflective.

"Of course," said Powell, without emotion.

He and Curt were not yet two locomotives on a collision course. Powell could see the tracks far enough down the line, though, to know that Lee would not disclose Lampley's information without some sort of guarantee. And he knew that Curt realized this also. A lot of things could happen to derail Curt's intentions. In the end, the decision would not be Curt's to make. In the end, he, as chief, would give the orders. Any deal with Lampley would have to be okay'd at the top. Though he and Curt were still traveling in the same general direction, Powell wondered when it would be necessary to place their friendship in harm's way.

"Go ahead and talk with them, buddy," said Powell. "No harm in talking, right?"

"Remember, there's no mention of hypnosis."

Lampley shifted his vision from the figure approaching on the grass to his lawyer.

"It'll only hurt you," said Lee. He waited for some confirmation from his client. Lampley nodded that he understood.

Robert Lee and Terry Lampley were seated on opposite sides of a concrete table, under some trees, in a shady corner of Rancho Park. In the distance, figures in white darted around a matching pair of tennis courts. The muted sounds of voices and popping tennis balls were interspersed with the chirping of birds. Two young mothers wheeled their infant children in strollers along a paved walkway. A group of old men played cards at a shaded table under the park office overhang.

Robert D. Lee had come straight from his afternoon court appearance and was dressed in a dark suit. Lampley wore gray jogging pants with a forest-green polo shirt. When the approaching figure was a few yards away, Lee got up from the table and extended his hand.

"Curt, we were beginning to worry."

"Sorry. Traffic was a bear." Curt shook Lee's hand, then moved toward Lampley, who remained seated.

"We couldn't have picked a nicer day," said Lee, trying to fill the uncomfortable gap in conversation.

Curt nodded, giving the young officer a half-smile. He thought Lampley looked nervous, a fish out of water. Not used to being the accused and having to trade information with the cops.

"Let's get some things straight from the beginning,"

said Curt. He'd taken a seat opposite Lampley and his lawyer. He rested his elbows on the table, gesturing with his hands as he spoke.

"This conversation, at least for now, is totally off the record. Anything that we say here will go no further, unless we all later agree that it should. What I propose is that Officer Lampley make a statement, or if you find it more comfortable, answer questions. I will take some notes, which nobody else will see. This whole thing will be outside Miranda. If after we talk, I feel that Officer Lampley's testimony might become necessary, then we can discuss the possible consideration for that testimony at that time."

Lee sat calmly listening as Curt laid out the rules of the game. When Curt finished, Lee removed his hands from in front of his mouth, pursed his lips, and said, "That pretty much puts us at your mercy, doesn't it? I mean, you get the information that you're after without giving us a thing. What's to stop you from using that information to bag the Butcher, then refuse to offer any consideration to my client? And that's not even discussing what that possible consideration might be."

"Fair enough," said Curt. "I can appreciate your position. And I would hope that you can appreciate mine. Any consideration given would have to pass muster with Francis Powell. It would also depend on the nature of Officer Lampley's information. One of us has to go first here. I do not have the authority to do more than hear you out, I give you my word on that." He paused, wanting the two men to believe his sincerity.

"Believe me," he said, "there's nobody in this town who wants to lay his hands on the Butcher more than I do. I think you can understand that. If there's a way to capture him, I'll do whatever is legally and morally within my power to do it. But right now, without knowing more, my hands are tied. If you take the position that you want a hard deal in writing before laying your cards on the table, well, that's just not going to happen."

Curt waited, watching for some wrinkle in the poker face Lee was hiding behind.

Lee said, "Will you excuse us for a second while I talk with my client?"

Curt got up and walked a short distance away, taking a position in the shade of a nearby tree, out of earshot of their conversation. After a few minutes, Lee motioned for him to return.

"Officer Lampley," said Lee, "will agree to your terms. Outside Miranda. Totally off the record." Lee flashed a nervous smile. "I trust you appreciate the fact that should you arrest a suspect based on Officer Lampley's information, that you will be required to supply the probable cause for that arrest in court. You will need Officer Lampley to do that, of course."

Curt nodded. It was a built-in safeguard, of sorts, for Lampley and his lawyer. The law required that the prosecution, upon demand by a defendant, prove that there was probable cause for the defendant's arrest. If Lampley's information led directly to the arrest of the Butcher, Curt would need Terry Lampley as a percipient witness to testify in court.

"Okay," said Lee. "Terry, why don't you start from the beginning."

Curt listened as Lampley related the events of that evening. Neither lawyer interrupted, letting the young officer tell the story in his own words. Lampley's expression rarely changed during the telling. His voice was uncertain at the start, even cracking at times. But once he got going, the facts came across clearly and with little emotion. Just the way a good police officer would testify in court.

When he had finished, Curt was certain in his own mind that Terry Lampley was telling the truth.

"How do I know," said Curt, "that the pin you supposedly saw on the car seat and the one you saw in court are the same? You mentioned nothing about seeing a pin initially. It couldn't be that clear in your memory. Maybe they were just similar?"

Lampley looked at his attorney, who nodded for him to answer.

"You don't," said Lampley. "All you have is my word that the two pins are the same."

Curt didn't respond. He stared into the young officer's eyes, waiting for him to blink. He didn't.

"I assume," said Lee, "that you've checked Ms. Sills' property, and that you have yet to come up with the brooch. Otherwise, we wouldn't be sitting here." A self-satisfied, smug expression flashed across his face.

Curt had checked the inventory of Jamie's property, and the brooch had not shown up. That didn't totally eliminate the possibility that it still was there, somewhere in the boxes of property that had been sent back East to her relatives. He had some family members going through the stuff, double-checking for the brooch.

"We're still looking into that," said Curt.

He felt certain that the brooch was gone. That it wasn't going to miraculously appear in some box. He had a gut instinct about Terry Lampley's honesty. Lampley held the key to the brooch, the key to finding Jamie's killer.

Curt asked, "And the license number of the car?"

Lee pulled a piece of notepaper from his breast pocket and placed it on the table. It was folded, and Lee held it folded with his index finger as he spoke.

"I've written the license number, the make of the car, *and* the registered owner's name on this piece of paper. You strike me as an honest man, Curt. Let's hope, for Officer Lampley's sake, that I'm a good judge of character."

He flicked the paper to Curt's side of the table.

"We've given you the Butcher," said Lee, getting up from the table along with his client. "What you *do* with him is your business."

He'd taken the gray out of the sides and let it grow longer in the back. He was toying with the idea of a short ponytail, maybe it would make him look younger. It was all part of the transformation he'd felt himself undergoing. Preparation. For when he and his Crystal would finally be together.

Nestor had called her a second time because he couldn't stand not to. He couldn't help himself, and had decided to just give in. After all, what did he have to fear? If the cop had made him, someone would have been out to see him already. And nobody had. He had nothing to worry about.

Still, he was getting itchy. Anxious about his promise to Crystal. She would expect him to follow through. And he did have someone in mind, like he'd said. This one would be his best. Another tale in the legend of the famous Barrister Butcher.

Nestor prepared the bridge for the oven, eyeing the group of women working in the corner, sensing their thoughts. They were watching him. Wanting him. They felt his transformation, he thought. They realized they were no longer looking at the old Nestor Stokes. He would go on forever, only getting stronger, better. It made him feel giddy, like he wanted to do something crazy, out of control.

The door to the lab opened and the office manager entered.

"Nestor," she said, crooking her finger at him and gesturing for him to come. He hated when she did that, especially in front of the others.

"There's someone here to see you," she said.

He wasn't expecting anyone . . . ?

"I'll be right there," he said, setting aside the crown and toweling the fine plaster dust from his hands.

"No need to hurry, Mr. Stokes."

Nestor didn't recognize the voice. He turned, and when he saw the face that went with the voice he felt his heart explode into a thousand shards, ripping at his internal organs.

He recognized the face. The one from the television.

It was Curt Denmark.

Twenty

Curt gestured with a shake of his head toward the interview room.

"That's our big bad killer," he said.

He was seated at a desk a few yards from the interview room. Inside, Nestor Stokes was rocking back and forth in his chair, his lips barely moving, mumbling incoherently.

"He's a nut," said Powell, approaching the one-way glass and staring at Stokes. "A fucking nut case."

"Nestor Jedidiah Stokes," said Curt, reading from a two-page D.M.V. printout. Registered owner of a 1987 Toyota Corolla, California license 1HAL497."

"Just like Lampley said."

Curt said, "He lives in a trailer park near the freeway between the Valley and Newhall. By himself. No kids, no relatives that we know of. Divorced."

"Join the club."

"Works at Valley Dental Labs in North Hollywood. Been there for nearly ten years. Moonlights as a rent-a-cop, night watchman in one of the high-rises in Century City."

"So he has a gun."

"Not sure. I sent Foley and Barnes out to the trailer with a search warrant."

Powell continued to stare at the suspect through the one-way glass. "What's he doing?"

Curt put his feet up on the corner of the desk, his hands webbed behind his head.

"He's been that way since we got here. Wouldn't talk. I advised him, and all he said was he didn't want to talk. Then once we got here, he went into a sort of trance. He's been doing that shit for the last hour."

The phone rang and Curt picked it up. It was Ernie Foley.

Foley said, "Curt, you definitely got a weird one there."

Curt nodded his head, watching Stokes rock back and forth.

"Guy collects newspaper articles about serial killers. They're all here, in notebooks. Even the Butcher. There's also a couple of videos, which Jake felt obliged to inspect. He thought they might be porno and he didn't want to miss a chance to see a little tits and ass. I think he was disappointed when all they turned out to be were tapes of that Pelotas woman talking about the Butcher."

"What about a gun?"

"No such luck, Curt. No pin either. Sorry. Forensic's on their way. Maybe they'll come up with something. We'll keep looking, though. Jake's outside rummaging around in the garbage underneath the trailer."

"Keep at it," said Curt.

"Yeah, right," said Foley. "Oh, and one more thing. The guy's got stuffed animals laying around all over."

"Animals?"

"Yeah, like on the walls inside a hunting lodge. Except these are smaller. A cat, and what looks like a squirrel. Mounted. They look almost real, except they don't move.

He's got some stuff here that looks like what you'd need to stuff'm. I'm no expert, but I can't figure any other use for the stuff. Cans of powder and glue. Styrofoam bodies. It's kinda weird."

"Taxidermy," said Curt.

"What? Oh, yeah. Guess you're right. Anyway, you want us to scoop these things up?"

"Not yet. Stick around until Forensic gets there. We'll go over all the stuff later.

Curt hung up, still thinking about the stuffed animals.

He had run Stokes' criminal record and had come up with nothing, except for a petty theft that had occurred several years back. The computer record indicated that the petty had never been filed, the case having been disposed of instead by a city attorney hearing. Curt had contacted the city attorney's office in an attempt to find out if they kept any record of the hearing, though he knew from personal experience that such hearings were usually informal, often presided over by nonlawyer hearing officers. If there were a record made of the hearing, it would be no more than a one-page form with perhaps some handwritten dispositional notes by the hearing officer.

"Who's the P.D. sending over to represent this guy?"

Powell had left the one-way glass and was standing behind Curt, looking over his shoulder at the D.M.V. printouts.

"Paul Fitzimmons," said Curt.

"Great. Just what we need. Now you can be sure you'll never get him to say a word."

"Fitzimmons is a good lawyer," said Curt, staring at the computer printouts, hoping to see something he might have missed the first three or four times through.

"Fitzimmons is a fucking showboat."

"Hell, Francis. You're just pissed that he left L.A.P.D. and took all your little secrets with him."

"Can you blame me? We train the guy, spend all that time and money, then the first thing he does is get himself a law degree and join the public defender. Then he sits there and grills our guys on the witness stand, like he enjoys it."

"I think he does," said Curt. "Enjoy it, I mean. You just don't like the guy because he wins more than his share of cases."

Powell grumbled, then took a seat at the desk next to Curt.

"Shit, I thought Fitzimmons was leaving the P.D.'s office, anyway. What's he still doing hanging around. There must be millions of sleazeball criminals out there willing to pay that guy big bucks to represent them."

"That's a big move," said Curt. "As a P.D., he doesn't have to scrounge for cases. He gets a check twice a month, and doesn't have to worry about getting paid. My guess, if he *is* thinking about leaving, he's waiting for a big case, something to get his name in the paper, to launch him, if you know what I mean."

"Well," said Powell, glancing at Stokes, "he might have just gotten his ticket out."

The phone rang again and Curt lifted the receiver, listening without speaking. After a few moments, he thanked the caller and hung up. He crossed his arms, dropped his head for a split second in thought, then looked up at Powell.

"What?"

"That was the C.A.'s Office," said Curt. "The only record they've got of Stokes' city attorney hearing are some notes from the hearing officer. They read them to me. A shoplift from a supermarket that turned into a fight.

Apparently Stokes never appeared at the hearing. But a lawyer appointed by the mental health court did. Stokes couldn't attend because he was in Camarillo State Hospital at the time."

"A fruitcake."

"At least for a while. The C.A. dismissed the case. They don't know what happened to Stokes."

"Mental Health would have a record if he were committed."

"Perhaps. Sometimes it doesn't go that far. They might have held him for a couple of days, then released him. It depends how bad off he was."

"This gets better and better, Curt. We make this off-the-record deal with Lampley, which leads us to some mysterious gold brooch and some guy that lives by himself with his stuffed animals in a trailer out in the middle of nowhere, and who's crazier than shit, with a lawyer who will milk this fucking case for all it's worth so that he can go out in private practice and make a million bucks, drive a Ferrari, and wear thousand-dollar cowboy boots made from some endangered species."

"There was no *deal* with Lampley," said Curt.

"You know what I mean. Lampley's gonna have to testify if we have any hope of convicting this asshole. And that's assuming he is the asshole we think he is. I tellya, I'm not so sure. And if *I'm* not sure, rest assured that Paul Fitzimmons will have a jury feeling the same way."

Curt looked Powell in the eye. He could see that Powell had something else on his mind. He was working up to something.

"Is all this bullshit to get me in the mood, Francis? Are you trying to get me ready for when you decide that you're not going to deal with Lampley?"

"I didn't say that."

"No, you don't have to. I can see it in your face, Francis. I know you."

The two men stared at one another for a few moments. Powell was the first to look away.

"That's it, isn't it, Francis? You have no intention of cutting Lampley any slack. Politically it would be too damaging. You're going to deliver Lampley to Isaacs and Poindexter on a silver platter. Save your own skin. Like you said, the Monroe Davis incident has taken the pressure off finding the Butcher. And nobody really cares, do they, about someone going around killing lawyers."

"I never said that," said Powell, stung by Curt's insight.

"No, Francis, you're right. You never said that."

Curt got up and left the room.

Paul Fitzimmons waited patiently inside the glass-enclosed cubicle of the attorney conference room. His curly light brown hair slightly receded along the sides. He kept it in a close-cropped Afro. On his face, a pair of brown aluminum Revue frames took attention away from his eyes, which appeared as indistinct shapes of dark and light behind the tinted lenses. He stood six foot five and had, until recently, been mostly muscle. Lately he had been concerned about putting on some extra pounds, and had been playing pickup basketball in the park in an effort to rid himself of the extra weight. He wore a lightweight tan poplin suit, the jacket of which was draped over the back of his chair. He'd rolled up the sleeves of his dress shirt and had loosened his tie.

His eyes wandered down the long narrow tables that spanned the length of the room, at the lawyers and probation officers speaking with the county jail inmates.

To him, the attorney conference room was just part of

the job, merely one cog in the criminal justice wheel, which grinded along day to day, meting out a form of expedient equity more concerned with statistics and the clearing of court calendars than any lofty philosophical ideals.

Not like when he'd joined the P.D.'s Office. For those first few years, he had actually felt like a lawyer, the type of lawyer he'd envisioned himself becoming when he was a kid. But then came his father's hospital bills, and the funeral expenses. Then his mother had taken ill. Three years of law school had seemed an unacceptable luxury at the time. He'd needed to make money, and L.A.P.D. looked to be the quick-fix answer. Then, as now, it had all come down to money.

He'd been promoted to a grade-four spot in the P.D.'s office, trying serious felonies, death penalty cases, back-to-back. Winning more than he should have. And for what? For the personal satisfaction of knowing that he was more skilled than most of his associates? That through his diligence, expertise, and hard work, he was thought of as one of the finest criminal defense attorneys in the county?

It no longer seemed worth it. He hadn't trained himself, worked the long hours, to end up punching a clock, being transferred from courthouse to courthouse at the whim of some politician or ass-kisser, watching the best attorneys in the office, his friends, turn into old men before their time.

He'd gone as far as he could. If he was to continue handling the pressures of trying high-grade felonies, of holding clients' lives in his hands, he was determined to be paid what he thought he was worth. To taste a bit of the good life before the system wore him down, burned him out.

"Visitor for Stokes?"

Fitzimmons looked up, lifting his hand in the air, notifying the deputy at the desk that he had requested the visit.

He watched as the inmate, his newest client, made eye contact from across the room and slowly walked over.

"I'm Paul Fitzimmons from the Public Defender's Office. Have a seat."

Stokes looked confused, like he wasn't sure where he was. He slowly sat down.

Fitzimmons felt there was something wrong with the man, the glassy-eyed stare, the uncomprehending expression. But he'd seen it before—the untrusting defendant testing the waters before jumping in.

"Our office has been appointed to represent you, Mr. Stokes."

Fitzimmons referred to the court documents that he'd placed on the desk.

"They have you charged with three counts of murder. I suppose you're aware of this?"

No answer. Stokes remained perfectly still, staring through the lawyer, his mind elsewhere.

"Do you understand me, Mr. Stokes?"

Still no answer.

Fitzimmons moved to the side, waiting to see if his client's eyes would follow.

"I hear you," said Stokes. He came out of his trance, turning his head and locking on Fitzimmons.

"Good. That's good. For a minute there, you had me worried."

Fitzimmons began to wonder whether this would turn out to be the great case he thought it would be. When word came down that they had a suspect in the Butcher investigation, he had volunteered for the assignment. Not that there wasn't a good chance he would have received the case anyway. But he wanted the Butcher. It was the biggest case in L.A. since the Matador, maybe even bigger. There would be press coverage at every court appearance. Mini news conferences conducted in the hallway outside the courtroom before and after court. The *Times* and *L.A. Magazine* might even run a biographical piece on him.

Just the sort of thing he needed to launch his career in private practice.

"Jesus came to me," said Stokes. He was looking directly into the lawyer's eyes. "Last night."

"Uh . . ." Fitzimmons squirmed in the chair, unable to find a comfortable position.

"You believe me, don't you, son?"

"Uh, well, if you say so, Mr. Stokes."

The feeling of elation that Fitzimmons had experienced at being assigned the case was quickly dissipating. Stokes was staring at him with killer eyeballs, fixed, like shiny black marbles. There was a slight, almost imperceptible tremor that was shaking his head, and the corners of his mouth were moist with drool.

And then in a whispered hiss that was loud enough to get the attention of the inmates sitting behind him, Stokes leaned across the table and blurted, "It's all a pack of lies! The Lord is my savior. I am Jesus Christ! His son on earth. It's all a pack of lies!"

Stokes began rocking back and forth, mumbling the same words to himself, over and over.

Fitzimmons looked up. Two burly sheriff's deputies were quickly moving toward him.

"You come with us," said one of the deputies, grabbing Stokes by his right arm while the other deputy took hold of the left. "Counsel, you'll have to come back to finish your interview."

Fitzimmons nodded, silently watching as the two deputies escorted his client back inside the jail.

"I am Christ the Lord," shouted Stokes. "You are forgiven, my children. You are all forgiven . . ."

Fitzimmons wondered if Stokes were merely running a number, or whether he had truly flipped out. He'd had clients in the past who figured that a stint in the mental hospital looked better than life in prison or the gas chamber. Most didn't get away with it though. They couldn't keep up the routine long enough to convince a judge to stay their criminal proceedings and commit them to a department of corrections mental facility such as Patton or Atascadero.

Fitzimmons wondered if Stokes fit into that category. After all, the man was looking at the death penalty three times over. Maybe he thought he'd run a game on the court with this Jesus business.

Yet, Stokes did have a prior commitment to Camarillo. A history of mental health problems. The man had heard voices in the past.

Fitzimmons scribbled the words, "Possible NGI 1368?" on the inside of the file. A plea of not-guilty-by-reason-of-insanity was definitely a possibility. Especially if the shrinks came back with anything close to that. With Stokes' prior commitment, an insanity plea would definitely carry some weight in court, even if it went solely to the issue of his present mental state, his inability to understand the legal proceedings and aid in his own defense.

But an NGI plea would mean no trial, at least not for a while. And no trial meant no daily meetings with the media, no articles in the *Times* or *L.A. Magazine*. Little or no publicity to launch his career as a high-priced criminal defense lawyer.

Fitzimmons retrieved his pen and crossed out the notation in the file. He smiled, thinking about the irony of Nestor Stokes, the Barrister Butcher, falling into his lap at this particular time, and how lucky it was that Stokes had been placed on this earth to be his ticket to success.

Whether the crazy asshole realized it or not.

Twenty-One

She'd lightened her hair, soft highlights that brightened under the harsh studio lights. She thought it made her look younger. She could see her reflection in the thick lenses of Lamont Poindexter's glasses when he turned to face the camera.

The director counted down, "Three, two, one . . ."

"Good evening, ladies and gentlemen. And welcome to another edition of *Real News for Real People*. Today our guests are no newcomers to *Real News* viewers. First, to my right, community leader and well-known political activist Rev. Lamont Poindexter." Crystal offered her hand to Poindexter, who gently shook the fingertips.

"And on my left," said Crystal, turning, "Also making a return visit, attorney Gerald Isaacs, who represents Monroe Davis in his multimillion-dollar lawsuit against the City of Los Angeles and the L.A.P.D." She shook hands with Isaacs, who surprised her by grabbing her hand, then leaning over and planting a kiss on her cheek.

Isaacs smiled and said, "Thank you for inviting me, Crystal."

Crystal quickly regained her composure, saying: "Now gentlemen, before we go any further in our discussion, I must make an announcement to our viewers, one that I'm sure both of you will be very interested in."

Poindexter looked only mildly concerned, adjusting his huge frame on the narrow straight-backed couch. Isaacs recrossed his legs, picking a piece of lint from the crease of his slacks. He looked as if he hadn't heard Crystal's last statement, or didn't care.

"*Real News* has learned that the confidential informant who provided information to L.A.P.D., which information enabled them to arrest Nestor Stokes in the Butcher murder investigation, is none other than Terrence Lampley, the L.A.P.D. officer charged in the Monroe Davis brutality case."

Crystal paused for only a second. She could feel the men at her side begin to move around, charging the air between them with their discomfort. She was tempted to take a better look, to enjoy their expressions of surprise and outrage.

"Informed sources tell *Real News* that information provided by Officer Lampley constitutes the bulk of the case against Nestor Stokes. That without Lampley's testimony, the prosecution will have very tough sledding indeed, trying to convict Stokes of the Butcher murders. Perhaps you, as a lawyer, would like to comment on that, Mr. Isaacs?"

Isaacs uncrossed his legs, brushed at his slacks yet again, then recrossed them. He shot his sleeves, fingering the cuff of his shirt, trying to buy more time. He told himself to start out slowly, not to jump to any wild conclusions.

"That's a very interesting development," he said, smiling and adjusting the knot in his tie. "This is the first I've heard of any connection between the two cases, Crystal. Leave it to you and *Real News* to scoop the competition."

He smiled, trying to laugh. It came out as a sort of groan.

"You are correct, Crystal," Isaacs continued. "Under the law, if a confidential informant provides information leading to the arrest of a suspect, and that informant is or could be a percipient witness to events relating to the probable cause for arrest or the crimes themselves, then the defense is entitled to know the identity of the informant and to have that informant available to testify in court."

"Well," asked Crystal, "doesn't that mean that the prosecution would have to deal with Officer Lampley as a suspect in the one case and as their star witness in the other?"

"You've hit the nail on the head," said Isaacs. "If Terrence Lampley is, as you've reported, the basis for the prosecution's case against Nestor Stokes, then they'll need Lampley's full cooperation if they hope to succeed in making the charges stick. If I were Lampley's lawyer, I wouldn't be at all anxious to have my client cooperating with prosecutors and law enforcement without some quid pro quo, as we say in the law."

"You mean a deal?"

"Exactly."

"Reverend Poindexter, how would you feel about offering Terrence Lampley a deal in return for his testimony? Convicting the Butcher is obviously an extremely important and serious consideration. Surely, we cannot just let this man slip through our fingers?"

"Ms. Pelotas, I'm not privy to your confidential sources. As Mr. Isaacs stated, this is the first that anybody has heard of this. I'm skeptical, I don't mind saying, of this latest development. Officer Lampley has been interviewed and reinterviewed. His statements are part of the public record. Nowhere do I recall seeing or hearing that he had any knowledge related to the so-called Barrister Butcher until now. Now, when the screws are being turned tighter, he all of the sudden comes up with this." Poindexter smiled and shook his head. "I'm skeptical, to say the least. I wouldn't be at all surprised if Chief Powell and his cronies have a hand in this."

"Could you be more specific?"

"What I'm saying is that this smacks of a last-ditch effort to get Lampley off the hook. It's the perfect reason for Francis Powell and the D.A. to offer Lampley the deal they've always wanted to offer him. Now they can claim that they need Lampley's testimony to convict the Butcher. Lampley will get off with a slap on the wrist, the Butcher will be prosecuted—by Chief Powell's close and longtime friend, I might add—and everybody, or so Francis Powell thinks, will be happy. It's the type of racist political ploy that I had hoped not to see. It won't work, I can tell you that. My people will see through this bit of legal skulduggery. We won't stand for it."

"Mr. Isaacs?"

Isaacs smiled. He leaned closer to Crystal, his eyes momentarily dropping to her plunging neckline.

"I agree with Rev. Poindexter," he said, reluctantly lifting his eyes from her cleavage. "The people of this city are not so naive as to allow this to happen. This will be a rallying point for my client, Mr. Davis, and for all oppressed people. I intend, at the first available moment, to press Francis Powell and Otto Durning for a statement regarding this development. The citizens have a right to know where their leaders stand on this issue."

Curt couldn't believe what he was hearing. Once again Crystal Pelotas had beaten everyone to the punch. It would have all come out eventually, he knew that. But now there was no time to plan, to try and structure a response.

Issacs and Poindexter would waste no time in hammering the issue with their supporters. The same supporters who were clamoring for Powell to step down. If Francis Powell had ever harbored even the slightest thought of dealing with Terry Lampley, that idea was now as good as dead. Lampley would never testify. The case against Nestor Stokes would cease to exist.

The bottle of Absolut, his regular evening companion, sat on the table in front of him. The voice of Crystal Pelotas continued to fill the air, but Curt's mind had drifted to other thoughts.

A strange feeling, unexpected, was coming over him. Not the morose depression, the sense of ultimate failure that he would have expected. Instead, he felt almost giddy. So light-headed that he thought he was drunk. But he looked at the bottle and realized that he wasn't. It wasn't the vodka that was causing him to feel this way. The vise of obsession that had been pressing down on him for so long had finally broken, shattering into pieces, leaving him with a sense of freedom for the first time in as long as he could remember.

It is all useless, isn't it?

All the effort, the diligence, the hard work. All the worry and concern. The self-doubt, the guilt. It was all for nothing. This thing had a life, a dynamic of its own. It had been vain of him to think that he could control it. He'd committed the classic sin of hubris, believing that the events of his life could be effected by self-will.

The demons and the lunatics, the psychopathic rippers and molesters, were destined to rule the world. He could see that now. All he could do was look out for himself, lower himself to their level, to the level of the sociopath and psychotic, if he cared to continue living.

And he wasn't so sure of that.

Isaacs and Poindexter were right. Powell would feel the pressure. He already had. He'd already let it be known that Lampley was untouchable. No deals, no promises. Lampley was to be the sacrificial lamb. It was written in blood on the walls of Powell's office, indelibly etched in the chief's mind.

It was the perfect out for Francis. He'd harbored doubts about Stokes' guilt from the beginning. About the truth of Lampley's convenient memory. This was the perfect reason for not doing what he had never desired to do in the first place. After all, they were only lawyers, Philbin, Berkowitz, and his Jamie. Who gave a shit about the world losing a few lawyers?

Perhaps it is time to just walk away?

The case against Stokes might get past a sympathetic judge at the prelim, but would certainly be dismissed at trial. Without Lampley, Paul Fitzimmons would make sure that the prosecution never got as far as an opening statement.

Curt had come up with a tie-in for Berkowitz and Jamie. Stokes had been involved with Berkowitz and with Jamie's firm. Philbin's records were scattered all over, and some had even been destroyed by a fire at his home. But Curt had little doubt that the connection was there. Still, it wasn't enough to merely show that Nestor Stokes was a disgruntled client or adversary of Bernie Berkowitz and Taylor & Crockett. There were scores of those.

Curt had counted on Lampley. He'd counted on Stokes saying something, making an admission of some sort, to help tie him to the murders. He'd hoped for something from S.I.D. to scientifically connect Stokes to the victims and the crimes.

But now he had nothing. Nestor Stokes had been charged and arraigned on the murders. A preliminary hearing date had been set. All of the forces of the criminal justice system had been set into motion. The giant, noisy, barely efficient machine, with Curt sitting astride its hood, clanked and churned and chugged its way, irretrievably heading for the precipice, unable to stop. All was lost. Except for the personal doubt that still lingered inside him.

He owed it to Jamie, he thought, to determine the truth once and for all. It would be his final parting gesture to a world gone insane. There were no more rules, no artificial boundaries within which he had to operate. Just emotion. The passion he felt for her still bubbled inside. He owed that much to her, before he bowed out. His world was spinning out of control. A remnant of a former great society now reduced to ruins. A tourist attraction for future generations of madmen and their offspring.

He needed to confront the man. He didn't know what he expected to hear, but he needed to hear it for himself. The words taking on a mythical quality, fueling a false hope. The final chapter. And then his work would be finished.

Curt tossed down the rest of his vodka and grabbed his coat. He left the house, the TV still blaring its advertisements for toilet bowl cleaners, feminine hygiene sprays, and attorneys guaranteeing million-dollar settlements.

He backed out the driveway knowing that what he was about to do was unethical. And he laughed at the thought. As if ethics had had anything to do with Francis Powell's decision, or the sacrifice of Terry Lampley—or the creation of endless demented killers.

Nothing was unethical.

The term had been rendered meaningless, moot. Nothing more than the sleight of hand by lawyers clothing ruse and deception in legal artifice. The chimera of a society designed by men who were filled with their own importance.

Curt headed downtown. He needed to see the man, to talk to him. And he wasn't sure why, or what he would say.

It would be his last involvement with the case, his valediction.

He needed to confront Nestor Stokes, face to face.

He sat in the back, away from the others. The smelly bodies, the horrid breath. Great muscular animals pressing against one another, taking their secret silent pleasures.

He could barely see the screen, and he craned to get a better view. His Crystal was there, though, looking beautiful. She had done something to change her hair.

Nestor heard the groans and catcalls from the others. He was tempted to tell them to be quiet. Animals. Their sex out of control, howling and grunting what they would do to her, grabbing themselves and slobbering lasciviously. As if someone like his Crystal would show them even the slightest interest.

Isaacs, the slimy attorney, was back. The same one he'd seen before and on the advertisements. Nestor didn't like the way the attorney was looking at his Crystal. He had even kissed her, holding on to her hand, taking liberties. And then looking down her dress in front of everyone. It demeaned his Crystal, and she was helpless to do anything about it. The lawyer was just staring, his hormones out of control, like one of the animals sitting next to him. It made Nestor glad that he'd already chosen.

But what were they talking about?

Nestor was aware of heads swiveling back at him as his name was mentioned. He was trying to put it all together: the cop who was in trouble, the attorney . . .

The face of the young cop who had stopped him flashed quickly in his mind, along with what he'd heard of the beating. He had seen pictures of the black man, bloodied and bruised, and the cop who had been charged with the beating, in the paper the next day. Nestor had been looking for the woman, for something to cut out for his scrapbook.

He hadn't put the face of the young cop together with the name. At least, not until now.

"Stokes! Stokes! Visitor for Stokes!"

Nestor got up and squeezed between the group of inmates, feeling hands moving up his legs, grabbing at his genitals. He quickly shuffled toward the deputy.

"You gotta visitor, Stokes. Attorney room." He motioned to another deputy who opened the door to the TV room.

Nestor followed the line painted on the floor, keeping to the side, always moving. He wondered who could want to see him at this late hour. His public defender hadn't been around in a while, and when he came, it was always during lunch.

Nestor began mumbling to himself, softly, as he approached the attorney room. He handed the deputy the visitation slip, keeping his eyes on the floor, still shuffling his feet.

The deputy made a notation on the slip, placed it in a pile on his desk, and said, "He's over there. In the corner."

Nestor looked up, squinting, trying to make out the haggard and uncertain face on the far side of the almost empty room. Then he felt something warm in his stomach, a good feeling, a tingling that shot into his chest and arms, making him feel electric.

He shuffled across the room toward the face, mumbling, and thinking to himself that Mr. Curt Denmark was about to make a very serious error in judgment.

Twenty-Two

The questions were still there, but the answers no longer seemed important. Curt felt they had the right man in Nestor Stokes, even though the evidence against him was less than overwhelming. Stokes was the Barrister Butcher.

Not that Stokes had even come close to admitting as much. He hadn't said much of anything, unless you could call his chanting—the rocking back and forth, mumbling incoherently—communication.

Curt had felt it, though. Looking into the madman's eyes, seeing some small glint of recognition at who he was, why he was there.

After all, hadn't the killing stopped since Stokes had been arrested? Didn't the man fit the profile of the crazed serial killer, keeping his scrapbooks as a record of his crimes? Hadn't Terrence Lampley placed him close to the scene of Jamie's murder, and in possession of the gold brooch?

"Mr. Stokes," Curt had asked. "You know who I am, don't you?"

No answer. A flick of the eyelid perhaps giving him away. Curt was unsure.

"I need to ask you a question," said Curt. "Some questions."

Still no response. Stokes rocked forward, then back. Lips moving. Occasionally a recognizable word, never a complete sentence.

"The woman in the parking garage. I need to know."

Still rocking.

"Mr. Stokes, do you understand what I'm saying?"

The rocking stopped. Stokes dropped his head to his chest, then slowly lifted it. His eyes seemed on fire, and at the same time, vacant.

"I am the Lord," he shouted.

The deputy at the desk looked over, but didn't move. They were used to him.

Curt was speechless, unsure of what to do.

"The Lord giveth, and the Lord taketh away. I am the Lord!"

This time the deputy got up and walked over.

"Everything okay here?"

Curt looked up. There was something blurry about the deputy. He blinked, but the image didn't clear.

"You okay, Counsel?"

Curt thought for a moment, then nodded.

The deputy remained, evaluating the situation, wondering if he should do something. He decided to go back to his desk.

Stokes was there, looking at Curt, looking through Curt. The eyes, unblinking, fixed. Madman's eyes. Killer's eyes.

Curt got up and started to leave.

"I am the Lord," Stokes yelled. Then he laughed, his maniacal voice filling the vacant room.

Curt looked back.

Stokes was silent, seated in the chair, rocking back and forth.

The drive back from County Jail was as if it had never happened. Curt had driven through the evening traffic like a machine, his mind hovering then drifting, like a hummingbird, not pausing long enough for him to get a fix on his emotions.

He tried to sleep. But the images of Stokes and Jamie swirled in his dreams, and he found himself wide awake, staring at the alarm clock. He puttered around the house for a while, making coffee, staring into the early morning darkness.

He sensed that this day would bring a resolution of sorts. But not the sort of ending he had expected when he agreed to take on the Butcher investigation.

At first light, he put on his cool weather riding gear and headed for the road, letting the bike carry itself down the serpentine canyon into the Valley. He lost track of time, working the pedals methodically, not feeling the straining muscles in his legs, the increased beat of his heart, the shortness of breath. Like an engine, perfectly tuned, emotionless.

When he returned, it was well into morning. The sun had crested over the mountains and the temperature had jumped ten degrees.

Francis Powell was already there, standing in the driveway, leaning against the door of his car. Powell's driver stood about fifty yards away, on the other side of the property, tossing stones into the canyon.

"Francis," said Curt, walking the bike into the garage. The clatter of his cleats echoed on the smooth cement floor and accentuated the curtness of his greeting. Powell remained where he was, following Curt with his eyes, waiting for more.

Curt said, "I suppose you heard?"

"First thing this morning."

Powell didn't seem angry. More confused than any-thing else. Curt felt Powell's eyes on him as he sat down on the driveway and removed his cycling shoes.

"Why, buddy?"

Curt didn't look up. He inspected the sole of the shoe, then removed an Allen wrench from his gear bag and began adjusting the screw that held the cleat in place.

"Why not, Francis? What was there to lose? You'd already made up your mind. There was no convicting Stokes without Terrence Lampley's testimony. The case was going nowhere."

"But Jesus, Curt. How do you think this is gonna look?"

"To tell you the truth, Francis, I don't give a shit how it looks."

Curt got up, and in his stockinged feet, padded over to the front porch. He turned on the spigot, slurping water from the hose.

Powell followed him, standing at the slope of the drive-way, watching the runoff from the hose stream down the pavement into the street. If his initial expression had been one of confusion or misunderstanding, it had now changed. Powell's face showed the tension of a man on a mission, the duty-bound bearer of bad tidings.

"I accepted your resignation this morning, Curt. My office will release a formal statement later this afternoon."

Curt allowed himself a smile, more for Powell's benefit than any happiness or relief he might have felt.

"All business, eh, Francis? That's good. You do what you have to do." He turned off the hose, then tossed the end into the garden. "Ya know, Francis. The guy never said a fucking word about the case. Not one fucking word, the whole time I was there."

"He didn't have to, Curt. You'll be lucky if the state bar lets you off with a reprimand. You just can't go talking to defendants without their lawyers knowing about it. Jesus, you know that."

"Yes, Francis. I know that."

Powell lowered his voice. "And you don't care, do you?"

Curt felt something pop inside his head.

"Now you've finally got the picture. You see, Francis, I'm tired of banging my head against the wall trying to get things done that I should've realized by this point in my life are never going to get done. I'm tired of being the one always having to do the right thing when I'm not even sure what the right thing is anymore. I've had it. With Nestor Stokes and with the law—and with you, Francis. At least Stokes is nuts. He's got an excuse. A reason for what he does. What's your excuse, Francis? What reason do you have? And don't give me that bullshit about weighty responsibility and the public good. I've heard that routine already.

"Just look at it this way, Francis. I've given you a gold-plated out. As if you needed one. Now you've got an excuse to do what you intended to do all the time. Go ahead and blame the whole damn thing on me. The case against Stokes has been screwed because of my actions, right? Just lay it off on me. You remember how that's done, don't you, Francis? You're good at it. Just ask Terry Lampley."

"Curt, that's not fair. You know . . ."

"Don't talk to me about what's fair, Francis."

Curt turned and headed inside, slamming the door behind him.

Twenty-Three

"Is that him?"

The receptionist nodded her head. They were both looking out the window. They'd seen the ambulance pull into the lot, and the driver helping the stooped slender balding man into a wheelchair.

"He don't look so bad to me."

"They got him pumped full of stuff," the receptionist said.

"Even so, he don't look so bad. You sure he's the Butcher? Don't look like no killer to me."

The aide and receptionist followed the attendant with their eyes as he pushed the wheelchair up the ramp toward the main office. A few seconds later the buzzer sounded inside. The receptionist pressed a button under her desk and the outside door opened. The ambulance attendant held the door open as he pushed the wheelchair through. Two of the more burly male nurse's aides were already there, waiting to escort Nestor Stokes to his room.

"You go ahead and get him situated," the ambulance driver said. "I'll take care of the paperwork."

Stokes didn't say a word. His chin rested on his chest, and if his eyes weren't opened in narrow slits, he would have looked as if he were asleep. There were leather restraints on his wrists and ankles.

The two women at the front, along with the driver, watched as Stokes was wheeled down a long corridor then disappeared around the corner.

"They send only one of you with that guy?"

The driver smiled. "My partner's in the van. No sweat though. They shot him full of juice at the hospital. He didn't utter a peep the whole way here."

"Still," said the receptionist, looking over the transfer paperwork, "he being the Butcher and all, I'd be a little worried."

The driver smiled. "They never did prove that, did they? I mean, that he actually killed those people."

"Didn't have to," she said. "There ain't been nobody else that's died since they got him. That tells me a lot, even if those stupid judges don't think so."

The receptionist looked over the documents, typing information as she read.

"LPS commitment out of 95A," she said, entering the information on her computer. It says here that criminal proceedings were dismissed?"

"Part of the deal," the driver said. "They had to dismiss charges against the guy cause the prosecution screwed up. Didn't have much of a case anyway, or so I heard. His lawyer agreed to the conservatorship as part of the deal. A locked convalescent facility. Seems to me that's one helluva deal for doing three murders."

The receptionist looked up from her computer. "I thought you said they never proved he did it?"

"Did I say that?"

The driver smiled, signed off on the transportation paperwork, and headed out the door.

* * *

"Now, how do those feel?"

Paul Fitzimmons stood, wiggling his toes, wondering if he'd ever get used to the weight and size of the boots.

"Pretty good," he said, shuffling his feet.

"Go ahead, walk around."

He slowly paced the floor, aware that the other customers were watching him. He felt like he was walking on a board that was tilted forward. He could feel the top of the boots rubbing against his calves.

"They feel great," he said, without conviction.

The salesman, sensing his uncertainty said, "You have to break them in. It takes a while. This your first pair?"

Fitzimmons nodded. He was standing in front of the shoe-mirror, admiring the boots. He lifted his pants leg, checking the hand-embroidered design and the soft, slate-colored leather.

"You won't find another pair like that," the salesman said. "One-hundred-percent pure sea turtle. Very rare."

He was getting the hang of the things now. Walking tall, like Gary Cooper or John Wayne, he thought. Maybe even Clint Eastwood. A stranger to be reckoned with.

The salesman said, "That your car out front?"

Fitzimmons followed the other man's eyes.

"The red one?"

"Yeah, the Dino."

Fitzimmons nodded.

"Beautiful car."

Fitzimmons smiled, still thinking about the boots.

"I'll take'm," he said.

"You want to wear them out?"

He could feel the stiff leather pinching his pinkie toes.

"Maybe I'll take them home," he said, sitting down and

pulling on the back of the boots. "Break'm in for a while before I wear them outside."

The salesman smiled. "Let me help you."

He straddled one leg, then the other, his backside to Fitzimmons, heaving and pulling until both boots popped off.

"They're a little hard to get off at first. But you'll get the hang of it in no time."

Fitzimmons nodded and put on his loafers while the salesman rang up the boots.

"Cash or charge?"

Fitzimmons placed his American Express card on the counter.

"Paul Fitzimmons," the salesman read, his eyes darting from the card to Fitzimmons, then back to the card. "Aren't you the guy, the lawyer that had that case. What was it, the Matador or something?"

"Nestor Stokes," said Fitzimmons. "The Barrister Butcher."

He subconsciously took a step back, unsure whether he'd be viewed as famous or infamous.

"Yeah, that's right. What ever happened to that guy?"

"It's a long story."

Fitzimmons flashed back the three months since he'd left the P.D.'s Office. Nestor Stokes had been his last case. It hadn't turned out to be everything he'd hoped for: A 1368 referral followed by a dismissal of charges after Curt Denmark's screwup. He would have preferred a long drawn-out public spectacle, a courtroom media event that would have thrust his name and face into the public eye.

Still, the result had been considered a coup by most. A legal victory of substantial proportions. Enough that he'd decided to ride the tide of success out of the public defender's office and into private practice.

"The guy got off, didn't he?"

Fitzimmons smiled, taking the boots and his receipt from the salesman. He had no idea where Nestor Stokes was being kept, only that his mental condition had progressively deteriorated and that he was locked up in some headshrinking snake pit somewhere.

"Yeah," he said, clutching the fifteen-hundred-dollar sea turtle boots to his chest and heading for his Ferrari. "He beat the case."

This one looked to be just right. Dark as night, with full red lips and an ass to match. She was just sitting there, alone, dangling one shoe over the rail of the stool, the muscles in her thigh and calf flexing beneath sheer charcoal-colored nylon stockings.

The bar at the Hilton was empty, except for a couple seated in a booth near the door. Robert D. Lee decided to make his move, joining the woman at the bar.

"Quiet night," he said.

She didn't answer. Just pursed her lips, those huge soft black lips, in a sort of pout, then smiled, turning up the corners of her mouth.

She knows, he thought.

"Can I buy you a drink?"

She nodded.

He got the bartender's attention and pointed toward her drink.

"Thank you," she whispered.

Her voice was like satin, deep and full. A soft throaty sound. He imagined what it would sound like whispering in his ear. Then she placed one hand softly on his thigh, the other fingering the lapel of his suit. Her eyes locked on his as she spoke.

"I love this," she said, running her fingertips up and down the lapel. He could feel the pressure of her hand on his thigh, the fingers slowly opening and closing, gently clawing at his leg.

"You must be very successful," she purred, her eyebrows rising ever so slightly, as if they both knew the reason she'd be interested in his answer.

"Listen," he said. "I've got a room upstairs. What say we finish our drinks up there."

She smiled, then opened her purse. He placed his hand on hers, seeing the sharp contrast of white on dark, feeling himself begin to stir between his legs.

"I'll take care of that," he said.

He watched her slide off the stool, slowly, tugging at the skin-tight dress, bending over and running her hands over her rear, smoothing out the wrinkles.

He quickly tossed some money on the bar. He felt himself throbbing now. He wanted to take her hand and place it between his legs. He imagined what she would look like without the dress, those long full thighs on either side of his head, his hands cupped around her soft black ass.

She was within inches of him as they waited inside the elevator. She stood in front, letting him press himself against her backside, pushing back ever so gently.

The elevator doors opened and she stepped off. He covered himself, trying to look casual. He felt like a human ramrod, unstoppable.

His mind was already ahead of her: opening the door; in the room; watching her put on then take off the skirt and blouse like the ones before.

"You don't see too many white suits these days," she said, standing in the hall, letting her hand run down the front of his jacket. She had positioned her leg between his, pressing against him.

"A real Southern gentlemen," she said, with a knowing giggle. "That's what you look like."

He opened the door to the room. As they entered, she placed her hand between his legs from behind and squeezed, and he knew he'd picked the right one.

Gerry Isaacs wondered how he could be so unlucky. Three months earlier he'd been riding the crest of the wave, the city had been his for the taking.

He sat gazing out the picture window of his twentieth-floor Century City office trying to decipher the outlines of familiar buildings in the brown haze.

On a square piece of mirror in front of him he had four neat lines of white powder, like road dividers showing him the way.

He placed the plastic straw in his nostril and snorted one of the lines, his head methodically following in practiced motion.

The word had come through the grapevine. The indictment was a sure thing. He'd known about the investigation for the last few months. Someone in the chain had decided to rabbit. They were falling like dominoes now, each with a story to tell about someone else. His turn had finally come.

He bent over and did the second line, letting the cocaine electrify his brain. He could hear the muffled sounds of car engines and horns coming from the street below.

That was the way they worked, wasn't it? They found the weakest link then milked it for all it was worth, before moving on down the line, adding additional pieces to the picture. He was there now. His face in the partially completed puzzle. One of the others had fingered him, an attorney, a secretary . . . it didn't matter. He'd been named.

It wouldn't be hard for them to piece it all together now. First the staged auto accidents, then the lawsuits and cross-complaints. The depositions and interrogatories back and forth between multiple defendants. And all the time, the lawyers milking each case, doing what needed to be done to add more parties to the litigation, bring in more lawyers for more discovery, more court appearances. It had been a very sweet deal. The unsuspecting insurance companies paying off like slots in Vegas. The money-making legal machine running on all cylinders.

But someone had gotten wise to the operation.

He snorted the third line, sniffing the errant grains of white powder, leaving only the last solitary line on the mirror.

The coke was giving him courage.

What did he have to fear? It would be years before the case came to trial. If it ever even got that far. They'd offer him a deal. After all, he had stories to tell, guys bigger than him up the line. He was just a small fish. What could they want from him?

Still, there was Monroe Davis. Those government guys stuck together. The case was working its way slowly through the courts. A thorn in the government's side, he thought. Something they might want to eliminate before they cut him any deals.

Isaacs did the last line, then leaned back in the chair, letting his head rest against the cushion. Davis was to be his swan song, his ticket out of the practice of law, at least the practice as he'd known it. Thirty-seven-million dollars. That's what he'd asked for in damages. One million for each time Terrence Lampley had swung his baton.

But things were falling apart.

Monroe Davis had been picked up again, and this time it was no mere probation violation. The cops said he'd been identified in a convenience store robbery. They had a video of the whole thing on a surveillance camera. The media was having a field day with that. The supermarket tabloids ran headlines like, DAVIS TO SPEND MILLIONS IN PRISON, or HEY MONROE, SAY IT AIN'T SO. Or, the one that had even made the Carson show, TAPE OF ARMED ROBBERY: MONROE DAVIS——THE SEQUEL.

Isaacs eyed the baggie of white powder, thinking about doing one more line to put him over the edge. He reached for the baggie when he heard a knock at the door. He quickly stuffed the cocaine under one of the sofa cushions and stood up, steadying himself before answering the door.

There were three men dressed in suits standing in the hallway. The first thing that struck Isaacs about their appearance was how young they looked.

"Mr. Isaacs," said one of the suits. He held a small leather case in front of his face, letting the case flap open exposing a shiny metal badge.

"Agent Spaulding," he said by way of introduction, even-toned, almost without interest. He gestured toward the men with him. "These are agents Danforth and Howard. FBI. We have a warrant for your arrest. If you would, sir . . ."

Isaacs stepped back and the three FBI agents walked inside. One of the agents motioned for him to turn around, and he felt handcuffs being placed on his wrists. He was then directed into the waiting room, where the one who'd cuffed him steered him to a chair, then assisted him in sitting. They were so nice, so damn courteous.

The receptionist and office staff looked on, pointing and whispering. Isaacs tried to look away, wondering how this could have happened.

A few minutes passed, during which Isaacs had wanted to say something, to deny his involvement in any wrongdoing. He kept his mouth shut, though. Just as he'd advised hundreds of his clients.

Then a voice from down the hall. The first agent. Spaulding. Almost playful.

"Look what we have here."

Gerry Isaacs closed his eyes, knowing what was to come. He wished he'd done that extra line before they'd gotten there.

When he opened his eyes, the young FBI agent was standing in the doorway, smiling, his arm outstretched. Dangling from his fingertips was the baggie of cocaine.

Twenty-Four

Colin Archer stood at the edge of the set, answering questions, barking orders, and continually checking his watch. With only five minutes before showtime, he made his decision.

"Crystal, Isaacs isn't going to show. We're going with the Madonna piece."

Crystal Pelotas was in her usual chair, receiving some last-minute touches to her makeup.

"Did you try calling?"

"Three times. Nobody answers."

She shook her head, causing the makeup artist to suddenly pull away.

"Sorry," she mumbled.

"We've got that piece that her agent sent us. On the guy that makes Madonna's bras. You know, those metallic pointed numbers. It's filler, but we're pinched for time. We'll run that instead of the Isaacs interview. Say he was sick."

Crystal didn't answer. She was thinking about what could have happened to Gerry Isaacs. Isaacs' arrest on fraud and narcotics charges was already old news. He'd bailed out and was awaiting trial in federal court. The police brutality case against Terrence Lampley was still getting coverage, the trial being just around the corner. Isaacs had filed his multi-million-dollar lawsuit against Lampley, L.A.P.D., and the city, and was orchestrating daily publicity around Lampley's criminal trial in the hope of pressuring the city into a pretrial settlement of the civil suit.

His sudden absence struck Crystal as strange indeed. It wasn't like Gerry Isaacs to pass up an opportunity to trumpet his cause to a television audience.

Not without a very good reason.

Since his run-in with Powell, Curt had been spending his days going on long early-morning bike rides, then taking a shower and spending some time on the deck out in back, alone with his thoughts. He'd spend most afternoons at the cemetery, sitting on the small concrete bench that overlooked the knoll where Jamie was buried.

Another place to think and be alone. He was getting very good at being by himself, had even begun to prefer it. He knew it was unhealthy, this insulation from others. He could no longer find the strength, though, to fight it.

Like a litany of grief, the images marched through his mind, day after day. The weeks had blurred together into a single funereal scene: seated on the bench, head in hands, whispering to Jamie his words of apology, failed explanations.

The final courtroom scene swirled in his psyche, mocking him: Stokes seated at the counsel table next to his lawyer. Chanting, rocking.

Fitzimmons hardly had to argue:

"See for yourself, your honor. My client is barely able

to understand what's going on around him, let alone assist in his own defense."

They'd brought in another special prosecutor to take his place, mop up. And that's exactly what he did. Faced with two psychiatric reports that claimed Stokes was grossly psychotic and delusional, the prosecutor didn't have much to argue.

Fitzimmons had said, "This is hardly a case of a defendant malingering, faking his psychosis. This man has a history of mental illness. Thirteen sixty-eight requires this court to suspend criminal proceedings until he has recovered sufficiently to aid in the preparation of his defense. If that time ever arrives, your honor."

And of course it never did.

The Great Curt Denmark had managed to fuck things up once again. The more he thought about it—finding Jamie in the parking garage; the 1368 sanity hearing; his unauthorized visit with Nestor Stokes leading to the dismissal of charges—the more he saw himself as an actor in a play, his part preordained, his thoughts and destiny predetermined.

Stokes and the others kept hounding him, their images intruding on his thoughts even at the cemetery.

On this day, he arrived a little later than usual. He'd had a flat on the road, which delayed his leaving. He approached Jamie's grave. Just a concrete block, no headstone, the traditional year not yet having passed.

Curt stood over the spot, hands thrust into the pockets of his windbreaker. He always remembered the way she was, the two of them together, that day in the canyon when he'd decided that the thing he wanted most in life was to spend the rest of it with her.

He turned away, about to have a seat on the bench, when he noticed the white envelope. It had been wedged underneath the concrete plaque and behind the flowers he had placed there the day before.

The first thing that struck him was how callous and insensitive it was for the funeral home to place a message, perhaps even a bill, in such a fashion. He quickly realized that it couldn't be that.

He bent over and picked up the envelope, surprised at its weight. He held it up to the light for a moment, then opened it.

The message inside had been composed of letters cut from magazines, then pasted on a piece of white writing paper. Four numbers and a street name. He recognized the location in Marina del Rey. The number thirty-two had also been pasted on the message, just below the street name.

There was another envelope, smaller, inside. He opened it, letting its contents tumble into his palm. He saw an amber flash as the object glittered in the sunlight, blinding him for a moment.

His heart leapt at the sight of the golden cat.

He quickly looked around, sensing that someone was watching.

There was no one.

Just the hiss of lawn sprinklers in the distance and the sound of an airplane overhead. He felt something jump to his throat, making it difficult to breathe. He tried to slow his heart, which seemed to be pumping uncontrollably. He forced himself to inhale deep, slow breaths.

The pin still lay in the palm of his hand, its sapphire eyes glittering in the sun.

There was only one explanation for this, he thought, gripping the brooch tightly in his fist. Only one person who could be responsible.

He hurriedly made his way back to the parking lot, got in his car, and headed for the Marina.

The address was a condominium that fronted the water. A narrow strip of grass and a small walkway were all that separated the back of the structure from the slips where the boats were docked.

There was a security entrance to the building off the street, and another less conspicuous door in the back near the boats.

Curt parked his car on the street, then checked the numbers of the condominium units on the listing in the front of the building. The name "Isaacs" was printed in small white letters next to the number thirty-two. Curt felt his pulse pick up again. He wondered what sort of cruel hoax the lawyer had in mind.

The entrance to the building was locked. There was a phone near the resident listings. Curt picked it up, searching, quickly reading the directions. He punched in the manager's number and after a few minutes of trying to convince her who he was and that he wasn't there to rob, rape, or murder any of the tenants, he was buzzed through.

He waited, as directed, in the lobby. Within five minutes, he heard the hum of the elevator descending.

The manager, a slender woman with wire-rim glasses, long brown hair, and a large German shepherd held tightly on a straining leather leash, stepped off the elevator.

Curt showed her his L.A.P.D. identification, and whispered silent thanks that he hadn't decided to do something dramatic like throw it on Powell's desk in protest.

"He done anything wrong?"

They were both on the elevator, going up.

"Routine police business," said Curt.

The third-floor hallway split off in opposite directions. "Thirty-two is this way," she said.

Curt followed to the end of the corridor, then around the corner. They stopped in front of unit thirty-two.

"You want I should knock?"

"I'll take it from here," he said.

He waited a moment before the manager got the hint and headed back to the elevator. Curt made sure she was gone before knocking.

No answer.

He waited a few seconds, then knocked again, this time louder.

Still no answer.

As a last resort, he tried turning the doorknob, not wanting to have to go down and bother the manager again. To his amazement, the door opened.

He stepped inside, feeling his feet sink into soft plush carpeting. He was in a small foyer that opened into the living room. The wall opposite the entrance was all window. The sliding glass doors were open and he could smell the slightly sour smell of sea air and gasoline fumes wafting in from the boat docks below. Blue sky and palm trees filled the rectangle framed by the sliding glass doors, like every tourist's picture-postcard of Southern California.

He closed the door and listened. Silence, except for the muted sounds of voices outside, and the distant roar of planes in the flight pattern over LAX.

"Hello," he shouted. "Anyone home?"

No answer.

He stepped further into the living room. To his left there was a small kitchen, a bachelor's setup: refrigerator, three-burner range, dishwasher, sink, and built-in oven all efficiently placed in an area the size of an average closet.

On the counter was a microwave oven, and near it, a plate containing a half-eaten piece of toast. The newspaper was spread out on the kitchen table, along with a ceramic coffee mug, still partially full of cold coffee, with the name GERRY printed in block letters.

There seemed to be something wrong with the whole setup. Outside, the sky was an incredible shade of pure blue, cloudless. A soft breeze brought salty ocean air inside, ruffling the drapes and lifting, ever so gently, the newspaper on the table. It was a perfect morning. The type of day that California was famous for, and the reason the Marina was chock-full of people living sandwiched together like sardines.

But there was something wrong . . .

Curt slowly made his way toward the hallway.

At the end of the hallway were two doors. He pushed at the first. It opened into a small bedroom containing a desk and some shelves. It was empty.

He paused a moment before placing his hand on the doorknob to the second bedroom. He tried to steady himself for what he thought he might find. The face of Gerry Isaacs, as he had seen him with Crystal Pelotas and on his television advertisements flashed in his mind.

He opened the door slowly.

No Gerry Isaacs. Just another sliding glass door leading to a small patio. The door was closed, and the room smelled of stale air. Stale air and something else. A smell he was all too familiar with.

He turned to his right. A large free-standing armoire occupied almost the entire wall. A trickle of red liquid ran from the base of the closed armoire doors, dripping onto the carpet, spreading in a slow, frothy pink stain.

Curt pulled one of the armoire doors. It made a creaking sound as it swung open.

The smell hit him first. Like copper and putrifying flesh.

Then the expression on Gerry Isaacs' face: eyeballs popping, lolling at the edge. Surprise mixed with disbelief.

Then the familiar black hole in the forehead, and the bloodied gore where the mouth was supposed to be.

Gerald Isaacs had been hung on a hook attached to the back of the armoire. He had on a shirt and tie, along with a perfectly tailored English wool suit. His business card protruded from the oozing purple hole of his mouth.

The message on the card read: *". . . And then there were none."*

Twenty-Five

"In an investigation that has had more twists and surprises than we can keep track of, the Barrister Butcher case has taken yet another bizarre turn with the violent death of attorney Gerald Issacs."

The screen changed from a frontal view of Crystal Pelotas to the sidewalk outside Gerry Isaacs' Marina del Rey condominium. Crystal provided the voice-over for the crime-scene footage.

"The body of local attorney Gerald Isaacs was discovered yesterday evening hanging inside the closet of his Marina del Rey condominium. Isaacs, you will remember, had represented Monroe Davis in his multimillion-dollar claim against the City of Los Angeles.

"He was pronounced dead by paramedic units at the scene. Cause of death, a gunshot wound at close range to the forehead.

"Investigators have yet to release a formal statement, but rumor has it that they're considering Isaacs' death the latest work of the Barrister Butcher.

"Interestingly enough, Nestor Stokes, the man originally charged with the Butcher murders, was reported missing early yesterday morning by administrators of the

Shady Acres Convalescent Home, the facility where Stokes had been placed following his commitment by the mental health court.

"A spokesman for Shady Acres stated that Stokes' absence was first noted when he failed to appear for breakfast. He had been kept in the locked wing of the facility, but according to officials, must have slipped past the guards in the early hours of the morning. Law enforcement officials have announced a statewide manhunt."

The screen flashed a booking picture of Stokes, with a telephone number below.

Curt got up from the sofa and headed outside, taking his vodka with him. He'd had his fill of Nestor Stokes, Gerry Isaacs, and the rest of them.

He'd given L.A.P.D. a complete accounting of having recovered the message at the cemetery, and subsequently discovering Isaacs' body. The media had been harassing him ever since. He'd turned down interview offers from Crystal Pelotas and others, and eventually had taken his phone off the hook.

The news programs were running lengthy features on the Isaacs' killing, rehashing the entire case, going over the list of Butcher victims, the arrest of a suspect, the decision not to prosecute, and Stokes' ultimate release to the convalescent facility.

The names were inescapable, like bothersome gnats on a hot summer's evening swirling about his head. Fitzimmons, Isaacs, Lampley, Lee . . . His own name was inevitably mentioned: the former Butcher investigator who had resigned for personal reasons.

Personal reasons?

Both Terrence Lampley and Monroe Davis were interviewed by all the local television stations. Each was looking for a new lawyer.

Davis had been interviewed in the courtroom holding-tank downtown, awaiting trial on his new robbery charge. Even during the interview, he had been approached by a half-dozen lawyers, handing him their business cards, seeking to take over his case against the city. He refused comment on his pending criminal matter, claiming he'd been set up by the police.

Terrence Lampley, in a segment of *Eye-Witness News*, dropped a bombshell when he announced that his attorney, Robert D. Lee, had been arrested on charges of soliciting an act of prostitution from an undercover officer at the downtown Hilton.

Lampley went on to say that Lee, who was married with two children, had been released on fifteen-hundred-dollars bail, which he'd asked Lampley to post for him. According to Lampley, Lee was withdrawing from the Monroe Davis brutality case citing personal reasons.

Curt figured that Terrence Lampley might end up not needing a lawyer. Otto Durning had announced that the D.A.'s Office was reviewing the charges against the young police officer in light of the recent arrest of Monroe Davis. They were concerned, Durning said, with the questionable credibility of Davis as a prosecution witness.

Curt slugged down the rest of his vodka and returned inside for more. Crystal Pelotas was still on the TV, making her final comments:

"When will it end?" she said, staring straight into the camera. "Your guess is as good as mine, ladies and gentlemen. But one has to question the competency of our elected officials when, after finally capturing this demented killer, this psychopath, they are forced to release him on a legal technicality. Who are the people making such dangerous decisions? Who is to blame for allowing this maniac to continue perpetrating his gruesome, deranged rituals of death on perfectly innocent, unsuspecting citizens?

"The man is a crazed killer, barely human. What do we as citizens have to do to protect ourselves from this lunacy? And what did we elect our public officials for, if not to afford us even a modicum of protection from such vile creatures as Nestor Stokes?"

Curt stood mesmerized in front of the television. Pelotas looked and sounded like a front-running politician at a political rally.

He poured himself another vodka, knowing that for him, it was over. He wanted to just fade into the background, become one of the lesser supporting players. Out in front, striving for a few crumbs of glory, he'd been fair game for people like Pelotas and Powell, the survivors, clawing their way to the top.

He felt no relief at being replaced as the Butcher investigator. No solace even in the hope that Stokes had taken his last victim. He'd probably kill again. And if not him, Curt thought, then someone else. The nursery schools were filled with nascent Nestor Stokes, waiting for their time to come.

He knew as the days passed that the sorrow would become like an old scar, a bad knee or a twisted ankle, that acted up only when it got damp outside.

He'd get over it, though. He was sure of that. Not like before. He was beyond that now. The scar tissue, white and calloused, had become too tough, hardened against the ultimate abuse.

But the pain would always be there. To remind him, after a few drinks or a few good days in the sun, that he'd been marked, specially selected.

And when he raced down the canyon on his bike, feeling part of something bigger, something grand in the natural scheme, it would be there to greet him when he returned. The wretched unceasing ache of memory. A misery that he'd suffer the rest of his life, learning to live with.

But learn he would.

Curt thought about the Butcher's last message, the one he'd left on Gerry Isaacs' business card.

". . . And then there were none."

And he wondered what Nestor Stokes might be thinking right about now.

Twenty-Six

He stood in front of the department store window, his back to the street, staring at the TV. His Crystal was there, on the screen inside the window.

Ellie was in his arms, resting peacefully in the crook against his stomach. He stroked at her head while he watched his Crystal on television.

And then there were none . . .

He wondered if Denmark and the others would believe him. That the killings had ended. It didn't matter, though. He knew they'd still come after him. Perhaps he'd take his time about traveling up north. The patent lawyer would still be there. Give him something to look forward to.

He turned his attention from the TV, looking to his left down the street. Although he couldn't see it, he knew that just a few miles away, the commercial streets turned into residential neighborhood.

He could see the house in his mind's eye, the gates in front, the large double-doors with the stained-glass inserts.

He saw himself going over the gates, slowly approaching the house. She would answer the door dressed in something light and see-through. And she would know immediately who he was and why he'd come.

He stroked at the cat, only half-paying attention to the scenes of the attorney's house being shown on the TV.

His mind was on her, his Crystal.

Then she was back. The program was almost over. He was aware of people walking behind him, and his heart jumped when he saw himself on the screen. His face vacant and afraid. He pulled up the collar of his jacket, wanting the picture to disappear.

Finally it did, and Crystal was there again. Except this time she looked different to him. Angry and sharp, with words to match. He listened to her words, wanting to cover his ears, not wanting to hear. Not from his Crystal.

. . . *demented? psychopath? deranged? barely human?* . . .

He stroked harder at Ellie, trying to will the words away. But they remained, swirling in his head, stinging his ears.

maniac . . . lunacy . . . vile creature . . .

And there was his Crystal, a different person. She was the one using the words. Calling for his capture. His death, even.

How could she?

The heat spread upward, filling his chest with its anger. His head was on fire and felt as if it would explode.

He'd been betrayed.

He'd given her his love, his all. Everything he'd done had been for her.

And now this . . .

And then the anger subsided, hardened, forged into steely resolve. The blood pulsed through his veins with excitement.

The answer suddenly came to him. He could still have her forever. Just the two of them. Just like his Gracie.

Except they'd taken Gracie. Along with all his equipment, his chemicals, his Styrofoam bodies . . .

He blinked, and his eyes came to rest on a display just to the side of the television. A mannequin, dressed in a pair of shorts and tennis shoes, with a light-colored cotton top.

It would be perfect, he thought. Just the right size.

He started away from the window, Crystal's voice still in his head, her image floating before him.

He would buy new chemicals, he thought. He'd need lots of them, in large quantities. And a new skinning knife, the largest and sharpest he could find. And a length of steel chain, perhaps hung from the tree in her backyard?

Yes, he thought. It would work. It would be his crowning glory. Better than the others. Legendary.

He quickened his pace, anxious to find his place in front of the house, where he'd watch and wait for his Crystal.

Yes, he whispered, smiling to himself. They'd be together soon.

He'd have his Crystal.

Forever.

Part Three

Twenty-Seven

In the corner, where the black soot-encrusted concrete walls came together, a mound of mismatched clothing sat atop two stubby legs stradling the metal drainage grate, releasing a steady stream of yellowish liquid in the general direction of the drain. Within a few feet of the grate, and currently being splashed by the stream of urine, a chromed shopping cart lay on its side, spilling its load of clothes or rags (or clothes that looked like rags) in a sort of cornucopia of urban blight.

Curt drove past the bum making his morning preparations and pulled into an empty parking space. The entire underground parking lot reeked of gas fumes and exhaust, mixed with the slicks of oil and puddles of vomit that stained the concrete floor. Occasionally the sour stench of urine would waft its way through the structure, adding its distinctive taint to the aroma of automotive and human waste.

He could have been walking through a flowered meadow high atop some incredibly pastoral mountaintop for all Curt was aware of the surroundings. He had decided that spending the entire day wallowing in alcohol and despair was making a permanent checkout a bit too attractive an alternative. Some built-in safety mechanism had clicked in, warning him to try something else. A red flashing light, barely noticed.

So now he pushed himself out of the house in the morning and went through the motions of being a lawyer: get in the car, drive downtown, see the clients, appear in court, say the magic words.

He knew it wouldn't work in the end, though. He knew he was just postponing the inevitable. He'd been fooling himself, camouflaging his true feelings behind the facade that he was sufficiently scarred and hardened to withstand anything. Acting as if control and logic would ultimately win out.

It was becoming painfully apparent that it wouldn't be that easy.

He couldn't put it behind him, not even for five minutes. When he took his morning shave he thought of them. Staring at his face in the mirror he saw them. In a room full of people and sounds, they were still there.

On the way into town he blasted the radio. The faces remained, though, in the expressions of the other drivers, in the reflection of the sun off the windshield, in the lyrics of a song they had listened to together. They were always there. Taunting him. Beckoning him to join them. It would be so easy that way.

Curt packed his things, moving as if in his sleep through the maze of custody hallways and locked doors, back to the courtroom. He would finish his business, making small talk with the court staff and attorneys. Act like he was back on track. Sage, knowing nods would be exchanged. Keep it on the surface, safe: *"I'm doing O.K.,"* or *"Just taking it one day at a time."* That's what they all expected to hear. Don't get in too deep. Nobody wants to see the scars, let alone the open wounds festering beneath the skin.

"Life goes on . . ."

Isn't that what they say?

By four o'clock he was firmly ensconced in his familiar position in a far corner of the bar, hunched over a double vodka. His clients were barely a memory. Ancient history. Names on files that had become indistinguishable from hundreds of other names. Clients whose identities had blurred together over the years. Ephemeral. Hazily recalled characters from one of his vodka-induced stupors. Too numb to remember. Too frightened not to stay numb for as long as possible.

The bar at Mistral was crowded. From where he sat, Curt could view the entire restaurant only if he swiveled completely. He was satisfied to show them his back, work on his vodka.

The San Fernando Valley restaurant served a great New York steak and even better *pommes frites*. Not much more than a storefront on Ventura Boulevard, the Sherman Oaks eatery consisted of about a dozen small tables. A massive oak bar occupied over half of the restaurant.

Curt had walked in thinking he'd have a drink, maybe two, then dinner. He was finishing up his third Absolut. The idea of dinner had fallen down some deep, dark hole. He could barely see it. He'd order his next Absolut, he thought, with a couple of olives. Even a drunk needs his nutrition.

"Denmark, I thought that was you."

Curt felt the hand on his shoulder. He looked over the other shoulder, twisting his body.

"You don't answer your messages."

Crystal Pelotas stood only two feet away. Behind her, looking at Curt with only half-interest, was a young man, perhaps in his late twenties, dressed in a pair of taupe linen triple-pleated trousers and a dark silky turtleneck. His hair was streaked blond and ruffled in that calculated way you see on magazine models. The guy looked like a cover-boy for *GQ.*

"I got the messages," said Curt, reaching for his vodka. "You just don't give a shit, is that it?"

The place was noisy enough so that you could fire off a small-caliber weapon and probably not raise too many eyebrows.

"I'm not interested in furthering your career, if that's what you mean."

"Too painful, huh?"

There it was, that sly smile, the one she used on TV. Probing the wound, Curt thought. This bitch was evil—and took pride in it.

"What would it prove? That Nestor Stokes is a madman?" Curt could feel the anger bubbling to the surface. "Tell the world something it doesn't already know, Crystal. Oh yeah, I almost forgot . . . You're not interested in investigative journalism, are you? You don't give a shit about informing the public. You're strong suit is titillation. Get'm fired up or frightened. Pander to the baser instincts. 'Real News for Real People?' " Curt laughed, shaking his head. "What incredible bullshit. You oughtta sell your shit at the checkout stands of the local supermarket."

The *GQ* guy looked uncomfortable with the conversation. He whispered something to the maître d', who cast his gaze over the restaurant, nodded, and motioned with an outstretched palm that it would be another five minutes.

Mr. *GQ* then whispered something in Crystal's ear. She turned, her lips moving briefly, then raised her chin to receive a kiss. Mr. *GQ* shot Curt a quick unwelcome stare, then moved toward the other end of the bar.

Curt said, "Your son, home from college?"

"Not funny, Denmark. I wouldn't have thought it possible, but it seems your personality gets even worse when you're drunk."

"You got it right there, lady. So why don't you go off with Mr. Big-Man-On-Campus and leave us common folks to our liquor." He started to turn back toward the bar. She caught him with her hand on his shoulder once more.

"I've seen him, you know."

Curt was confused, wishing just to be left alone.

"Stokes," she said, monotone. "He came to my house. Wants me to interview him on TV."

Curt sighed, wondering when it would ever end.

"You don't believe me, do you?"

"Why should I?"

"I don't blame you. You and I, we have different agendas. But I'd be a very bad judge of character if I'm wrong about you this time. You want him as much as I do. Think about it, Denmark. Just me and Stokes—and you."

She arched a brow, a slight smile turning up the corners of her mouth. Curt saw the silvery glint of anticipation in her eyes. Like a fisherman who has felt a nibble and is about to set the hook.

"What do you need me for?"

"A little spice to the pot. Stokes doesn't expect it. The guy is mad, but also madly in love with me."

Curt smiled. "There's no accounting for taste."

"A crazed fan," she said. "A bit more crazed than most."

"You aren't afraid of what he might do?"

"Like I said, Denmark, the guy is in love. It's worth the risk, anyway. I'll have a cameraman there; Stokes has okay'd that. And you'll be there, if you decide to come." She glanced at her date. "You want to bust him after the interview, that's fine with me. Better, even. It'll make great theater: The serial killer pours out his heart just before being arrested by his victim's lover. The whole fucking thing on tape. Jesus, Denmark . . . It'll be great!"

"Not interested," said Curt. He wasn't sure how much of this was bullshit. It would be like Pelotas to set up something like this without Stokes ever showing.

"I think you are," she said. She motioned to Mr. *GQ* "What do you have to lose, Denmark?" She took a step back. "I'll call you again when he gives me a time. Think about it." She smiled, then turned and walked away.

Fat chance, Curt thought. Nestor Stokes had remained invisible for months. He'd never risk something like this. He might yank the reporter's chain, wanting attention. All those crazy assholes loved the attention. But risking exposure on national television? No way.

Curt tossed down the rest of his drink. As he walked through the restaurant he intentionally avoided looking her way. Pelotas could only lead to trouble, digging up the past.

And he already had enough of his own problems dealing with that.

Twenty-Eight

"That's absolutely amazing, how you do that. That animal doesn't take to no one, not even me, unless she's hungry, and even then, if I get too close she'll take a nip."

The plump elderly woman tisk-tisked a few times, shook her head and marveled at the furry ball undulating under the hand of Nestor Stokes.

"I think they smell it," he said. "Some sort of innate sense. Maybe instinct. Not really sure. They know who their friends are, though."

"You must have some of your own," she said. "At home."

He hesitated. For a few moments he'd lost himself in the pleasure that stroking the cat's arched back afforded.

"Used to," he said. He stood, watching the calico mound of fur slide around his ankles, rubbing itself against him.

"Well, it's all just too amazing for me. Haven't seen that old Tom in weeks. Now you show up, a perfect stranger, and here he is just one big ball of love. Amazing!"

Stokes had been watching the woman for several days. He knew she lived in a small three-bedroom tract house about a block away. He knew that she lived alone, except for her two dogs and an assortment of cats. He knew that she took walks every morning to the park where she let the dogs, sometimes the cats, run free. She always brought her knitting, and always sat under the same tree.

In the evenings he'd watched her through the kitchen window, cooking her small meals. She ate from a tray set up in front of the TV, he could hear the sounds. Then she quickly washed the dishes; there were only the few. Afterwards she'd go back to the TV. No visitors, barely a phone call. Alone. All by herself.

Nestor knew she wouldn't answer the door, not to a stranger. After all, this was still L.A. Graffiti covered the walls and buildings of the neighborhood, attesting to the never-ending battle between the Crips and the Bloods. The rival gangs spent the evenings shooting at each other from passing cars, and drinking in the same park that now seemed so peaceful. The old woman had learned when it was safe to go out and when it was not. She'd learned to be cautious, and to avoid confrontations with strangers. She was necessarily overly conscious about self-protection, but not altogether coldhearted.

"You live around here?"

Nestor smiled. "Used to." He looked away wistfully, inviting her to ask more. When she didn't, he said, "Got laid off. Been just trying to make ends meet lately. Odd jobs, you know."

She nodded, her brow furrowed with concern.

This is almost too easy, he thought. For a split-second he felt sorry for the lonely old lady, nobody to talk to.

"I work for food," he said. "If there's anything around the house you might need done."

She hesitated, but for only a moment. "I don't know," she said. He knew she wanted to help, but was afraid of getting too close to this stranger who had a way with cats.

"I understand," he said. "Nice meeting you, and your cats." He turned and started walking.

"I could use some work in the yard," she said, as if asking a question.

Nestor smiled, then looked down at his shoes, shuffling his feet.

"That'd be fine, ma'am."

They walked back to her house. The station wagon was still parked in the garage in back, where she always kept it.

"I'll be out back," he said. "Tools in the garage, I suppose?"

"Take what you need." She seemed happier now. She was moving about the kitchen like a young girl, making preparations for dinner.

I will, Nestor thought, I certainly will. He busied himself in the yard, pulling weeds, cultivating the earth beneath a bed of marigolds. He thought about the old woman, and he thought about his Crystal. Everything was set now. Just like he knew it would be. He had what he needed to complete his plan.

Nestor was aware that his Crystal was not being completely honest with him. He knew she just wanted to use him. The old Nestor would have resented that. The old Nestor didn't understand, though. It wasn't Crystal's fault. She couldn't help herself.

But soon that would all end. Soon he'd have her all to himself, the way it was meant to be. He'd play along with his Crystal for the time being. It made him so happy to see her smile, to listen to the excitement in her voice when he called.

He listened to the old lady singing in the kitchen. An old love song he hadn't heard in years. He made his mind blank, clearing it for the task that lay ahead. He'd visualized it a hundred times. What he would do, how she would be. He was almost there.

Soon it would be over.

Soon.

Twenty-Nine

Another restless night, sleeping alone, dreaming dreams he was sure he'd remember, but forgot the following morning. What was left from the previous night's slumber was a bit of nervous stomach, a wired feeling that, after a few failed attempts to return to sleep, caused Curt to roll into the beginning of the new day in the darkness of the night before.

After making a pot of coffee, he threw on a pair of jeans and a heavy hooded sweatshirt, and went out to the patio deck. The metal chairs and table were still wet with dew. He walked right up to the edge, placing his cup on the wood railing and thrusting his fists inside the pouch of his sweatshirt against the cold.

Curt knew last night's turbulent sleep had everything to do with Jamie and Darren, and the mess he'd made of things. It seemed he'd spent most of his life a spectator to the administration of the American justice system gone wrong. It had all turned out so twisted. Worse than that, he'd been left with nothing, not a single thread to hold on to, to help pull him through.

About sixty yards away, where the hillside sloped toward an outcropping of boulders, Curt spotted a lone coyote, loping toward the patio, nose down, sniffing the wild brush. Coyotes were not uncommon in the canyon, especially in the early morning. Curt had seen, on occasion, packs of three or more foraging in the twilight gloom, looking for breakfast, perhaps a squirrel or rodent that they could fight over.

The vague gray-black outline of the animal moved closer, bounding three and four steps at a time, then stopping, sniffing. It was unusual for them to come this close. Many of the hillside homeowners had patio decks similar to his, and the coyotes and other wild animals had acclimated their lifestyles to their human neighbors.

Curt remained perfectly still. He watched the steam from his coffee rise off the cup and drift in the opposite direction of the coyote. The coyote moved carefully. Curt could now see that it carried something dangling haphazardly from its muzzle. An animal of some sort, brownish-gray with patches of white. Perhaps a rabbit, one of its floppy ears securely within the killer's jaws, the rest of the small body swaying back and forth as the animal picked its way over the brush and rocks.

The wary predator stood motionless, staring directly at Curt, the dead animal still hanging from its mouth. It was close enough for Curt to see the steam curling from its nostrils. Close enough for the animal to be aware of the scent of human fear tainting the morning air.

Curt was now sure that what hung from the coyote's muzzle was in fact a rabbit, its body without movement except for the occasional jerking of the coyote's head. A cotton-puff tail showed flecks of bright red. The coyote's eyes, like black holes, glistened in the morning fog. It lifted its head, baring its pointed teeth, as if to show off its capture: the victorious hunter fresh from the kill, its sacrifice still warm in the mouth, only moments from the terminus of life.

Curt must have been daydreaming, looking away, or inside himself, for when he returned his attention to the coyote, it was gone. If he were superstitious, he would have thought this a very ominous beginning to the day. An object lesson in life. Law of the jungle. Kill or be killed. More likely, he mused: kill *and* be killed.

He remembered now what his dream had been about. It was the blackest of comedies, filled with scenes of death, corpses bleeding into one another, eyes staring without understanding—questioning him. The cold concrete floor of the parking garage. Trembling fingers awkwardly poking at the body of the woman he loved, knowing it was useless, knowing he'd failed yet another of those who had given themeselves to him. He drifted back. Darren's tiny body motionless on the street, eyes staring blankly back at him and asking, "Why?"

Jamie and Darren. Bodies contorted and mutilated in ways that only violence begat.

Curt's coffee was cold. He could feel the chill on the outside of the cup. He tossed the remnants over the railing and went back inside. Despite the warming rays of the sun beginning to lap over the crest of the mountains, bathing the patio in light, Curt felt unbearably cold. Chilled to the bone.

Barrymore LaFontaine—early sixties, flaming red hair, rouged cheeks, full red lips—sat perfectly still, looking straight ahead, knees together, both feet on the floor, back ramrod-straight. One hand rested on his knee, the other held a paperback novel within inches of his face. He was the only person in the hallway outside Division Fifty of the

Criminal Courts Building who was reading. Curt had taken only a few steps off the elevator when he spotted him.

Jamie had a friend, a producer-type, who had asked her for a favor. The friend had asked Jamie to help LaFontaine, who he said was an actor who had a little problem with the law. As Curt found out after a couple of phone calls to the city attorney and the fraud section of L.A.P.D., Barrymore LaFontaine had been arrested and charged with grand theft. The theft being of money, which Barrymore LaFontaine had obtained by cashing his mother's social security checks for the past ten months at the local Alpha-Beta. Actually, the cashing of the checks was not the problem. The problem came about because Barrymore LaFontaine's mother had been dead for nearly two years.

Curt had promised Jamie that he'd see what could be done about resolving LaFontaine's case. He learned from the C.A. that Alpha-Beta was out a little over two thousand dollars, but was primarily interested in getting restitution. The city attorney just wanted to get rid of the case without pissing anybody off. Curt figured he'd be able to work a deal to pay back the money, maybe have LaFontaine do a little community service, then come back to court afterward and get the charges dismissed.

At least that was his plan. He wanted the day to go smoothly, because his mind was not into taking on new clients, at least not this morning. And LaFontaine had the extra baggage of reminding Curt of Jamie every time he looked at the man.

"Mr. LaFontaine," said Curt, looking down on the pompadour of red hair and noticing some tiny dots of red on the actor's forehead where the dye had stained his scalp.

"Ahh, Mr. Denmark." LaFontaine slipped the paper-back into the inside pocket of his sports jacket and stood, extending his hand. Curt thought he remembered seeing LaFontaine on television in a bit part. A western came to mind, but he couldn't fix the name.

"I should have told you to meet me downstairs," said Curt. "It's less crowded, and the clientele is a bit more pleasant." Curt looked around at the throngs of pimps, hookers, petty thieves, hypes, and gangbangers. This morning, two overweight bearded Hell's Angels in black leather, chains, and greasy dirt-encrusted motorcycle boots, stood in the corner near the snack bar wolfing down hot dogs and belching.

A couple of Mexican kids practiced the barrio slouch: shoulders drooped, upper torso cocked backward, thumbs hung over the waistband of oversized khaki trousers. The gangbangers all wore perfectly pressed white T-shirts, and black hairnets, which gave the appearance of a spider's web at the top of their forehead. Spotless black Nike tennis shoes completed the outfit.

"Why, Mr. Denmark," said Barrymore LaFontaine in his best stage voice, "these are my people. The people of the world. I am but a poor player amongst them."

LaFontaine had one hand extended as he made his speech. Curt now remembered where he had seen LaFontaine. The elderly actor had been a regular on a show that he used to watch with Darren. A game show of sorts. Actors would play parts, always very hammy, and the contestants would guess what person in history they were depicting. LaFontaine had been a favorite of the show's producers since the basic philosophy of the show was that it was impossible to overact, the hammier the better, and Barrymore LaFontaine fit the bill perfectly.

Curt pulled LaFontaine further down the hallway, noticing that both the barrio brothers and the greasy bikers were giving the actor hostile stares.

"I'm going to try and talk to the city attorney," said Curt. "I assume that you're not contending that the money from those social security checks was rightfully yours?"

LaFontaine puffed his chest. "Why, that's *exactly* what I'm contending, Mr. Denmark! Those checks were sent to my mother. In her name. For years I cashed checks at the market and nobody said a word. Now, just because I cashed a few after she passed away, they consider me a criminal." He extended his arm, fully enmeshed in his stage persona. "I am an *actor*, Mr. Denmark. I am a respected member of my profession . . ."

"Wait a minute," said Curt. "First, it wasn't just a few checks, it was ten. Second, the only reason you're here in the local system instead of in federal court is because the supermarket paid those checks. They are out the money. Mr. LaFontaine, believe me, you do not want to fool around with this thing. You do not want to get the feds involved in this. Consider yourself lucky that we're here, in state court, where we can handle this matter without some U.S. attorney or federal judge chomping at the bit to put you behind bars.

"And that's another thing," Curt continued. "I don't know where you got the idea that cashing somebody else's social security checks is legal, because it definitely is not. Especially when that person is dead! Now you tell me, Mr. LaFontaine. You want me to go into court and lay that dribble on the city attorney and the judge, see how they take it? Because if you insist that I do that, I will. I just want you to know that it's not me who'll end up with their ass in jail. And believe me, Mr. LaFontaine, a guy like you, great hair, all madeup and everything . . . A nice guy like you does not want to spend five seconds in jail."

Barrymore LaFontaine looked around for somewhere to sit. He turned away from Curt and walked a few steps to a graffiti-scarred wooden bench, wiped a milky puddle of liquid off the bench with his handkerchief, and sat down. He then reached into his breast pocket and removed a small silver flask, unscrewed the cap, and slugged back whatever it was that was inside. He then offered some to Curt, who declined, but not before detecting the strong odor of alcohol.

"By the way, Mr. LaFontaine," said Curt. "That's also illegal here."

LaFontaine muttered that he understood, and stowed the flask back inside his pocket. He removed a small cannister of breath spray and spritzed himself three times.

LaFontaine said, "Do the best you can, young man." He appeared deflated. Curt noticed for the first time that the actor was wearing a toupe, and that the middle portion of his hair was a slightly different shade of red than the sides. Close up, the artifice behind the actor's persona was clearer: the wrinkles around the neck and eyes, the sagging chicken gullet jowls, the blue-red alcoholic's veins spreading their spidery tentacles from his nose into puffy clown cheeks.

"I thought I could get away with it," he said. LaFontaine was mumbling to himself, staring at the scarred linoleum floor. "I haven't been working too steady recently. Not much call for someone like me. Especially when they know you like to take a little nip every now and then." He shook his head. When he looked up, it was with watery eyes. Curt thought he wasn't acting this time.

"I just thought I could get away with it," he said, his voice cracking. "You know how it is?"

Curt nodded that he did.

Barrymore LaFontaine's words echoed in Curt's mind the rest of the morning, and were still there after he'd finished the actor's case in court. After speaking with the city attorney, Curt was able to send LaFontaine on his way with the promise that he'd do what he could to see that the actor did not go to jail, but that restitution would definitely have to be made to the market. LaFontaine, the new LaFontaine, seemed happy with the arrangement, especially after considering the possibility of sharing a cell with three rather large, rather angry, rather sexually frustrated hardened criminals.

Before leaving the courthouse, Curt called in for his messages. There was only one, but that one stopped his heart. The soft, sexy, rather nonchalant tone. The voice so familiar: Crystal Pelotas saying that the meeting with Nestor Stokes was set for that evening, her place, at midnight.

Thirty

He should just call Francis Powell, he thought, and let the pros take care of it. Powell would station undercover units inside and outside the house. Stokes wouldn't stand a chance.

So why was he sitting here, inside the car, slumped behind the wheel, gazing down the street, waiting?

There was a van parked in the driveway. It had the television station logo painted on the side. The cameraman, Curt thought, perhaps an additional technician. Curt couldn't remember exactly what Crystal Pelotas had said about who Stokes wanted present at the interview. No cops, though. And no additional people milling about, gawking.

It was eerily quiet in the street outside the house. Curt figured that Pelotas and the cameraman had to be inside, waiting. Waiting for Nestor Stokes to just come tooling down the street, pull into the driveway, get out, and walk up to the front door.

Incredible, Curt thought. Like the frigging pizza delivery boy! It was crazy. Could Stokes be that stupid? Would he put himself in jeopardy just to give one final interview?

Pelotas claimed the killer was in love with her. Obsessed. That he'd do anything to be with her, to get her attention. Curt had his doubts, though. Nestor Stokes had been very cagey thus far. He'd parlayed his claimed insanity into a civil commitment from which he had easily escaped. Walked right out of the facility. He'd managed to stay one step ahead of those who were looking for him, despite the fact that his picture had been front-page news for months.

The sun had long ago made its final descent behind the mountains that cradled Laurel Canyon Boulevard. The house and street were reduced to indistinct outlines vaguely illuminated by a single porch light from a neighboring house.

Crystal Pelotas lived in a rambling 1950's style ranch bungalow on a narrow winding street just off Laurel Canyon. The street inclined steeply and ended in a cul-de-sac. Crystal's home was at the far end of the cul-de-sac, with a view of Laurel Canyon Boulevard from the front windows.

The house stood on a promontory and backed against the scrub and underbrush of the foothills. It was shrouded by several large oaks rising from the depths of the backyard. Their gnarled limbs hung over most of the wood shingle roof and provided a canopy for the backyard.

It was eleven-thirty. Curt had been seated in his car for nearly thirty minutes. He wanted to be there when Stokes arrived, get a jump on the killer. He wondered if Crystal had mentioned anything to Stokes about his being present for the interview. It would be just like her, he thought, to say something. Then again, maybe she'd decided it would make for better theater seeing the look of surprise on Stokes' face when Curt showed up.

Powell would have told him to stay out of it. Francis would have handled the whole thing, nice and neat. That was the problem. Curt didn't want neat. He was beyond that. Nothing that had happened since Jamie's death had been nice, or neat. It was as if he owed this to himself, to her. He didn't want to just read about Stokes' capture in the morning paper. That was too sterile, too far removed from reality.

He would do this himself. However it turned out, this was one thing that he had to personally resolve. He'd been plagued by the *would've* and *could've* demons. *If only he'd done this . . . If only he'd acted differently . . .* It was time for him to take control—or to destroy himself in the process.

A quarter to twelve . . .

Curt lowered the volume on the tape player: Annie Lenox singing about love, or death. Curt wasn't quite sure.

Come to me, run to me, do and be done with me . . .

In the end, did it really matter? Love. Death. Curt could no longer distinguish between the two. How welcome it would be, he mused, to just loosen his grip, let himself relax. Feel himself slip under the glittering blue ice.

Dying is easy, it's living that scares me . . .

Still no sound from the house, except the chirping of crickets. The street was empty, ghost-like. Two dogs sniffed around an overturned trash can across the road.

Maybe Stokes had thought better of exposing himself to capture. After all, this meeting was totally unnecessary. Stokes could always continue his secret communications with Pelotas, receiving the attendant publicity without risking arrest.

This was all probably an elaborate joke at his expense, Curt thought. Jerk the lawyer around, watch him twist in the wind.

Then, suddenly, the sky behind the house exploded in white. A brightness that caused Curt to squint, shading his eyes with his hand. The night fog, illuminated by the intense light, swirled between the branches of the oaks like smoke from some netherworld inferno. Insects, like tiny phosphorescent shooting stars, twinkled in the smoky mist, their paths momentarily caught in the reflection of light on the vaporous night air.

How could he have been so stupid?

If it had occurred to him to come early and wait for Stokes, it certainly would have crossed the killer's mind to do the same. Stokes had beaten everyone to the punch. He'd made sure that Crystal Pelotas held to her promise about not calling the cops. He was already there. Inside the house. He'd been there the whole time. And he knew Curt was outside, waiting.

Curt's worst suspicions were confirmed when he approached and found the front door to the house wide open. He could hear voices coming from inside. Familiar sounds. A television or radio.

He should have brought a gun, he thought. Hell, he didn't even own one. Yet he started looking around the foyer, just inside the door, as if a weapon would suddenly materialize. He'd been so consumed with the thought of confronting Jamie's killer that he'd blanked everything else from his mind, including self-preservation. An image of a grimacing Francis Powell standing over his grave and muttering flashed through Curt's mind.

A table lamp illuminated the small living room: two couches, a glass coffee table, and scores of pictures on the walls, most depicting Crystal Pelotas arm-in-arm with some celebrity. The celluloid Crystal was everywhere, but there was still no sign of the real Crystal, nor of Nestor Stokes.

There was a large projection television in one corner of the living room. Its enormous screen dominated the room. The screen was angled away, and the images seemed vague and distorted. Curt moved closer, pausing for a moment as his eyes adjusted to the oversized characters. He recognized something in one of the voices, and took a step back, squinting at the hazy image.

It was Barrymore LaFontaine. He was there on the screen, standing behind a long saloon bar, serving drinks to the cowpokes. Curt recognized the TV western as one that had been popular several years back. The cable stations were reprising some of the old shows, running the same episodes over and over, usually late at night.

Curt was dumbfounded. It was LaFontaine, all right. Curt's most recent client looked a bit younger, hair not quite as red. He sported a handlebar moustache as he poured whiskey into a row of shot glasses. Curt flashed back to the corridor outside the courtroom, the greasy bikers and the gangbangers eyeing LaFontaine, unsure what to make of the weird guy wearing makeup. The pompadour red hair. The actor's easily deflated bravado. The tears of a defeated old man.

Curt pulled himself from the screen. He didn't have time for this. Nestor Stokes was somewhere in the house, he could feel it.

He made his way toward the French doors leading to the backyard, where he found the usual upscale Southern California scene: pool, cabana, gas barbecue, a beach towel casually draped over a chaise lounge. The yard was bathed in the same bright light that had first drawn his attention, but there was still no sign of its source.

Gingerly, Curt opened the door and stepped out. The silence enveloped him. There was no movement, except for the leaves of the giant oaks whispering in the breeze.

With the fingers of his left hand he traced the contours of the house as he slowly walked to the side. The chirping of the crickets had stopped. There was no sound except for the two dogs barking in front, and the muted dialogue of the TV western.

Curt reached the corner of the house. The next step would take him around to the other side. He hugged the house with his body, not knowing what to expect. He turned the corner and started to take a step, then stopped, feeling his heart drop to his stomach. For several seconds he could hear nothing, not the television or the dogs, nothing except the beating of his own pulse, throbbing like a bass drum in his head.

He knew what he was looking at, what he had glimpsed. His mind registered the images like individual frames of a film viewed slowly, frame by frame. The whole scene had not yet made itself clear. He couldn't make sense of it.

She was there, in the tree, suspended in midair by some sort of chain that glinted in the television lights. It was Crystal Pelotas, her arms stretched to her side, the chain wrapped around her body then draped over one of the tree limbs. Curt had to shield his eyes from the light, looking high into the tree to see her. She wasn't moving.

The television lights stood off to the side, their high-intensity beams trained on the tree. Crystal hung inside the leafy branches, motionless, like some grisly death-ceremony tableau.

It was after he took a step toward the tree that Curt spotted the other body, sprawled at the gnarly base of the tree's trunk. A few feet away, a video camera lay on the grass, angled up toward the limbs of the tree.

In the silence, Curt heard the faint whir of the camera's motor and saw the red light near the lens. A branch from the tree had been wedged against the camera's trigger to keep the film rolling.

It was all starting to make sense. This was some sort of show. Nestor Stokes had planned the whole thing. His final farewell performance.

Curt heard a faint cry. When he looked up he saw Crystal's lips tremble, then her head jerk in a groggy spasm. Her makeup streaked her cheeks like a ghoulish fright mask. Her eyes opened, fluttered, then caught his. Her eyes opened wider, unblinking. She was staring at him, trying to tell him something . . .

Then there was a cracking sound, and Curt felt a terrible numbing pain. A blackness began to spread from the back of his head. He felt himself falling forward, dizzy, out of control.

Everything went dark.

Thirty-One

He thought: *I must be dreaming.* He would just close his eyes, maybe roll over and the whole thing would end. But it didn't. When he tried to roll to his side, there was something wrong. He couldn't move his arms. An object, hard and sharp, pressed against his face. He needed to wake up, get out of the dream.

Curt opened his eyes again, this time realizing that it was no dream. His feet were bound and his hands were loosely tied behind his back. He lay facedown on a concrete paver. It started to come back to him in waves washing over his consciousness. He'd come to Crystal Pelotas' house looking for Nestor Stokes. He'd been stupid enough to believe this was something he could handle himself. Stupid enough not to think that Stokes wouldn't have this deadly encounter perfectly planned like he had the others.

". . . And now, ladies and gentlemen, this story must come to an end."

Curt turned his head. Stokes stood several feet away, holding a knife in his fist as if it were a microphone. The blade of the knife glistened under the TV lights. Slender and shimmering, almost delicate. It looked like some sort of stiletto or surgical instrument.

Stokes moved closer. "The great police investigator, Mr. Curt Denmark." Stokes laughed, quietly at first, then threw his head back and howled at the moon like an uncaged wild animal.

Curt remembered Crystal, hanging in the tree. He lifted his head, then felt it thudding back to the ground. It was as if a great lead weight were resting on it. Beads of perspiration accumulated on his forehead, running down his nose, burning his eyes. His vision had gone blurry, and he tasted blood dripping down the back of his throat.

He tried turning again, this time barely catching Crystal's figure in the corner of his vision. She hung there, wrapped in chains, motionless. Curt forced himself to put some order to his thoughts. He needed to remember exactly what had happened, what he'd done to bring himself to this point. He managed to roll on his side, facing Stokes.

"Ahh, Mr. Denmark," said Stokes, bending over and holding the tip of the knife against Curt's neck. "I'm glad you decided to accept my invitation." Stokes flicked the tip of the blade, breaking the skin. Curt felt something warm running down the center of his chest.

Then Stokes got up, as if he were on stage, and walked slowly toward the camera. He positioned himself so that he was in the foreground of the picture, with the body of Crystal Pelotas visible behind him.

Stokes spoke into the camera, "Our first guest tonight, I'm sure you'll all recognize." He turned and walked to the base of the tree. The chain had been wrapped around one of the branches. Stokes released the tension on the chain and slowly lowered Crystal's body to within inches of the ground.

"Ahh, my sweet Crystal." Stokes gently stroked her face, running his hand down her neck and softly over her breasts. He whispered, "My sweet Crystal's been a bad girl, haven't you?" He was fingering her nipples, not sensually, but like a haberdasher testing the quality of the fabric.

"Yes," Stokes murmured, "this will do very nicely."

Curt saw movement off to the side. Crystal's cameraman, whose body had lain motionless within inches of the camera, moved his arm, then his head. In a split second, Curt made eye contact with him. Not enough time for either man to know what the other was thinking, but long enough to see the fear in the other's eyes.

"We'll save you for later," Stokes said. He moved in front of Crystal's lifeless body and delicately placed his lips on hers. He then took up the slack in the chain, using the weight of his body to raise her back into the branches of the tree.

After securing the chain, Stokes turned toward the camera. "The world has underestimated Nestor Stokes," he proclaimed. "It is not I who is mad." He gestured, waving the knife dramatically in the air, like an actor in an amateur stage production. "It is the world that's gone mad. Not Nestor Stokes." Stokes dropped his head, and Curt could barely hear the last words. Stokes stood for a moment, his chin resting on his chest, his shoulders heaving. When he next lifted his face to the camera, Curt saw the tears, the contorted, tortured, incredibly sad expression of suffering.

"It is not Nestor Stokes," Stokes said softly, his voice cracking, "who caused the madness." He seemed in a trance, locked in some awful memory, unable to escape his past, his destiny.

Curt knew there were only moments left. If he didn't act now, it would be over for all of them. He pulled his legs against his chest and rocked himself to an upright position. The rope around his wrists loosened so that there was enough play for him to steady himself with his hands. His ankles remained securely bound, though. He glanced at Stokes, who stood, trancelike, rocking back and forth in front of the camera.

Curt was within five feet of Stokes, but he might as well have been a mile away. With his ankles bound together, it seemed impossible to stand upright. How long could this last? he asked himself as he tried to find some leverage that would allow him to get to his feet before Stokes emerged from his trance.

"Vengeance is mine, sayeth the Lord . . . All God's children . . ."

Stokes was coming out of it. His head bobbed and his eyes popped open as if he'd been startled from a deep dream.

Curt made one last try at throwing himself upward. He landed unsteadily on his feet, wobbling from side to side like one of those inflatable punching dolls. Stokes was only a few feet away.

Stokes turned, calmly, as if this final act was just part of a scene he'd played dozens of times before in his mind. The corners of his mouth turned up in a smile. His eyes crossed in a demented parody of the game small children play on their parents. Stokes raised the knife over his head and let out a scream that silenced even the barking dogs.

In that moment, Curt saw the knife arcing toward him. He saw Crystal's legs twitch, shaking leaves from the tree. And he had a sudden recollection of himself bent over

Jamie's dead body. Curt summoned all the strength he had left. He turned his body so that his side faced Stokes, then launched himself head first. In that partial second—his body a projectile carving an arc toward its target—Curt saw the glint of the blade, then felt something stinging, yet smooth, trace a delicate swirl on his chest. He heard Stokes scream, then felt himself, like a baby, resting his head on the killer's chest, plunging forward into nothingness.

Epilogue

There was a bowl of fresh fruit on the table. Peaches and nectarines, a kiwi, strawberries out of season, a bunch of ripe bananas, several types of apples and grapes. There were pitchers of chilled orange and grapefruit juice. Two silver carafes of coffee sat atop warming stands alongside china cups and saucers. On a large plate in the center of the table, assorted danish, coffee cakes, muffins, and cookies were available for the taking.

Despite the abundance of food, nobody was eating.

"I'd like to see the tape again."

The others seated at the table silently nodded.

"Run it from the beginning, John."

John Swain got up and walked to the VCR. He rewound the tape, pressed the play button, then returned to his seat.

Herb Krantz sat at the far end of the polished rosewood conference table. This was supposed to be his show, his decision. He'd reviewed the tape once already, and frankly could not believe what he'd seen. As he looked around the room, it appeared to him that the others were also somewhat stunned by the events depicted on the tape.

"Stop it there for a minute, John." Krantz leaned forward, trying to make out the details on the screen.

"That's where I came to," said Swain, gesturing toward the screen with the remote control. "I tried to move the camera without Stokes noticing."

"Yes," said Krantz, considering what might have been going through Swain's mind at the time. "Miraculous, John. Incredible." He motioned for Swain to advance the tape.

Krantz said, "You oughtta get a damn Emmy for this, John."

Swain just smiled. He'd already started to think along those lines, himself. "Lucky for us that Stokes planned on filming the whole thing, otherwise we wouldn't have got that first part."

Colin Archer sat next to Crystal Pelotas. Both watched the drama on the tape unfold for the second time. Archer was less than pleased about what had happened. Crystal had promised to let him in on any developments concerning Nestor Stokes. The tape was dynamite. Biggest show of the year, maybe of the decade. And he'd had absolutely nothing to do with it. All he could do now was watch in amazement, along with the others, and wonder how any of them had escaped alive.

"Uh, Herb, this next part we might want to edit a bit."

"Wha? Oh, yeah, sure." Krantz had been mesmerized by the image of a naked Crystal Pelotas filling the screen. He was surprised just how built his little newscaster was. Of course he'd heard the rumors about her sexual appetites, but he'd never personally had anything to do with the woman. Not because he hadn't wanted to, though.

Now here she was, hanging from that tree, naked as a jaybird. Jesus, this was great stuff. He looked over at

Crystal, who was averting her eyes from the screen, doodling on a notepad.

Great body, Krantz thought. And what a pair of tits!

"Stop the tape, John."

Colin Archer got up and walked to the television screen. "See, that's where we lose Denmark for a second. Then he's back, that blur flying through the air." Archer fiddled with the VCR, trying to improve the picture without success. It was all part of his attempt to take control of the editing process, trying to salvage some personal credit for the ultimate presentation of the tape.

"That silvery glint, there," said Krantz, pointing. "The knife. Jesus, it looks like Stokes got him."

The others nodded, everyone's attention riveted to the screen.

Swain, the cameraman, said, "I didn't see him coming. Just afterwards, after Stokes was hit. That part's on the tape. Then I blacked out again."

Krantz again gazed at Crystal.

"If this is too much for you to go over so soon," he said, "we'll all understand, Crystal." His eyes dropped from her face to her breasts. He was having difficulty forgetting the images from the tape.

Crystal looked up from her notepad. "Herb, that asshole came this close to carving me up." She made a gesture with her thumb and forefinger. "If it wasn't for Denmark, you'd be looking for a new host right about now, and I'd be six feet under feeding the worms. Sure, it still kinda shakes me up when I watch the tape, but there's no way in hell that we're not going on the air with this story. I want the whole show devoted to this, not just an extended segment. Colin's already got Francis Powell lined up. We're still working on Denmark."

"Good," said Krantz. "As far as I'm concerned, you've

got your show." He cleared his throat. "Of course, the tape will have to be edited. We'd never get that nudity past the censors, and I don't think Crystal would be too happy to have herself plastered across the screen like that."

Krantz chuckled, waiting for the others to join in. Even Crystal smiled.

"We'll introduce John, lay out how this whole thing got started. How John got knocked out by Stokes, then regained consciousness, laying on the ground, running the camera."

"And Powell can fill in what happened afterward," said Archer. "The injuries, the arrest, and so forth."

"What about Denmark?"

"He doesn't answer his calls," said Crystal.

"Have you offered him more money?"

Crystal Pelotas smiled and slowly shook her head. "He doesn't care about money. Denmark's a hardcase. This was some sort of personal vendetta for him. Now that it's over, I doubt whether anyone will see much of the guy. The last thing he'd want to do is go on national television to discuss what happened."

Krantz thought about the part of the tape showing Denmark's attack on Nestor Stokes. Stokes had been holding the knife, and Denmark's hands and feet had been bound. It was an incredible stroke of luck that Stokes didn't turn in time to plunge the knife into the lawyer's body. To Krantz, it almost looked as if Curt Denmark hadn't really cared whether he lived or not.

"The man's a hero," said Krantz. He got up and the others did the same. "See about getting him on the show." He walked through the doorway toward the secretarial area. "Triple the fee if you have to."

Pelotas and Archer nodded as they walked past, heading for their offices. Krantz put a hand on John Swain's shoulder. Swain had removed the tape and placed it safely inside a canvas shoulder bag.

"Listen, John. I need you to do me a favor."

Krantz was guiding the cameraman out of the conference area, down the hall toward the elevators. He still had his arm draped over Swain's shoulder.

"Sure, Mr. Krantz. You name it."

"Herb, John. You can call me Herb. And again, your work on this thing has Emmy written all over it."

Swain smiled.

Krantz whispered, "You could make me a copy of that tape, couldn't you, John? Before it gets edited, I mean.

Swain paused for only a split-second before saying, "Sure, Mr. Krantz." He smiled. "I mean, *Herb.*"

Francis Powell sat opposite Crystal Pelotas behind the news-anchor desk. On the wall behind them the *Real News for Real People* logo glowed bright gold and blue.

". . . and by the time your officers arrived, Chief Powell, Mr. Denmark had already taken control of the situation?"

"Well, Crystal, as you know, having been there, Curt, I mean Mr. Denmark, had managed to render Nestor Stokes unconscious. We're still investigating the entire incident, but as far as we know, Mr. Denmark, in an unbelievable exhibition of bravery and personal sacrifice, was somehow able to knock Stokes to the ground. Stokes, we believe, hit his head on something hard, a rock or part of the tree trunk. Mr. Denmark then telephoned us. The rest, as they say, is history."

Crystal looked away from Francis Powell, directly into the camera.

"Let me just say, ladies and gentlemen" she started in a calm voice, "that while I was a participant in the grisly events depicted on the tape that you've just seen, I was unconscious during much of what happened. Perhaps, in hindsight, that was a good thing. I can tell you this much, though. There is a man out there, maybe watching this very broadcast, who deserves my thanks."

Crystal paused for dramatic effect.

"Mr. Denmark, if you are watching, I'd just like to say thank you. That's from me and John Swain, my camera-man, and everyone on the set of *Real News*. You are a true hero in our book."

Curt got off the couch, walked to the television, and turned off the picture. He grabbed the vodka bottle, his glass, and headed for the patio.

It had rained that morning, a light, steady drizzle. Just enough to make everything smell moist and damp for the rest of the day. In the twilight the mountains and scrub of the canyon took on a mottled brown hue, heavy and wet, like a paint-by-the-numbers oil portrait.

Curt leaned back in the aluminum deck chair and put his feet on the railing. He rocked back and forth, balanc-ing on the two rear legs of the chair.

So now he was Crystal Pelotas' hero? That made him laugh. The woman was still playing to an audience. After all she'd brought on herself and the others, she just couldn't resist the spotlight. Curt knew he would remain Crystal Pelotas' hero for about as long as it would take the viewing public to lose interest in the story. Then Pelotas would drop him and move on to the next bit of sensation-alist bullshit that passed for news these days.

He hadn't done it for her, anyway. As far as Curt was concerned, Pelotas and Stokes were made for each other. He found the image of Nestor Stokes carrying around a life-size Crystal Pelotas doll, one of his own making, more humorous than shocking.

But Pelotas had been right about one thing. She'd intimated that it was almost as if Curt had not cared about his own safety. She'd called this apparent selflessness *heroism*. Curt, though, had another word for it.

Pelotas had been only partially right. He was willing to risk his life, but not to save the reporter or her cameraman. Curt wanted Nestor Stokes for himself. And he hadn't much cared whether he lived or died in getting him.

Maybe now, he thought, they'll stop calling. Pelotas and her ilk had filled the tape on his message machine. The media hyenas were crawling over each other, thrusting money in his face for his story.

But that was it, wasn't it? In the end, it was *his* story. He was the one who would have to learn to live with what had happened to Jamie, just like he'd struggled to adjust to Darren's death. It was *his* problem. Another suitcase in the emotional baggage that Curt Denmark would carry with him for the rest of life.

Nestor Stokes was again in custody. The process was to be repeated once more, with new players. Stokes would be charged with whatever crimes the District Attorney could make stick. The judicial system would grind out something approximating justice, whatever that turned out to be.

But Curt would have no part in it, except as a witness if the case were ever brought to trial. An unwilling participant in another of the city's legal media events. A courtroom circus. More grist for the media mill. Crystal Pelotas, it seemed, worked in a limitless growth industry. There appeared to be no end to the public's voyeuristic appetite for violence, pity, and despair—as long as it was viewable from the comfort of their living room Barcaloungers.

Curt tossed down the rest of his drink, then closed his eyes. He could hear the traffic on Ventura Boulevard, and the sounds of small animals scurrying about the hillside underneath the deck.

He pushed the incidents of the last several months from his mind. In their place, he envisioned himself with Jamie and Darren. They were all together, happy. He could almost convince himself that it was true. That there was something worth looking forward to. That the rest of his life would be okay.

Almost.